She rested he
flowed throu
and fall bene.... .....
legs, he released a low groan.

"Take it slow," she cautioned. "Don't rush to get up."

In response, his lids partially opened, exposing hints of his soulful brown eyes. Suddenly to her, he didn't look like a guy who'd just fallen from his horse. He transformed into a drop-dead gorgeous man who looked like he'd just awakened after spending a pleasurable night tangling in the sheets.

Her gaze landed on his mouth. His full lips were made to deliver slow, deep toe-curling kisses. As her thoughts drifted toward the possibility of what those kisses might feel like, her own lips tingled. The unsteady thump of her heart against her rib cage snapped her back to reality. What was wrong with her? She needed to help the poor guy, not fantasize about kissing him.

As his eyes started to close, she gave him a small shake. "No, don't do that. Open your eyes. Hey, can you hear me?"

He rasped out, "I hear you just fine, Sun Angel."

Sun Angel? The guy was seeing celestial beings? That wasn't good. She shook him a little harder. "Don't go anywhere. Stay with me."

Dear Reader,

Welcome to Bishop Honey Bee Farm, located in Bolan, Maryland. As the sign just outside town says, "Friends and Smiles for Miles Live Here." If you've visited before, welcome back!

In *A Honey for the Beekeeper*, Bishop Honey Bee Farm book one, you'll meet Brooke Bishop and Gable "Dell" Kincaid. Brooke dreads coming back to the family bee farm every year to fill in as temporary beekeeper. Gable is escaping the music industry at the property next door that he's turning into a hobby farm. Plastic shopping bags whirling in the air and a fall from a horse brings them together and ignites their plan for a casual fling, aka the perfect distraction from their pasts. Nothing can go wrong with that...or could it?

Revisiting tragedy or heartbreak is never easy, but Brooke and Gable will discover the resiliency of the heart, the value of family and how love makes us stronger.

While you're in town, you'll also get a chance to see the Tillbridge family and the friends and acquaintances introduced in the Tillbridge Stables and Small Town Secrets series. And yes, the infamous *Bolan Town Talk* is still keeping up with the latest "news."

Brooke and Gable are waiting for you. I hope you enjoy their story and the upcoming books in this new series!

Hearing from readers makes me smile. Visit www.ninacrespo.com and say hello. While you're there, sign up for my newsletter. It's my favorite place to share about my books and upcoming appearances, and don't forget to follow me on social media. I look forward to seeing you there.

Happy reading!

Nina

A HONEY
FOR THE BEEKEEPER

NINA CRESPO

SPECIAL EDITION

Harlequin®
SPECIAL
EDITION™

Recycling programs
for this product may
not exist in your area.

ISBN-13: 978-1-335-40234-9

A Honey for the Beekeeper

Copyright © 2025 by Nina Crespo

Harlequin Enterprises ULC
22 Adelaide St. West, 41st Floor
Toronto, Ontario M5H 4E3, Canada
www.Harlequin.com

Printed in Lithuania

MIX
Paper | Supporting
responsible forestry
FSC® C021394

Nina Crespo lives in Florida, where she indulges in her favorite passions—the beach, a good glass of wine, date night with her own real-life hero and dancing. Her lifelong addiction to romance began in her teens while on a "borrowing spree" in her older sister's bedroom, where she discovered her first romance novel. Let Nina's sensual contemporary stories feed your own addiction to love, romance and happily-ever-after. Visit her at ninacrespo.com.

Books by Nina Crespo

Harlequin Special Edition

Bishop Honey Bee Farm

A Honey for the Beekeeper

The Fortunes of Texas: Digging for Secrets

Expecting a Fortune

Small Town Secrets

A Chef's Kiss
The Designer's Secret
Second Take at Love

Tillbridge Stables

The Cowboy's Claim
Her Sweet Temptation
The Cowgirl's Surprise Match

Visit the Author Profile page
at Harlequin.com for more titles.

To Love, Life, Breath and Inspiration
for always providing the light and leading the way.

Chapter One

"Ugh, no. What is that?" The brunette in a fashionable blue dress backed away from the line of tables laden with fancy hors d'oeuvres.

One of her stiletto heels caught on the carpet, but a tall, dark-haired guy in a navy suit caught her by the waist before she fell.

Seconds later, an older woman rushed over to them from across the banquet room located in an upscale neighborhood's clubhouse. Guests attending the engagement party, as well as the catering staff, moved out of her way. She and the newly engaged brunette could have passed for twins, decades apart, but the expression on her flushed face defined who she was—protective mom gearing up for a rampage.

"What's happening?" she demanded. "What's wrong?"

With a look of distaste, her daughter pointed. "There's a bug in the food."

Uh-oh. Brooke Bishop, serving iced tea at a guest table, slipped past concerned onlookers to get a better look.

On the buffet, a lone bee buzzed between a large wheel

of honey-glazed brie and a centerpiece with orange roses, sunflowers and purple asters.

Poor girl. Drawn to the honey and the flowers, the last thing the bee was interested in was bothering anyone. Had she drifted in with the guests or hitched a ride on the bouquet?

The mother of the future bride-to-be looked past the rescuer in the navy suit to another dark-haired guy, her future son-in-law. "Don't just stand there. Do something."

Just as the future groom-to-be started to respond, navy suit guy jumped into action. "I'll get it." He grabbed a cloth napkin, prepared to swat the bee into oblivion.

Before getting lost at the party, the forager bee had probably been collecting pollen and nectar to take back to the hive. On its journey, it had bravely faced multiple dangers and would continue to do so until the end of its life. But that ending wasn't happening yet.

"No, wait!" Brooke snagged an empty wineglass and a reserved sign from a nearby table. Hurrying back to the buffet, she elbowed him aside. "I've got you," she whispered to the bee. "Just land."

Relief poured through her as it settled on the white tablecloth. She put the glass over the bee then carefully slid the card stock paper underneath both. With the precious insect sheltered from harm, she left the room, walked through the poshly decorated common area of the clubhouse and out the front door. A couple of yards away on the expansive lawn, she released the bee into a fall breeze that held the warmth of the Florida sun and a hint of ocean brine. A sense of lightness filled her as she watched it fly away.

As a young girl, before she'd understood honey bees instinctively knew their way home, whenever she'd spotted them drifting through the flower field at her family's bee farm in Maryland, she'd believed they were lost. Capturing the bees, flower buds and all, she would return them to the apiary. Surprisingly, she'd never gotten stung.

Brooke's mother used to say her eldest daughter had a way with bees.

"Hey, bee charmer."

Startled to hear the childhood nickname her mother used to call her, Brooke looked over her shoulder.

Her coworker, Nellie, stood on the palm tree-lined sidewalk. "The boss sent me to find you. But instead of going back, I think we should make a run for it." The blonde, wearing a white shirt, black pants and a matching dark apron, joined Brooke on the grass. Her usual impishness reflected on her tawny brown face. As coworkers, they'd only known each other for a few weeks, but Nellie's wry sense of humor had quickly moved her onto Brooke's friend list.

Brooke faced her. "Why? Did something more menacing than an innocent honey bee wander into the party?"

"Definitely. Momzilla's transformed into the Mother of Dragons from *Game of Thrones*, and she's raining down complaints like fire. Now everyone's on edge, including the boss. And I really feel sorry for her future son-in-law. He's catching hell for not leading the charge during the so-called bug attack. There's no mystery what'll happen to the next bee that shows up." Nellie made a cutting sound as she sliced her finger across her throat.

"Oh really?" The heat of irritation scorching Brooke's brown cheeks felt powerful enough to set her dark curly ponytail aflame. "So it's acceptable for everyone at the party to gobble down a wheel of honey-glazed brie triple the size of a human head, but it's not okay to protect the bees that helped provide it? Obviously, they don't have a clue how important bees are to the environment. Well, guess what? There won't be any bee killing on my watch. And if the boss or Momzilla don't like it, they can kiss my—"

"Okaaay," Nellie interrupted, holding up her hands in surrender. "I get the message. No unaliving bees. Not that I would. Now I understand why you were so into Jack, the bartender who worked the party with us last night. You're both nature freaks. He climbs mountains and you have a thing for bees."

"I wasn't that into him." But he *had* gained points for understanding the importance of bees. "We were comparing job experiences. He used to work for the same employment agency I do."

"Is that all you talked about?" As Nellie tucked a strand of hair behind her ear, mischief filled her eyes. "If I'd been in your shoes, I would have compared a lot more than job experiences. Are guys like him the norm with that agency? Cuz if they are, sign me up."

Amusement dissolved Brooke's irritation. "Yes, I've met cute guys along the way, but that's not why I decided to work with them. Epic Jobs is *the* place to find the best temporary job opportunities."

Since connecting with the boutique employment service three years ago, she'd been hired as a house sitter from coast to coast, sailed the Caribbean as a crew member on private yachts, been a kitchen assistant for a personal chef in Nantucket, and worked as a stable hand at a luxury dude ranch in Texas.

But working as a cater waiter wasn't an agency assignment. She'd spotted the position on an employment website. It was the perfect gig to pad her bank account, and it didn't interfere with her *real* job of the moment—housesitting on the other side of Jupiter Beach. The homeowners were on an extended work vacation in Brazil. After that, she would remain in the area for another house-sitting job and then work at a beach resort during the winter holidays.

Being near the beach this winter would be a definite perk. Last year, she'd been trudging through snow to her front desk job at a ski resort back East. Enjoying hot cocktails at a local spot, and spending time with an even hotter ski instructor, had made up for freezing her buns off.

"Girl, I envy you." Nellie sighed dreamily. "All that excitement and adventure."

"Sure, adventure is a part of it. But for me, the excitement is exploring places I've never been before and learning new things."

"And no major responsibilities. You gotta love that, too."

"No major responsibilities?" Brooke choked out a laugh. "Are you kidding me? It's not all fun and games."

During one of her house-sitting assignments, torrential rains ripped off part of the roof of the house. Another time, a teenage neighbor learning to drive decimated the homeowner's mailbox. And once, a relative of the homeowners showed up uninvited with a parrot, dressed a little too similar to Pennywise the clown from the horror movie *It*. He'd wanted to stay in the pool house for the weekend. Yeah, that didn't happen. She'd dealt with all of those situations and more as a house sitter, and some of her non-house-sitting assignments had also been far from drama-free. Just as Brooke started to explain the reality of working temporary and seasonal positions, the door to the clubhouse opened and the groom-to-be stalked out.

Talking to himself, he walked past them to the parking lot to a blue car and got into it on the driver's side.

Nellie arched her brow. "What's he doing?"

"He probably just needs a moment." Or the guy planned

to escape. After witnessing his future mother-in-law in action, Brooke couldn't blame him.

He started the car then revved the engine.

Nellie's brows rose higher. "I don't think his fiancée will like whatever moment is happening now."

Brooke nudged her toward the entrance. "We should go inside."

"This reminds me of a movie I saw where the groom bolted on his wedding day."

"Don't you mean the one where the bride ran away?"

"No, the groom. It was a sci-fi thriller. He was eaten by an alien as he ran from the altar." Nellie cackled with glee. "In the end, the bride married the alien from a rival galaxy who ate the alien that chomped down on her fiancé."

Brooke resisted the urge to make sense of the odd plot twist. Her friend's taste in movies veered toward the weirder the better, direct-to-streaming titles.

"Are we telling anyone about Mr. Runaway Fiancé?" Nellie asked.

"Nope." This was real life, not a movie plot. Having grown up in a small town, Brooke knew how easily speculation could open the floodgates of chaos and confusion.

In the banquet room, their boss, a usually upbeat woman in her forties, looked as if she'd taken a few spins through the unhappy customer blender and been spit out. She gave them a get-back-to-work stare.

Brooke and Nellie split up and circled the room, pouring beverages and clearing away plates at the tables.

As Brooke bussed dishes, her conversation with Nellie about Epic Jobs came into her mind. Most people tended to have their own ideas about what it was like working short-term assignments versus holding down a steady full-time job. Some, like Nellie, thought it was great. But others, like Brooke's younger sister, Harper, believed anyone who qualified as an adult should be leading a *normal* life that didn't fit into a backpack and a duffel. At age twenty-five, Harper, who was two years younger than Brooke, ran Bishop Honey Bee Farm along with their aunt, Ivy.

Brooke's decision not to return to Maryland five years ago after graduating college had surprised Aunt Ivy and disappointed Harper. Two years later, after being laid off from her nine-to-five marketing position, once again Brooke chose not to return home to the farm and embraced temporary work instead. This decision had caused a huge rift between her and her sister. Harper had accused her of not caring about anyone but herself. Of course, she cared about Harper, Aunt Ivy and the farm. Otherwise, she wouldn't bother returning home once a year to fill in as beekeeper.

As the memory sparked renewed frustration in Brooke, she dropped a tray of dishes harder than intended on a corner stand. Globs of honey-glazed brie splattered on her fingers. Releasing a sigh, she slipped a napkin from her front apron pocket. Getting through to Harper was as difficult as trying to make this crowd understand they shouldn't harm bees. It was even harder to believe they had ever experienced happier times as sisters. The only thing they seemed to have in common now were differences.

And the most painful moment of their lives.

As Brooke wiped brie from her hand, sorrow almost as palpable as it was twelve years ago, when she and Harper lost their parents, rose inside of her. Before that terrible accident took away their mom and dad, she'd never envisioned leaving the farm, but now, she didn't even go home for Thanksgiving or other holidays, and she couldn't begin to imagine living there. But she did want Bishop Honey Bee Farm to thrive.

Momzilla hurried past Brooke, pulling her out of her thoughts. "Where is he?" the woman said. "He knows we're on a tight schedule."

Brooke met Nellie's gaze. The alarmed expression on her friend's face reflected what went through Brooke's mind. *Oh crap. Did the groom-to-be actually make a run for it?*

As the guests began murmuring amongst themselves, he strode in. Sighs of relief flooded the space.

Moments later, the engaged couple stood at the front of the room with their beaming parents. As toasts were made to their happy future, the bride-to-be kept glancing at navy suit guy drinking shots at the corner bar, and he stared longingly at her in return. Her fiancé, standing beside her, looked trapped.

As Brooke observed what was happening at the front of the room, she shuddered at the thought of being stuck in a situation she didn't want to be in. Thankfully, unlike the unhappy trio, she wasn't facing a till-death-us-do-part scenario, only a three-week visit. Twenty-one days at the farm was more than enough.

Chapter Two

Jacksonville

Gable Kincaid sipped a glass of whiskey at Lou's Uptown Lounge, a small establishment featuring live music. It was a Sunday night, and casually dressed customers, escaping the chilly weather outside, occupied every stool next to him as well as seats at the surrounding tables.

On stage, his friend Theo played a familiar pop song on the piano. He ended the number with a flourish, and as the applause died down, he keyed the opening chords of an R & B classic.

Most of the people in the bar, including Gable, hadn't been born when the Motown ballad was released in the sixties, but many of them knew the lyrics and sang along with him. Soon, the multiple voices drifted to silence, leaving just Theo's smooth, soulful baritone.

Gable had met Theo six years ago at a club in Atlanta where they, along with other up-and-coming musicians, played on slow nights of the week. Both in their midtwenties, they'd related to each other's dreams of making it big. Theo was the one who'd encouraged him to make the switch to country music after hearing him perform an impromptu cover of a chart-topping song during a mic check.

At first, Gable rejected the idea. As a pop and R & B performer, he'd already been struggling to get noticed in a sea of musicians hoping to be discovered. Crossing into a genre where some people didn't consider Black country music artists the norm was even harder. Still, Theo persisted, and Gable caved in, adding a couple of country songs to his sets. The audience's reaction had been overwhelmingly positive.

Heartened by the reception, Gable started posting videos of his shows on social media. Most of the responses had been, "Give us more!" but a few ignorant comments claimed he didn't have the right to invade "their" genre.

The haters didn't know their history. Black country music artists weren't a new thing. Gable's deceased great-uncle Wes, a country music enthusiast, had introduced him to the music of some of the trailblazers when he'd stayed with him one summer years ago in Maryland.

Performers like Lesley Riddle, whose innovative style of guitar picking helped shape the sound of country music. The "Harmonica Wizard" DeFord Bailey, who'd been a pioneer member of the Grand Ole Opry, and Linda Martell, the first commercially successful Black female country music artist. She'd made her on-stage debut at the iconic country music venue in the late sixties. They, as well as others, paved the way for today's musicians, including Gable.

Confident in where he belonged as an artist, he'd blocked the haters and continued singing country music. Over time, he reaped the rewards of more online followers and larger audiences at his live shows. These days, it felt more than just right to slip on a cowboy hat and sing the style of music that truly spoke to him. According to his talent manager, Keith Carson, a potential deal for an extended play album was on the horizon.

As Gable thought about that possibility, eagerness grew inside of him. The release of an EP with just a few songs would allow a record company to test his marketability. If it did well, the door could open to a debut album and even bigger opportunities.

A vision of his stage name, Dell Kincaid, on album covers, topping music charts and on lighted marquees flashed in his mind. But a sudden dose of reality dimmed his excitement. None of that would happen if he didn't finish the audition recording Keith needed from him, showcasing his talent as a singer and songwriter.

Cheers and applause erupted at the end of Theo's performance, and genuine happiness lit up his friend's light brown face. "Thank you. That was my last song of the night, but stick around. The group Back Alley Velvet will be on in fifteen minutes." As Theo stepped off the stage, he spotted Gable, and they acknowledged each other with a heads-up nod. On his way over to the bar, multiple people stopped him. From Theo's widening smile, they were complimenting his set.

Theo performing again and receiving a positive reception from the crowd was good to see. Almost two years ago, after Theo's girlfriend, now wife, Melonie, had gotten pregnant, he'd chosen to focus on his growing family and given up the dream of making it as a singer. He'd also relocated to Jacksonville for a better paying job.

After the move, Gable lost touch with him, but a few months ago, they reconnected. During one of their phone conversations, Theo had admitted how much he missed playing music for an audience, and Gable encouraged him to return to what he loved. Gable also took the extra step of checking in with his music connections about opportunities for Theo to perform in Jacksonville.

As luck would have it, Keith's administrative assistant was acquainted with Lou Bingham, the owner of Lou's Uptown Lounge. Lou had been looking for a manager/performer to work a few nights a week, and Theo was perfect for the job. He'd started a little over three weeks ago.

Theo reached him at the bar. "Hey! You made it."

"Of course." Gable exchanged a handshake-bro hug with him. He'd performed at a small club in Savannah the night before. Instead of returning home to Atlanta, he'd flown to Jacksonville that afternoon to catch up with Theo. Despite having a lot on his plate, seeing his friend had remained at the top of his must-do list. "You sounded good up there."

As Gable settled back in his seat, Theo stood beside him. "Good enough, but my pipes are a little rusty." He pointed at Gable's empty glass. "Next one's on me. What are you drinking?"

"Crown—straight up."

Theo signaled the bartender. He ordered a club soda with lime for himself and a refill for Gable. "So how's everything going with you? Tell me about the record deal."

"I don't have one yet. Keith's still working on setting up meetings with a few A and R reps." The delivery of their drinks paused the conversation. "And actually, it's a good thing nothing's happening right now. I haven't nailed down the songs to showcase for an audition. I'm just not feeling what I'm working on."

"Are the songs the issue or is your head the problem?"

Gable couldn't deny the latter. Worrying about if he'd get the chance to impress an A and R representative *had* messed with his concentration. "Both."

"I can't fix what's going on in your head, but I can help you with the songs. Are you in a hurry to get back to your hotel?"

"No. I'd planned on hanging out here until you got off work. I thought we could grab some food. You can pick the place."

A brief electric guitar riff and drum taps reverberated through the bar. Back Alley Velvet, a pop rock band, warmed up on stage for their performance.

Theo downed the last of his drink. Wincing a little, he rubbed his chest as he set the glass on the bar.

"You okay?"

"Yeah, I must have lifted something the wrong way and strained a muscle. I have to focus on the club right now, but once we close at ten, you and I can sit down at the piano and figure out your problem. After that, you can treat me to breakfast. There's a twenty-four-hour restaurant that's close to here."

Gable hesitated in leaping at the chance. Melonie wasn't thrilled about Theo working at the bar or performing again, and he wasn't her favorite person. She blamed him for her husband's renewed interest in music. Still, he could use the help. He was on the verge of a huge opportunity and couldn't afford to mess it up.

"Are you sure Mel will extend your hall pass?" Gable asked.

"I'm good. She won't be too upset if I stay out for a few more hours."

"Just remember you said that when you're sleeping in the doghouse this week."

Theo chuckled and clapped him on the back. "Maybe so, but I owe you. Seriously, after all you've done for me, the least I can do is help you out."

Later on, after the bar closed, Gable sat down at the piano on stage. It wasn't his instrument of choice, but his guitar was back at the hotel. After warming up with a few simple chords, he started singing an untitled song he'd written about a guy taking his shot with a woman he'd spotted on the dance floor. The music as well as the lyrics flowed better than when he'd been working on them at his apartment in Atlanta.

Sitting in a chair next to him, Theo nodded to the beat. "It's good. I like it, but maybe you should change the lyrics up and raise the chord an octave at the end of the second line." He grabbed a pen and scribbled musical notes and lyrics on a bar napkin.

Their back-and-forth conversation was reminiscent of the days when they used to give each other input on their music. After trying so hard to make the song work, Theo's perspective revived him like a breath of fresh air.

Gable moved to the next song he'd written. His confidence waned in the middle of the arrangement, and he purposely ended it with an off-key chord. "I can't figure this one out. I've tried changing the tempo and the chorus, but it's still not right."

"No, the song is fine. It's your delivery. Trade places with me." Gable got up, and Theo sat down in front of the piano. "Your first song was about hooking up with a woman. But this one is about being in love with her and not wanting to lose the relationship. It has a different feel to it."

Theo rubbed his palms together then laid his hands on the keys. He played the flowing melody and sang, *"What I'm feelin' for you I just can't hide. I'm standing here for as long as it takes…for a chance at something real…my love."* He delivered the song with a raw believability that Gable not only heard but felt. He sounded like a man fighting for a relationship.

Theo stopped singing and playing, and a group of employees who'd been listening to them while cleaning the bar whistled and applauded.

"Rusty pipes?" Gable huffed a breath. "Are you kidding me? This is your song. It was meant for you."

"No. It's yours. You wrote it. Now you just need to own it in here." Theo thumped himself in the middle of his chest. "Just remember a time when you found love and didn't want to lose it. For me, that's Mel. My life wouldn't be the same without her."

From the way Theo nailed the song, he clearly cared about his wife, but Gable couldn't resist asking, "What about your love for music? We used to talk about cutting albums, being headliners, winning awards." He glanced around the bar. "Is working here enough for you?"

"Absolutely. Would I jump at the chance of being a headliner at Coachella? Of course I would, but for me, being famous isn't what it's all about." Theo softly played the chords of Gable's song. "I have my wife and son, a good job that allows me to support my family, and now I have this place where I can connect and share my music with an audience a few nights a week. Thanks to you, I have the best of all worlds."

In the wee hours of the morning, as Gable lay in bed back at his hotel room, Theo's suggestions for all of his songs were on his mind. They'd stayed at Lou's until after midnight and then talked about music and life at the restaurant for a few more hours. Now that his creative block was resolved, he couldn't wait to get back home and perfect the song that Theo had sung so well. The song now had a title. "Chances."

He'd written "Chances" months ago after his two-year, on-again, off-again relationship with his girlfriend, Lyla, had ended. She'd wanted to take their relationship to the next level, and he'd been honest with her. He cared about her, but building his music career was his priority. She hadn't wanted to settle for anything less than a real commitment, and he couldn't blame her.

Sure, he'd been disappointed about Lyla breaking up with him, but writing "Chances" hadn't come from a place of yearning for "something real." After witnessing Theo give up music to keep his relationship, he didn't want to risk falling in love and having to face that same choice down the line. Also angsty relationship ballads resonated with people. The inspiration for the song was purely about gaining attention and popularity with an audience, but was it a mistake for him to include the ballad on the audition recording? He'd never experienced true love in a romantic relationship. Could he pull off singing "Chances" as well as Theo had at the bar?

As Gable closed his eyes, a vision of Theo's scribbled recommendations drifted through his thoughts. He'd meant to grab the napkins before they'd left the bar. Maybe Theo still had them and could send pictures of the ideas he'd written down for his songs, especially about "Chances." Another image came into his mind. At the restaurant, Theo had looked a little wiped out. Working a double shift had taken a toll on him—that's what Theo had said and had reassured him everything was good. After a cup of coffee, he had been more alert. Hopefully, Theo was at home getting some sleep.

Later that morning, still groggy after the equivalent of a catnap, Gable hurried through the hotel lobby carrying his bag and the case with his guitar to catch the courtesy van to the airport. Thankfully, his early flight home to Atlanta was a short one, and he had the next two days off from his remote job as a loan approval specialist. The promise of crawling into his own bed in a few hours made passing the coffee bar on the way out a little less painful.

Outside, just past the glass doors, his phone rang. It was Keith. His talent manager lived on the West Coast. He never reached out this early. Was he calling him about an audition?

Gable dropped his bag on the sidewalk. As he stared at his phone in his hand, his heart rate ticked up. This could be the call he'd been waiting for…the one that would change his life and lead to an even better future.

Chapter Three

Six months later in Maryland

Gable pressed his foot on the accelerator, and the engine of his black crew-cab truck rumbled as it ate up the miles. The afternoon sun shining over homes and lush pastures bordering the two-lane country road warmed his face. A breeze coming through the partially opened window held the smells of rich earth, traces of livestock and leafy green trees signaling the firm arrival of spring and the promise of a warm summer ahead.

Going to the middle of nowhere right now is a mistake...

That's how Keith had described this sudden move to Maryland, but Gable disagreed. A few weeks ago one sleepless night, he'd stumbled across an online listing for a house in the small town where he'd experienced one of the best summers of his life with his great-uncle Wes Brunson. It had felt like a sign and a way forward...if that possibility even existed for him. What he faced now hadn't been the future he'd envisioned, especially after visiting Theo that night at Lou's. Prioritizing his music career over everything else had been a costly mistake.

Recollections shadowed by sadness and guilt emerged in Gable's mind. If only he could go back six months in time and change what happened. But he couldn't. Gripping the steering wheel, he shoved the regretful memories back into the mental box he'd reserved for them. Now, instead of popularity, he just wanted to find peace and forgiveness and acceptance that Theo was no longer in his life. A noisy harrumph pulled his attention.

Peggy, a local real estate agent, sat in the front passenger seat. She'd twisted her ankle and couldn't drive. He was taking them to the house he'd spotted online. He planned on renting it with an option to buy.

The older woman with frosted blond hair and a fair, age-defying complexion peered out the window over her dark sunglasses. "Well, look who's back."

Gable glanced to where she stared and then did a double-take.

A brown-skinned woman carrying a blue backpack walked in a field of wildflowers. Her yellow dress billowed and clung to her lithe frame. The same breeze ruffled her dark curls, flattening some of them to her cheek while the rest waved in the wind. He couldn't see her face, but he imagined she had a smile and a sparkle in her eyes.

Sun angel... An improvised melody teased in his throat, and he almost hummed it aloud. The spark of creativity caught him by surprise. What was that about? He hadn't felt the desire to sing in months. Goose bumps rose on his arms below the pushed-up sleeves of his gray pullover shirt. His jeans-clad legs tensed and he barely resisted stomping on the brake.

"Who's that?" he asked.

"Your neighbor." Peggy straightened the jacket of her bright pink suit and faced forward. "Or at least her aunt and sister, Ivy and Harper Bishop, will be. They run Bishop

Honey Bee Farm. They're good people—been here for years."

"And the woman in the field?"

"Brooke? She comes to town once a year for a few weeks to help out as beekeeper. She's a strange one. Going from place to place…" Peggy launched into details about Brooke. Most of which sounded like pure speculation.

Gable glanced in the side mirror. The field of flowers along with Brooke the Lost Wanderer—Peggy's description, not his—grew smaller in the distance. The way she held herself, graceful and confident, she didn't look like a misguided soul to him. What was that saying he'd spotted on a bumper sticker while driving from Atlanta three days ago? All who wander are not lost?

A short time later, he parked in the wide driveway of a two-story light brick home. Far from the road, hidden behind tall elms and maples, it was in harmony with its surroundings.

He got out of the truck, and a sense of hopefulness waved over him as his boots settled on the ground. His deceased great-uncle Wes's property had been sold years ago and wasn't available to him, but standing there, he felt hints of the peace he'd experienced while visiting Wes's farm as a teen that summer.

"When did the owners move out?" he asked.

Hobbling with a cane, Peggy joined him at the front of the truck. "About two months ago. The Rosses, the couple that lived here, worked remotely, but the wife's company needed her back in New York. I think her husband was sad to go, but she couldn't wait to leave." As Peggy removed a set of keys from her leather portfolio, she shook her head. "Honestly, when I sold them the house, I had doubts about them staying here for long. Too many people move here expecting to live some idyllic small-town dream. It's great until they can't DoorDash a delivery from their favorite restaurant. But I suspect that won't be a problem for you?"

"Not at all. I already know what to expect." Gable hesitated. He hadn't told the real estate agent he'd been to the area before.

Sixteen years ago, when he'd turned into a rebellious teen after his parents' divorce, his mom had sent him to Wes. She'd hoped her uncle, who'd been the local farrier in Bolan, would be able to turn him around.

Gable caught the gleam of curiosity in Peggy's eyes as she waited for him to say more. Based on how she'd gossiped about Brooke, she wouldn't hesitate in adding his details to the local rumor mill. It was best to keep his business to himself for now. No one would connect him to the skinny fifteen-year-old who'd visited Wes, and his great-uncle had called him by his middle name, Dell.

Ignoring her invitation to elaborate, he asked, "Did the owners decide to lease the house because they're not in agreement about selling it?"

"No, not at all." She led the way up the stone path bisecting the front lawn and leading to the entrance. "Leasing the property for income now with the strong possibility of you buying them out in a month or two really appealed to them." Smiling brightly, she opened the door. "Welcome to your new home."

Gable stepped across the threshold and drank in the view of the wood-floored living room with a stone fireplace and dual staircase leading to the upstairs bedrooms. The panoramic view on the other side of the living room was nothing short of amazing.

As he walked to the floor-to-ceiling sliding door taking up most of the wall in front of him, Peggy went to the high marble counter to the left. Behind the counter with six high-back stools was a galley-style kitchen that could also double as a bar. From what he'd read in the online listing, it had a sink, small refrigerators for wine and food and a pass-through oven. The two archways bordering the sides of the space led to the main kitchen and dining room.

But the unique kitchen setup didn't compare to the view. As he took in the pasture and open fields, a vision of Wes, a tall thin man with a bald head and a stoic expression, drifted into Gable's mind.

As the older man had provided instructions on caring for the alfalfa crops, operating farm equipment and tending the horses, he'd never raised his voice. Even when Gable had tested his patience, Wes's temperament had remained like a placid, fathomless lake. The wealth of life knowledge the older man had possessed had run just as deep.

He'd never made it back to Wes's farm after that summer. They'd talked on the phone a couple of times after he'd left, but any major news about changes in their lives had been relayed by Gable's mom.

Wes had been thrilled to hear about him graduating high school and being accepted to college. Gable had been equally happy about his great-uncle, who'd lost his wife in his early thirties, finding love again and remarrying. Wes and his second wife had spent years together on the farm before relocating to California to be closer to her family. He'd heard from his mom that Wes had died a little over two years ago and his wife had passed soon after. He should have made time to see his great-uncle. Wes had done so much for him. That was another regret he couldn't undo.

As the image of his great-uncle faded from his mind, Gable released a long exhale. Wes had helped him gain a new perspective about his place in the world and set him on a different path that included music. When he'd returned to Atlanta, he'd joined a music club at school and learned to play guitar. Now he needed to rediscover his purpose again but without music as a part of it. Fame and fortune were no longer goals in his life because of Theo. After the pain he'd helped cause, he didn't deserve those dreams.

He faced Peggy. "You said the owners are fine with me making some improvements?"

"Absolutely." The real estate agent joined him by the sliding door. "Like the half-built gazebo out there to the left of the field. They won't object to you finishing that or making any other helpful additions or changes. All they ask is that you go over the plans with them first. Other than that, they want you to view this place as home. Speaking of home, you mentioned wanting to get your horse settled." She pointed to the right. "That dirt road provides access to the barn in the east pasture. I had the paddock mowed and the stalls cleaned."

His dappled gray, Pepper, was boarded at Tillbridge Horse Stable and Guesthouse, the establishment where he'd also been staying since he'd arrived two days ago. A stable hand was coming with his horse that afternoon. Maybe he would take Pepper out for a ride. It would be a good way to check out the property.

In the distance, a red vehicle parked near where the dirt road intersected with a paved one caught his eye. "Are those roads open to the public?"

"The dirt road is, but it dead-ends at this property. None of the locals use it. If anyone comes that way and you're not expecting them, they're lost. The paved road is private. It belongs to the Bishops, but they usually leave it open to the public. But don't worry. This house is far enough away, you won't hear the cars and no one will bother you, and that includes the bees." Peggy gave him a smile. "So what do you think? Would you like to see the rest of the house?"

Admittedly, he'd experienced some apprehension over renting the property sight unseen, but now, those traces of doubt disappeared. That was a good thing since he'd pretty much committed to the move. He'd cashed in some of his investments and emptied out most of his savings to pay for expenses while taking an extended break from his job. Pepper was on the way, and the moving company was delivering his furniture there in a few days. The house, the surrounding land, his neighbors—they were all better than he'd expected.

Gable's gaze wandered to Bishop Honey Bee Farm. Brooke was far in the distance still walking through the field, but he could see her clearly in his mind. The way she'd emanated confidence, beauty and grace would remain firmly planted in his memory. Surely, he'd meet her while she was in town. The possibility raised something he hadn't experienced in a while—anticipation. As he thought more about the possibility of meeting Brooke, strangely some of the invisible weight he'd been carrying for months lifted from his shoulders.

He looked to Peggy. "I don't need to see anything else. Let's review the leasing agreement. I'm ready to sign."

Brooke hitched the strap of her backpack higher on her shoulder and paused at the edge of the wildflower field. A gravel path led to her family's home yards away, a lemon-yellow house with white trim. In the distance to the right sat the apiary. On the left, one of the farm's white trucks was parked near greenhouses.

Aside from honey production, Bishop Honey Bee Farm grew high-quality blooms that were sold to local florists.

Ivy had added flower farming shortly after she'd taken over running the operation twelve years ago after Brooke and Harper's parents, Lexy and Dion Bishop, died in a car accident.

At the time of the tragic, life-altering incident, Ivy had been a single woman in her twenties. Setting aside her own grief over losing her sister and brother-in-law, she'd focused on her nieces, Brooke and Harper. Within days of the funeral, she'd moved from New York and accepted the responsibility of becoming their guardian as well as running the farm. Her keen business sense turned Bishop Honey Bee Farm into a profitable concern. These days, although Harper also had beekeeping experience, Aunt Ivy mainly focused on the bees while Harper handled the flower farming and most of the general operations.

As Brooke contemplated seeing her family after a year of being away from them, happiness warred with a feeling of dread. Instead of walking to the house, she turned toward the place that had always given her a sense of comfort. The apiary.

The bee hives—square, approximately waist-high, light-colored wood boxes—dotted the wide grassy field like tiny castles. Deep-body brood boxes, where the larvae of bees-to-come were sheltered and cared for by worker bees, were stacked near the bottom of every hive on a stand.

The hives with additional shallower boxes, or honey supers, on top of the brood boxes meant the bees were already storing precious nectar in the frames of wax comb inside of them. Over time, the nectar would ripen into honey. From the number of hives with their first supers, the farm could have its first taste of liquid gold in a couple of months.

Standing near the apiary, Brooke closed her eyes. The sound of gently rustling leaves joined the faint, low hum of the bees. Listening to one of nature's most soothing melodies diminished some of her unease. But she couldn't stay there forever. Aunt Ivy and Harper were expecting her, and she needed to fix the tire on her Jeep. She'd gotten a flat down the road from the farm. Taking care of it had been the plan, but her car jack was missing, and she had a pretty good idea where it was—somewhere in Florida.

Months ago in Jupiter Beach, Nellie had borrowed her Jeep to help out a friend stranded on the interstate. She'd assumed Nellie had put everything back where it belonged. Since then, she'd been to South Carolina, Georgia and back to Florida on job assignments. What if she'd gotten the flat miles away instead of close to home? Turning toward the house, exasperation made Brooke shake her head. As much as she liked Nellie, she had more than a few words for her friend about misplacing the jack when she called her.

Moments later, Brooke arrived at the front of the house. As she approached the steps to the wraparound porch, the front door opened.

Aunt Ivy, comfortable looking in a blue chambray shirt and jeans, rushed out. "You're here!" As she pulled Brooke into a hug, happiness glowed in her sepia-brown cheeks. "Why are you standing on the porch? Where are your bags?"

"I haven't been here very long. I just got to the house." Brooke sunk into her aunt's loving embrace. "Most of what I need is in my backpack."

Standing in the threshold, Harper released a derisive snort. Dressed similarly to Ivy, her sister's dark hazelnut-colored curls were neatly secured in a ponytail. "Don't you mean *everything* you own is in your backpack?"

Meeting her sister's judgmental coppery-brown gaze,

Brooke replied. "No. Not everything. Just most of what I own. I don't carry around unnecessary baggage."

"Of course you don't. That would be—"

Ivy interrupted. "Something we don't need to get into right now." Sighing, she looked between the sisters. "You two sound like you did when you were teenagers. Could you at least say hello and hug before you pick each other apart?"

She started it. As Ivy walked into the house, Brooke almost said what she was thinking aloud. But then she really would sound like a teen instead of a grown woman who didn't need to defend her choices to her baby sister. She actually did have a duffel with more clothes in the Jeep, but Harper's attitude had prompted her response.

Don't let Harper get under your skin. Brooke silently repeated the promise she'd made to herself on the drive up. During her brief visit home, she would stay in her lane away from Harper, focused blissfully on the solitary task of taking care of the bees, and her upcoming house-sitting assignment in the Hollywood Hills.

The large house in California had an infinity pool and a hot tub overlooking a spectacular view of the Los Angeles skyline. Permission to use them was a bonus that came with the contract. There was also a chance she might house-sit in Spain. A family living in Valencia was considering hiring her as a house sitter to look after their apartment along with their two cats for a month. If it happened, this would be her first house-sitting assignment abroad.

Thinking of her travels in five weeks, Brooke envisioned herself poolside enjoying a cocktail. Her happy smile was genuine as she exchanged a "hey" and a stiff one-armed hug with her sister.

She caught a glimpse of their aunt observing them from the foyer.

A sad worried expression came over Aunt Ivy's face, but it quickly transformed into a pleased look. "That's better. I need to talk to both of you. Meet me in the kitchen." Ivy breezed into the beige-tiled living room with light wood furnishings. As she walked past the salmon-colored sectional, she snagged a large white envelope from the coffee table then veered into the side archway.

Remembering the expression on Ivy's face just moments earlier, Brooke asked, "Is she okay? She looks a little stressed out."

Harper shrugged off the question. "She's fine. We've been busy, and she's been deep into organizing the farm's promotion for National Honey Month. She's probably just looking forward to taking time off."

Brooke dropped her pack by the door and took off her boots. Ivy normally left for vacation two or three days after she arrived. What could be so important that they had to meet as soon as she walked in the door?

In the kitchen, stainless steel appliances gleamed in the natural light and so did the white quartz countertops with vintage canisters that coordinated with the deep green cabinetry. Jars of wildflowers adorned the sills of the windows overlooking the side lawn. Through the window, the white cottage where the farm's offices and retail space were located was visible yards away.

Ivy waited at the end of the long kitchen table drinking a mug of coffee. Harper refilled her mug from the maker on the counter then sat to the right of their aunt.

After pouring herself a cup as well, Brooke settled in the seat across from Harper. During the pause, she took a reverent sip from her mug. The smell of dark roast coffee wafting in the air blended pleasantly with the earthy-sweet scent of the beeswax candle centerpiece on the table.

Harper peered at her phone. "I can't stay long. The business council meeting at town hall starts at two o'clock."

"You'll make it." Ivy glanced at the envelope on the table next to her arm and released a deep breath. "The easiest way to do this is to just say it. I won't be gone for just three weeks."

Concerned about her aunt's change in plans, Brooke asked, "When will you be back?"

"Oh, come on." Harper slightly rolled her eyes. "Is it really that big of a deal for you? I'm sure your next big excursion can wait."

Not getting under my skin... Brooke took a beat before she responded. "By big excursion, if you mean my next work assignment, I do have to be there by a certain time." She looked to Ivy. "How much longer should I plan to stay? A week? Ten days?"

"It won't be longer than a month," Harper interjected. She looked to Ivy as well. "You've already blocked off time on your calendar to meet with our restaurant collaborators in four weeks to discuss events for the honey promotion, or are you pushing the meetings further out?"

Once again, Ivy's gaze darted to the envelope next to her arm.

Brooke could only guess what was inside of it. Maybe the details for the honey celebration that took place every September?

Ivy cupped her mug a little tighter on the table. "Actually, I've bumped them up a few weeks. Brooke, you're meeting with Rina Tillbridge at Brewed Haven Café tomorrow morning."

Brooke knew Rina well. She was the owner of the café, and also the co-owner of Tillbridge Horse Stable and Guesthouse along with her sister Zurie and her cousin Tristan.

But Brooke had never attended meetings for her aunt in the past. Surprise kicked her voice up a notch. "I am?"

"Yes, you are." Firmness anchored Ivy's tone. "The plan for National Honey Month is in a file in the farm's cloud drive along with the calendar showing all of the meetings I've scheduled. You should look at both of them tonight. And the two of you will be taking over other responsibilities as well. I'm not coming back from my vacation. I'm leaving for good." She slid the white envelope forward. "As of today, I no longer have a stake in Bishop Honey Bee Farm. The two of you own it now, fifty-fifty."

Chapter Four

Speechless, Brooke looked to Harper. From her sister's alarmed expression, she honestly had no idea this announcement was coming. But how? Harper and Aunt Ivy worked so closely together. When it came to running the farm, they practically read each other's minds.

Swallowing hard, Brooke set her own shock aside. "This is sudden. Can we talk about it?"

"She's right," Harper exclaimed. "We have to discuss this. I need you. You're our head beekeeper."

"No, there's nothing to talk about. It's time." Love and determination were in Ivy's tone. She reached out and took hold of one of Brooke's and one of Harper's hands. "You really don't need me anymore. I was just supposed to keep things going until the two of you could take charge. That was the plan all along. You're ready." Looking between her nieces, she gave their hands a squeeze. "Now it's up to you to decide the farm's future and for me to decide what I want for mine."

The beep of a car horn sounded from the front of the house.

Ivy let go of their hands and stood. "My ride is here. I have to get to the airport. I don't want to miss my flight."

Their aunt retrieved a suitcase from the corner that

Brooke, as well as Harper, based on her similar stunned reaction, hadn't noticed was there.

Wheeling it through the kitchen, their aunt added, "Oh, and any information you can't find in the cloud drive is on my laptop on my desk. All of the files are clearly marked. I'm sure you'll be fine, but if something does come up, call and leave a message on my phone. But it might take a while for me to respond. I'm going on back-to-back cruises."

"No, but wait…" Harper jumped to her feet. She looked to Brooke for support as Ivy kept walking.

But as much as Brooke wanted to beg their aunt to stay, she couldn't. Just like she'd left home and discovered a life beyond the farm, didn't Aunt Ivy deserve that same opportunity?

Standing on the porch, Ivy gave them both brief hugs and kisses on the cheek.

There were so many things Brooke wanted to ask, but their aunt seemed in a hurry to leave.

Brooke settled on a few questions. "When you get back from your cruises, where will you go? Are you moving back to New York?"

"I'm not sure yet. I'll be staying with a friend until I decide. I'll send you the address. As soon as I find a place of my own, I'll arrange for my car and the rest of my things to be delivered." Ivy walked down the steps of the porch. After giving her suitcase to the driver from the car service, she paused before getting into the back seat of the sedan. Determination slipped from her face like a mask and only love remained. She gave them a tremulous teary smile. "You'll be fine. You know what to do. Just follow your instincts." Her gaze connected with Brooke's for a moment longer then moved away. She blew them a kiss. "Love you both."

"Love you more." At a loss of what else to say, Brooke

waved goodbye and blinked back her own tears. Aunt Ivy wasn't coming back? Was this actually happening?

The moment felt surreal as the sedan drove off with Ivy. Just a short time ago, her aunt had welcomed her home almost in the very spot where Brooke stood on the porch, and now she was gone, just like that. Her reasoning for giving up her partnership in the farm made sense, but why had she chosen to do it now and without warning? Maybe she knew they would try to convince her not to leave and she'd been afraid of giving in to them? Especially to Harper. Although Brooke had always had a share of the farm, Aunt Ivy and Harper had worked together as the active partners. Or at least they had been.

Standing next to her, Harper remained silent. The forlorn expression on her face reminded Brooke of when they'd suddenly lost their parents. Overnight, Harper had transformed from a pain in the butt, know-it-all thirteen-year-old into a heartbroken child wrapped in a fragile shell of uncertainty.

Recalling how they'd leaned on each other to get through the tragic loss, Brooke reached out to put an arm around her sister's shoulders.

Harper spun away from her and stomped into the house.

Sighing heavily, Brooke lowered her arm. Of course her sister didn't want her comfort. As an adult, Harper was still a know-it-all, and an even bigger pain in the butt, but she wasn't that scared teen anymore who'd needed her support.

Taking a moment to collect herself, Brooke went inside, dreading the discussion to come. She and Harper running the bee farm? They could barely hold a civil conversation. How were they supposed to make important decisions together? What had made Aunt Ivy think that leaving them in charge of the farm could ever work?

In the kitchen, her sister collected the mugs from the table and took them to the sink. With her back turned to Brooke, she washed the dishes and said, "I'll brief you when I get back from the business council meeting this evening. That should give you enough time to review all of Aunt Ivy's notes. As far as general operations, you should leave that to me. Now that you're the permanent beekeeper…"

Permanent beekeeper? Panic surged through Brooke and she broke out in a light sweat. It made sense to Harper that she would step into that role, but, no, she had plans. In a few weeks she would be house-sitting in the Hollywood Hills, lounging poolside, drinking cocktails. And she might have a chance to travel to Spain and explore Europe. She had a life. She wasn't giving up what she enjoyed to be stuck there running the farm with Harper.

As her sister kept talking, Brooke felt as if she was being pulled under by a tidal wave. "No, Harper, hold on."

"I know what you're thinking," Harper said, rinsing dishes and putting them on a drying pad on the counter. "Why am I putting myself in charge? Before you jump to conclusions, hear me out. We have a new groundskeeper and greenhouse supervisor, as well as new employees. Aunt Ivy has probably mentioned in her notes how she'd planned on cross-training some of them to help with processing the honey harvest.

"You'll have to make that choice now, and I really think you should take some time to observe and get to know the staff before you do. And you'll have a lot on your hands between handling the apiary and organizing the activities for National Honey Month. Why stress yourself out by stepping into a management role for the entire farm right away? I can do it until you're up to speed."

"I can't."

"Of course you can. You're a born beekeeper, just like Mom was."

My little bee charmer... As her mother's words reverberated in her mind, Brooke's heart beat a little harder in her chest. Just like Harper was no longer a teenager, she wasn't that little girl anymore, the one who'd wanted to be like her mom and chased bees. "Harper, you don't understand."

"I do understand. You're nervous about taking over responsibility for the hives."

"No, I know I can handle taking care of the hives. I don't want to be the new beekeeper." *You know what to do*... Her aunt's parting words brought sudden clarity. "I want out. I'm selling my stake in the farm."

"Selling?" Harper faced Brooke. "You're not serious."

"I am. I don't want to be here."

Disbelief filled her sister's expression. "Just like that, you're going to walk away from everything that matters?"

As usual, Harper wasn't hearing what she was saying to her, just her own point of view. Brooke reined in frustration. "Look, it's simple. You want to stay here, and I don't, so I'll sell you my share of the farm. You'll own this place free and clear, and you can run it any way you want. We'll both be happy."

"No." Her sister shook her head and crossed her arms over her chest. "I'm not buying you out. It's time for you to stop playing around and step up to take responsibility for *our* home. Didn't you hear what Ivy said? *We're* supposed to run this farm, not just me on my own. She made sacrifices and put her life on hold managing the business so we could have it. And what about our parents? The two of us running it now would be what they wanted. It's what they dreamed of when they bought this place. Bishop Honey Bee Farm is our family legacy."

"Legacy?" Scorn born from sorrow pushed a bitter laugh out of Brooke. Being given a so-called legacy but not having their parents wasn't the trade-off she would have chosen. She hadn't had a choice about what happened to her life twelve years ago, but she did now. "Aunt Ivy didn't say anything about this being our legacy. She said it was our turn to decide the farm's future, and I know that future doesn't include me. And I'm tired of you trying to make me feel like it should. My life isn't here, and it hasn't been for a long time."

"Your life?" Harper scoffed. "Stop trying to spin this situation like you're being inconvenienced or misunderstood. All these years, Ivy said I was being hard on you for not coming back home, but I was right. It's not that you just don't want to be responsible for anything. You're selfish and afraid to commit to real life. You want everything and everyone to work around what you want. You don't care about anyone else, and you definitely don't care about the bees."

A spark of irritation made Brooke cock her head to the side. "Excuse me?" Had Harper actually said she didn't care about the bees?

Growing up, who'd stuck by their mother's side learning about how to take care of the hives? Who'd spent hours in the extraction room helping to bottle the honey that had been harvested? Who'd traveled with their mom to farmers' markets and festivals to sell the honey and helped deliver it to nearby stores? *She'd* done all of that, not Harper. In fact, Harper had pouted so much over taking care of the bees, their parents had stopped expecting her to work in the apiary. And what about after the accident? Who'd followed the tradition of telling the bees about the loss of their beekeeper?

The resurging memory of going to the apiary and whispering the news to the bees about their mom's death released echoes of heartbreak. Returning to work in the apiary without her mom had been one of the hardest things she'd ever done, but even then, she'd never abandoned the hives. Once she'd left for college, one of the main reasons she'd returned to the farm was to help Aunt Ivy with the bees. Swallowing against the rising lump of sadness in her throat, Brooke turned to walk out.

"Where are you going?" Harper demanded. "We're not done discussing this." As Brooke kept walking, her sister huffed, "I swear, you're so predictable. Scampering away, as usual, when you can't handle reality."

The space between Brooke's shoulder blades tightened and she paused. It took everything she had not to turn around and deliver her own verbal jab about who wasn't facing reality. Harper had tied herself to the farm and hidden from what existed beyond it. She was the one who was afraid to commit to real life. But there was no point in sparring with her. It would only lead to them saying things they'd both regret.

Without turning around, Brooke responded, "Buy me out or don't. It's up to you. If you won't, I'll find someone who will."

In the foyer, she stuffed her feet into her boots. After snagging her car keys and a small cross-body bag with her phone from her backpack, she left. At the four-bay garage at the side of the house, she punched in the code to open the doors.

Harper's beige two-door compact and Ivy's blue one occupied the first two bays. A white crew-cab truck with the farm's logo on the doors—Bishop Honey Bee Farm written in script cleverly intertwined with bees—sat in the next one. The fourth bay for the other truck was empty. The new groundskeeper or greenhouse supervisor Harper had just mentioned were probably using it at the greenhouse.

She hopped into the available truck. As she sped down the driveway along the side of the house, she spotted Harper walking out the front door.

Brooke fumed. Scamper? Seriously? She'd never scampered anywhere, ever. Aunt Ivy had left them the farm and now they had decisions to make. Hers was to leave. It was as simple as that. Harper needed to come down from the mountain of sanctimony she'd planted herself on and deal with it. She was the one who was being selfish by trying to lay a guilt trip on her about wanting to live her own life instead of staying.

And why had Aunt Ivy just dropped this on them like this? Yes, she'd done her part, and she'd placed the burden of the farm where it now belonged—on Brooke's and Harper's shoulders—but did their aunt honestly believe they could figure this situation out on their own? Maybe she didn't. She must have realized selling was an option. Doubt needled Brooke's mind. Still, after all Aunt Ivy had done for the farm, would she be disappointed in her for not staying to help run it?

A heavy mix of uncertainty over Ivy's opinion along with frustration with her sister made Brooke want to press her foot on the gas and drive straight out of town. Instead, at the farm's open front gates, she made a left and then another one onto the paved road separating the farm from their neighbor's property. Farther down, she parked behind her red Jeep positioned on the shoulder near where the paved and dirt roads intersected.

The overcast sky miles away drew her attention.

She should have the tire changed long before those clouds rolled her way. Unfortunately, she would have to leave the Jeep there, drive the truck back home, then walk back for her vehicle. She still might get caught in the rain. Her shoulders dropped with a sigh. She really should have changed into a T-shirt and jeans for this, but there wasn't time.

Brooke grabbed her earbuds and phone from her bag. While she worked, she needed a break from thinking about Aunt Ivy leaving and Harper's accusations. After choosing a playlist Nellie had shared with her via a streaming app, she got out.

Just like her choices in movies, Nellie's taste in music veered toward eclectic, but unlike her film picks, her song recommendations were always on point. The list Brooke listened to now was an upbeat mix of hip-hop, R & B and country songs, many of which were from nonmainstream artists she wasn't familiar with, and she was loving the vibe. She'd gotten hooked on finding up-and-coming artists after attending a music festival in Texas a couple of years ago.

At the back of the vehicle, two metal storage bins were permanently attached to opposite sides of the truck bed. She opened one of them. It contained a smoker and pellets and other clean beekeeper's tools in a protective bag. Also folded neatly next to the bag was something that would really come in handy now. A bee suit. The white canvas, jumper-style garment, minus the gloves and the netted hood, was the perfect way to protect her clothing while she changed the tire.

Humming along to the music, she stepped into the bee suit, stuffed the skirt of the dress inside of it, then zipped and fastened it closed. It was a bulky fit around the middle and the tops of her hips, but she could still move around to get the job done.

The main thing she needed was in the bin on the other

side of the truck bed. The roadside kit containing a jack. As she unfastened the first latch on the second storage bin, she glanced at the neighbor's property. A horse trailer sat next to the barn.

She'd met the Rosses last spring, shortly after they'd moved in. The young couple could have stood in as the definition of opposites attract. While the husband had looked forward to living the simple life, his wife's main interest had been finding a scented air freshener strong enough to mask the "green" smell of the grass and trees.

During a phone conversation a few months ago, Aunt Ivy had mentioned the Rosses and how it seemed like they were finally settling in. She hadn't said anything about them buying a horse. That was a big step, and a sign they were adapting to living in the area. Good for them. The town gossips hadn't expected them to last a year living in a small town.

What a strange joke. The Rosses were still there…and Aunt Ivy was the one who'd left. In some ways it felt like her parents leaving all over again.

Pushing aside a sinking feeling of loss, Brooke turned her attention back to opening the bin. The first latch had unfastened easily but the second wouldn't budge. She applied more force.

Suddenly, the lid popped open like an exploding gift box. But instead of something fun like confetti, colorful paper butterflies or candy bursting out of it, empty plastic shopping bags took flight in a gust of wind.

Shit! Brooke sprang into action, snatching bags out of the air from near the fence surrounding the neighbor's field, and chased others down the road. Not wanting to risk losing them again, she stuffed them in her hip pocket.

One of the bags tumbled toward the intersection.

She almost caught it, but a strong breeze slipped the bag from her grasp and sent it down the dirt road. Movement caught her eye and she glanced up.

A few yards away, a man wearing a backward dark ball cap, a gray pullover and jeans rode a dapple-gray horse.

The plastic bag danced toward them in the wind seemingly to the beat of the song playing in her ears.

Spooked by the tumbling bag, the horse snorted loudly, raising its head as it shuffled sideways.

"Easy, boy." Expertly using the reins, the rider circled the dapple-gray horse away from the scary object, and the horse settled down.

A breath whooshed out of Brooke. *Whew!* That could have been ugly. Suddenly, another plastic bag whipped across the dirt road, and trepidation leaped inside of her as it jumped and twirled around the man and his horse.

Spotting the new threat, the horse whinnied and reared up, and its rider plummeted to the ground.

As the startled equine galloped in the opposite direction, Brooke hurried over to the guy and knelt beside him.

His ball cap sat askew, partially revealing his close-cropped black hair. His eyes were closed. His face, a combination of strong lines and angles, was accentuated by deep-brown skin and a shadow of dark hair on his cheeks and jawline.

She rested her hand on his chest. Relief flowed through her to feel its steady rise and fall beneath her palm.

As he moved his legs, he released a low groan.

"Take it slow," she cautioned. "Don't rush to get up."

In response, his lids partially opened, exposing hints of his brown eyes. Suddenly, he didn't look like a guy who'd just fallen from his horse. He transformed into a drop-dead gorgeous man who looked like he'd just awakened after spending a pleasurable night tangling in the sheets.

As her imagination grew a little more vivid, the unsteady thump of her heart against her rib cage snapped her back to reality. What was wrong with her? She needed to help the poor guy, not fantasize about him.

As his eyes started to close, she gave him a small shake. "No, don't do that. Open your eyes. Hey, can you hear me?"

He rasped out, "I hear you just fine, Sun Angel."

Sun angel? The guy was seeing celestial beings? That wasn't good. She shook him a little harder. "Don't go anywhere. Stay with me."

Chapter Five

Stay with her? Gable wanted to tell her he wasn't going anywhere at the moment. He was still trying to recover the breath that had been knocked out of him. *Damn.* He'd tried to make an emergency dismount but didn't make it out of the saddle in time.

"Please—" she gripped his hand "—just try to open your eyes again."

The urgency in her tone prompted him to do as she asked. He squinted against the sun escaping through the clouds. As she leaned in closer, blocking some of the light, the bright rays threaded through her curls like a halo. *Brooke the Sun Angel.* She was even prettier than he'd imagined. Her features, an alluring combination of distinct yet delicate, were brought out by her chestnut-colored eyes and her full shell-pink lips.

The melody that had come to him in the truck when he'd first spotted her played through his mind, and Gable gave himself a mental shake. He needed to forget about that song. He needed to find his horse. Gable moved to sit up. Pain fired through his left arm and shoulder, and he muttered a curse.

"How badly are you injured?" Her hand moved to his

chest near his unhurt shoulder. He lay there a bit longer, soaking in her gentle touch.

He'd landed mostly on his left side. Apart from the ache in his hip and his throbbing arm and shoulder, the only thing that hurt worse was his pride. He shouldn't have allowed himself to get bucked out of the saddle.

"I'm good." Protecting his left arm, Gable came to his feet, and she rose with him. He adjusted his ball cap. "I have to find my horse."

"He went that way, near my neighbor's house. The road is a dead end so he can't wander off." She glanced around. "How close are you to where you rode in from?"

"Real close. Just follow my horse. I guess I should be glad he knew the way home."

She gave him a quizzical look. "You live next door? Since when?"

"Since today. I'm renting the house."

"Oh."

The disappointment in her tone struck him like a small blow.

As thunder reverberated in the distance, she glanced at the sky. "We should get to your horse before the rain hits. I'll drive you to him."

"I can walk." Gable took hesitating steps, attempting to ignore the twinge in his hip.

She kept up with him. "You're hurt. You probably shouldn't handle a fidgety horse on your own."

"He's not fidgety. He got spooked."

"That's my fault. I'm sorry. Some plastic bags flew out of my truck. I tried to catch them."

So that's why he'd spotted her running back and forth across the road. But that didn't explain why she was wearing that lumpy-looking jumpsuit. "I'm sure you did. It was an accident, but I can handle my horse."

Brooke stepped in front of him. "I'm not doubting your horse skills. You're probably Nat Love's modern twin, but I feel terrible about what happened to you. I just want to help."

Her sincere expression dissolved most of his irritation, and the comparison of him to one of the famous heroes of the Old West almost made him laugh. Nat would have stayed on his horse. Gable glanced ahead. The barn looked even farther away. The pain in his hip had eased up, but not enough for him to pick up the pace. He needed to reach Pepper well ahead of the storm and get him into the barn. "I'll take that offer of a ride, but will you answer a question?"

"Sure, if I can."

"What's the problem with me being your neighbor? You seem disappointed I've moved in."

"Oh no, it's not you. It's just the couple that used to live in your house relocated here from the city. Some of the people in town made bets against them lasting here a whole year. I'd hoped the couple would prove the gossips wrong." The disappointment on her face was genuine. "I know that probably doesn't make sense to you."

"Actually, it does." After hearing Peggy practically gloat that her prediction of the couple not staying in town long had been right, it was refreshing to hear Brooke had cheered for them instead of hoping they'd fail. He turned and limped toward the paved road.

"Do you need to lean on me?"

Her offer was tempting. She was the perfect height for him to wrap an arm around her shoulders. But if he used her for support, he'd spend more time worrying he'd crush her than trying to get to the truck. "Thanks, but I can make it."

As they walked, a weird crackling sound made him glance between them. The end of a plastic bag peeked out from her side pocket. As he took in her outfit, it came to him. "You're wearing a bee suit."

"That's right." She smiled. "I guess someone told you that you're living next door to a bee farm?"

"Yes, Peggy, the real estate agent who showed me the house, did. So were you on the way to check on the bees when the bags flew out of your truck?"

"No. I was looking for a jack to change the flat on my Jeep."

Plastic bags. Her wearing a bee suit. A flat tire. Her story was growing more interesting by the minute, and it was also a good distraction from his discomfort. "Sounds like you use that suit for a lot of things."

"I do. Chasing plastic bags. Changing flat tires. Catching runaway horses. Helping hurt cowboys. And of course, a little beekeeping, too." A gleam came into her eyes, just as he'd imagined it.

He couldn't help but smile. "Have you come across a lot of hurt cowboys?"

"A few. But none while wearing this bee suit. You're my first."

A chuckle escaped from him. "I'm honored." Strangely, knowing he was her first made his chest puff out a bit.

"So, can I get a name? I'd like to know who I'm saving."

"Pepper."

"Is that your first name or your last?"

She wanted to know about him, not his horse. What was he thinking? "I'm Gable Kincaid. My horse's name is Pepper."

Amusement joined the gleam in her eyes. "Do you always introduce your horse first?"

"Since you mentioned helping me chase him down, I thought you should know his name."

She laughed. "Good answer. I'm Brooke Bishop, by the way."

I know. He almost said it aloud, but if he admitted Peggy had told him her name that might end their conversation or make it awkward. Being from the area, Brooke had to know the woman liked to gossip. She might wonder what the real estate agent had said about her. "Nice to meet you, Brooke."

"Nice?" Smiling, she gave him a knowing look. "You can be honest. If you'd had a choice between a peaceful ride on your horse or the bad luck of meeting me chasing plastic shopping bags in the middle of the road, I doubt you would have chosen me."

"I would have preferred meeting you on my feet instead of lying on the ground, but I'm still glad I got a chance to run into one of my neighbors."

Especially her. Meeting Brooke had been at the top of his must-accomplish list after moving into the house. Maybe falling off Pepper was the opposite of bad luck. Maybe in some strange way it was meant to be. No, believing something like that was as ridiculous as believing in fairy tales. If that's where his mind was going right then, maybe he'd hit his head a little harder than he'd realized.

They passed the Jeep with a flat tire and walked to the front passenger side of the truck parked behind it.

He felt torn about leaving the tire unchanged. "Between the two of us, we might be able to take care of your flat tire before we find Pepper."

"It can wait, and you're hurt." Brooke's demeanor shifted from amused to concerned. "Lean on the truck and take the weight off your leg. I need to move the seat back so you'll have enough room."

Bossy in a good way. He respected that. The self-assurance she radiated made it easy to imagine her managing simple challenges to complex situations with the same calm directness. No fuss involved.

As a musician, he'd run into his share of people on the road who'd thrived on drama. When Lyla had been with him, she'd leaned into the drama, maybe a little too much, viewing the messy antics as entertainment. Sometimes her reaction to it had made him wonder if she was being transparent with him about who she was. If he could trust what was true and what was false in their relationship or any of the ones he'd entered into afterward.

Funny. He'd only known Brooke a hot minute, but he didn't feel like he had to search for a motive underneath her actions. There was something real about her that made it easy for him to sit back, trust her and let her take the lead.

"There you go." Brooke moved out of the way then walked around the front of the vehicle.

A couple twinges hit him as he folded himself into the seat.

She got in on the driver's side then started the engine. "We just might make it to your house before the storm. How cooperative is your horse?"

"He can be ornery at times, and this barn is a new place for him. Hopefully, once we get him into the barn, he'll settle in."

As they drove down the dirt road, he gingerly rolled his shoulder. Nothing felt broken, but it hurt like hell, and the area below his shoulder blade stung. But worries about his injuries disappeared, as Pepper was nowhere in sight. The gate to the road leading to the barn was open. Had the horse gone to the enclosed paddock where the grass was safe to eat or wandered into the pasture? He hadn't gotten a chance to make sure there weren't any harmful weeds in the open field.

They drove through the gate and apprehension left him in an exhale.

Pepper, still wearing the Western-style saddle, grazed in the paddock next to the barn.

Brooke parked the truck and they both got out.

"How can I help?" she asked.

"If you can open the barn door, I'll lead him in." Gable went through the open gate of the fenced-in paddock. "Hey, Pep. You found your way home."

The horse snickered and shook his head, regarding him as if to say, "Took you long enough to show up."

He patted and rubbed the horse, looking him over from head to hooves to tail. Satisfied the gelding wasn't hurt, he clipped on the lead rope and walked him through the open sliding doors leading into the barn.

Brooke stood on the wide, rubber-floored aisle separating the four stalls with Dutch-style doors on one side from the grooming stall and a combination tack room/storage space on the other.

"How's he doing?" she asked.

"A lot better than me." His hip felt almost normal but his arm still hurt.

Brooke slowly approached the horse from the front toward its shoulder and extended her hand. "Hi, Pepper."

To his surprise, the gelding, who was usually standoffish with strangers, gave her hand a nudge. As she crooned to him, he moved closer to her then lowered his head, snorting softly as she petted him.

She smiled. "Someone told me you were ornery, but look at you, being super friendly."

Chuckling, Gable reached into his front jeans pocket and

took out a small plastic bag with alfalfa cubes. He handed a couple to Brooke. "Trust me. He's on his best behavior right now."

"Best behavior. Aww, I don't believe that one bit. You're always this way, aren't you?"

Pep ate up the attention she gave him along with the alfalfa cubes. Gable couldn't blame him. His horse had good taste on both accounts—her and the treats.

Thunder rumbled in the distance.

Pepper whinnied and his ears perked up.

"I think Mother Nature's giving us a nudge." Gable led Pep to the grooming stall, removed the bridle then cross tied him. On the left side of the saddle, he put the stirrup over the horn before loosening the latigo knot holding the cinch.

Brooke went to the right side of the horse. With a casual straightforwardness that obviously came from experience, she rested the stirrup and cinch on top of the saddle. "Do you want to brush him down before putting him in the stall?"

"Yeah, it'll help calm him."

"Where are your tools? I'll grab a brush."

"Thanks. Everything's in the cabinet on the right."

While she went to grab the brush, he took the saddle off Pepper. As soon as he held the full weight of it, fire seared through his left wrist and up his arm. *Damn.* Maybe he had done some damage. Gritting his teeth, he carried the saddle to the tack room and put it on the wooden stand. Massaging his arm, he went back to the grooming stall.

Brooke had already started brushing Pepper, who was more than content. His horse was in good hands.

Gable turned his attention to filling the hay bin and water bucket. "You're good with him," he called out. "Do you own a horse?"

"No, I've never owned one."

"So where did you learn to take care of them?"

"I worked as a stable hand at a ranch in Texas last summer."

The wanderer... Peggy had mentioned Brooke moved from place to place for work. "That sounds interesting. Did you like it?"

"I did. I met a lot of people, and I got in more than a few trail rides with the guests. Mucking stalls wasn't much fun, though, but that part of the job comes with the territory. Hey, I just checked Pepper's hooves. They're good. Is there anything else I should do for him?"

He joined her in the grooming stall. "No, that should do it. Thanks for brushing him down."

"My pleasure. He's a great horse."

"Yeah, he is."

As he went to untie Pepper, Brooke laid her hand on Gable's shoulder. "Oh no, you're bleeding."

"Where?"

"Your back." She stood behind him. "Something cut through your shirt."

As she gently touched a spot near his shoulder blade, a sizzling jolt of awareness ran through him.

She quickly took her hand away. "Sorry, I didn't mean to hurt you."

"You didn't." After taking a breath, he glanced at Brooke from over his shoulder. A small frown marred her brow. Curling up his fingers, he stalled the reflex to smooth it away, not trusting he wouldn't let his hand linger longer than necessary on her smooth skin or his sudden preoccupation with her lips. Were they as soft and lush as they looked? Gable mentally shook off the question. "It just stings a little."

Turning his attention to his horse, he untied Pepper then led him to the stall. Just as he got the horse settled, rain started pattering on the ground.

He joined Brooke by the barn doors. "We finished just in time."

"We might just make it to your house before the sky opens up."

"We can if we hurry. Come on."

Working together, they closed the barn doors. By the time they got into the truck, their clothes were damp. He got a little wetter when he got out again to shut the east pasture gate behind them.

Traveling down the back driveway leading to his house, the earthy fragrance of rain and the musky scent of horse filled the truck. Brooke didn't seem upset by the smell or that she'd gotten caught in the rain helping him. Strangely, in a way, it felt normal sitting there with her. As if they'd just completed the first part of a planned outing, and now they were moving on to the next anticipated activity. But they weren't. He'd taken up enough of her time.

He pointed to the garage on the side of the house. "You can just drop me off there."

"What about your back? Is there someone at home who can take a look at it?"

"No. I'm the only one who lives there."

"That cut is in a difficult spot for you to reach. It needs to be cleaned and bandaged so it doesn't get infected. I don't mind doing it."

"Are you sure? I've already held you up from changing your tire. I don't want to stop you from getting home before the weather gets worse."

"Trust me. You're not." Brooke parked in front of the

garage. She murmured almost imperceptibly. "Home is the last place I want to be right now."

According to Peggy, she'd just gotten into town when they'd spotted her in the flower field. What had gone wrong since then? Her desolate expression almost prompted him to ask, but Gable tamped down his curiosity. It wasn't his business. "In that case, I'll take the help. Thanks."

A smile took over her face. "No problem."

Brooke parked and they got out.

While he used the keypad to open the garage door, she removed a medical kit from the back of the truck.

He had a small first aid kit in his vehicle parked in the garage, and another one somewhere in the house, but they didn't compare to the large bag she carried on her shoulder.

Gable opened the door to a mudroom. He led her down the hall through a space with a washer and dryer then out near the kitchen that adjoined the empty dining room.

Realizing there wasn't a place to sit, he pointed to one of the archways in the wall at the side of the kitchen. "My furniture hasn't arrived yet, but there are stools at the kitchen counter on the other side."

She gave the large fully equipped kitchen with dark marble countertops a questioning glance. As she followed him through the archway, her face lit up with understanding. "Two kitchens. What a bonus."

"It is. This one also doubles as a bar."

"It's perfect for entertaining." She set the medical kit on the counter. "Wow. And so is that view."

He hadn't done a lot of entertaining at his apartment in Atlanta—just had friends over to watch a ball game or play music. Good memories of relaxing with friends marred by the regret of losing one of them surfaced. He replaced them with a vision of sitting near the window of the living room, singing and playing his guitar for Brooke. Still, sadness began to overshadow that image as well, and he swiped it all away. Music wasn't a part of his life anymore. He needed to remember that. His life was now on this farm, building a new future. But just like it had been with his music, he would have to devote his sole attention to the farm to get things up and running the way he wanted. He wouldn't have time for exploring anything like that with Brooke.

"May I use your bathroom?" Brooke asked.

Her question grounded him in the moment. He pointed toward the front of the house. "Down the hall on the right. Second door to the left."

Brooke paused. "I should take this off first." She pulled apart the fasteners and unzipped her jumper-style clothing. As she slipped it from her shoulders, her yellow dress was revealed, explaining the bulkiness underneath the bee suit.

Maneuvering the canvas fabric past her hips, she pushed it down with a shimmy. What was meant to be a practical movement became a hypnotic rhythm accentuating her curves. The skirt of her dress unfurling to almost midway down her satiny smooth-looking legs was the sexiest non-striptease he'd ever witnessed.

Dragging his gaze away, Gable cleared his suddenly parched throat. "Water. I should get some."

She laughed. "With all the rain, haven't you had enough?"

As he looked at her, the image of her taking off the bee suit still burned in his memory. "Not even close."

Chapter Six

Standing at the bathroom sink, Brooke wet her hands with cold water then pressed them to her warm cheeks. That look of longing on Gable's face hadn't been the equivalent of an invitation for the two of them to turn his living room into a clothing-optional space. Still, as the memory of his steady gaze taking her in from head to toe blazed through her mind, heat bloomed over her skin all over again. It felt as if she was standing in a room full of radiators on full blast instead of one with cool beige tiles.

Pain from falling off of his horse, that's what she'd spotted in his eyes. He was suffering from his injuries.

Staring at her reflection in the mirror, she blew out a deep breath and fanned her damp cheeks. *Go out there. Don't think of Gable as an ice cream cone you'd love to lick. Just bandage him up and go home.* That's all she had to do.

Go home. That last ultimatum felt like the hardest of all. If only she could just hang out with Gable for the rest of the day. He was so easy to be with. He also had a sense of humor, and she didn't sense any toxic BS from him. Or any of the unnecessary drama Harper was currently signal boosting her way.

Brooke saw Harper's scowling face shadowing her reflection. Her sister had taken judgment to a whole new level, claiming she didn't care about the bees. Instead of going there, her sister needed to accept they felt differently about the farm. Harper wanted to give her life over to it, and she didn't. In Brooke's mind, seeds of irritation started to take root again over their recent argument. No wonder she was fantasizing about Gable. It was a lot more fun thinking about him than her judgmental sister.

As she went back down the hall, she passed a room on the right. Walking by it earlier, she hadn't noticed the moving boxes, thin rolled mattress and guitar case against the wall. A dark Stetson hung on a hook at the top of the open closet door.

He'd traveled light, she could respect that. At least he had entertainment with the guitar. Was he the type who liked to play for a group of people or on his own? Did he sing as well? His deep voice had a certain richness and clarity as if it was made for the lyrics of a poignant ballad. A picture formed in her mind of him singing and playing the guitar near the fireplace and her listening to him. The pleasant fantasy soothed away her troubling thoughts.

In the main part of the house, he stood near the galley kitchen drinking a bottle of water while staring toward the large sliding glass door. He'd taken off the ball cap. She envisioned him wearing the hat she'd spotted in the closet. Yeah, she could see it. Gable looked like the type who knew how to wear a Stetson well.

As she approached, he remained preoccupied in his thoughts. Stillness emanated from him. He didn't have the equivalent of a Keep Away sign stamped on his exterior, but she sensed he kept himself carefully reined in. She couldn't deny this mysterious, unknown part of Gable made her even more curious about him.

He glanced to Brooke, and the intensity in his gaze made her pulse kick up, but something other than longing filled his eyes. What she saw was powerful, haunting and maybe a little sad. What was it? Worries about moving? It could be hard to leave one place for another. Or was it deeper than that? Something personal like issues with an ex-wife or a former girlfriend? Or maybe ex or former wasn't the case. Just because he was living in the house alone didn't mean there wasn't a significant other somewhere in the picture. The reality of that doused her curiosity. Not that it should matter. It wasn't like she was going to try and start something with him. She was cutting all nonessential ties with Bolan, like co-owning and running the bee farm, and not adding any new ones.

He blinked and it all went away. Gable pointed to a bottle like the one he held that was sitting on the counter. "I got some water for you. I forgot to ask if you wanted one."

"Thanks. I appreciate it." Brooke unzipped the medical kit. "Let's see how bad that cut is." As he positioned the stool in front of her then straddled it backward, the obvious hit. "Umm...you'll have to remove your shirt, unless that's a problem. I can cut away the fabric near that spot." She rummaged through the kit. "I have scissors...someplace."

"I can take it off." Gable lifted the hem of his shirt. As he reached back to pull it over his head, he took in a swift breath.

She helped him remove the garment, muting the part of her brain fixated on the muscles bunching along his back and shoulders. Keeping his discomfort at the forefront of her mind, she donned a pair of gloves and studied the two-inch cut ending with a slightly jagged edge. "It's stopped bleeding. I don't think you'll need stitches. It's not deep, but there's no telling what caused it. It could have been a piece of glass, metal or a sharp rock." She opened a sterile wipe for wounds. "Have you had a tetanus shot lately?"

"I have."

As she gently cleansed the cut, Gable twitched a little. Goose bumps emerged on his back and he released an unsteady breath.

"I'm sorry. I know this hurts." Hoping to distract him, she added, "I noticed the guitar in the other room. Do you play?"

His whole torso tensed. "No. I don't."

Then why did he have the instrument with him? Did it belong to someone else? His answer along with what he wasn't saying hinted at the duality she sensed in Gable. He was controlled on the surface, but whatever was causing him to tense up was just below that. What had happened to him?

He cleared his throat. "So how did you become the farm's beekeeper?"

Brooke paused in opening the tube of ointment in her hand. The bee suit, that's what had led him to believe she was the farm's beekeeper. Or was it Peggy? That woman loved sharing tidbits of information about people almost as much as she reveled in selling a house. Shifting her mind from what Peggy might have told him about her, Brooke contemplated a response to his question.

The delight and reverence in her mother's eyes whenever she'd interacted with the bees, that's what had attracted her to beekeeping. She'd wanted to be just like her. But she wasn't. The trajectory of her life didn't include living in Maryland at the farm.

Instead of sharing the backstory from her childhood, Brooke chose the simplest answer to his question. "My family owns the farm. Growing up, we had different tasks and that was mine. But I'm not a full-time beekeeper. I work temporary jobs, like house-sitting."

"Really? That's different. What got you into that?"

She applied the ointment. The warmth from his smooth skin, seeping through the glove into her fingers, tempted her to explore beyond the cut and trace over the muscles in his back. Brooke refocused on the conversation. "I fell into it after the marketing firm I was working for downsized..." She explained about Epic Jobs and told him about a few of the temporary assignments she'd worked over the years.

When she finished talking, he said, "Working different jobs like that takes talent. That's impressive. Not everyone could adapt to changes and be successful at it."

Hearing him take what she did seriously instead of viewing her choice of employment as an easy pastime pleased her. In the past, the guys she'd been interested in had viewed her job as a hobby or an amusing diversion. It was nice to feel validated. She smoothed down the edges of the waterproof bandage she'd applied to his back. "Thank you. I love the challenge."

"But I can imagine with all of the moving around, it must be nice having your family's farm as a home base."

Brooke hesitated. She'd never thought of the farm as her home base, but maybe on some level she had viewed it that way. The farm was the one place where she was always welcome and could return to if she needed...or at least it had been. Once she sold her stake in Bishop Honey Bee Farm, it would be Harper's home, not hers. The only thing she would have ownership of was her memories growing up there. Watching their mom experimenting with new honey recipes in the kitchen, knowing they'd get to taste the results. Their dad listening to music while cooking at the grill on a warm sunny day. Snowball fights in the backyard as a family and drinking hot cocoa afterward. Christmas mornings... Their parents had always worn matching elf hats and had been as excited to see her and Harper open their presents as they had been to tear into them. A hint of bittersweet nostalgia crept into her heart, and she quickly swept the memories away.

"Yes, but I don't spend a lot of time here. I like exploring other places." She stated it to herself as well as him. Preferring to switch the topic away from the farm, she said, "All done."

"Thank you." Gable stood. Turning slightly toward her, he slipped his shirt back on.

Trying not to notice his defined abs, she looked to his face. Aside from picking up on the slight wince, she noticed a collection of faint bruises on his shoulder. "Are you sure you're okay?"

"I'm fine. Nothing that a couple of ibuprofens won't fix."

Reaching into the med kit, she pulled out two hot-cold packs. "You might want to ice your shoulder." Brooke handed him the packs. As his fingers brushed hers, tingles of awareness bloomed where they touched. On a reflex her hand tightened, and Gable's did, too. Instead of letting go, she looked up at him.

He stared at their hands and then his gaze met hers.

Neither of them moved as she felt something wild and magnetic spark between them. Was she imagining it? Did he feel it, too?

Gable spoke first. "Icing my injuries—that's a good idea."

"And if that doesn't help, you should probably drop by to see Dr. Kyle. Her office is downtown, just off of Main Street. I'll be more than happy to check you out." His brow rose just as she caught herself. "Not me, I don't work there.

I won't be happy about it. I mean, I'll be glad you went to the doctor, and Dr. Kyle will be glad, too, because that's what she does…she's a doctor." *Stop talking. You're embarrassing yourself.*

Brooke opened her hand, leaving the packs in his. As the feeling of sparks dissipated, her hand felt oddly empty. She busied herself, closing up the med kit. "You should rest and put those packs on your shoulder. You might be good now, but you'll feel it later on if you don't."

"Thanks. I'll make good use of them."

Feeling a tad self-conscious under his steady gaze, she looked down. "And your knee, you should probably ice that, too."

"My knee is fine. My hip took the hit."

"Oh, that's too bad." Her gaze drifted to where he'd indicated. From his point of view, it probably looked like she was staring elsewhere. And she wasn't…not intentionally. "I should go."

"I'll show you out."

"No need." She walked through the archway leading to the main kitchen.

"Brooke."

She called back to him. "Seriously, I'm fine. I know my way out. You should stay off that hip."

"Brooke, stop. You're forgetting something." Aside from how to control her mouth, and her mind, and not embarrass herself?

She faced him.

Gable walked toward her. The bee suit and the unopened bottle of water he carried in his hands disappeared as she took him in—head to broad shoulders to lean hips, muscular-looking thighs and all the way down his long legs.

The space around her grew warmer. Yeah, he *would* look good wearing that Stetson. And she definitely needed that water.

Chapter Seven

A billow of steam followed Brooke as she hurried from the bathroom into the adjoining guest bedroom wrapped in a towel. She didn't want to be late for her meeting with Rina Tillbridge that morning. Having overslept, she'd only had time for a quick shower. She'd already styled her hair, simply pulling it back with a tie. Now she just needed clothes. *Crap! What am I going to put on?*

Rummaging through her backpack, she cobbled together an outfit. Dressing quickly, she put on jeans and a black top, and slipped on a pair of matching suede chunky-heeled sandals.

Standing in front of the mirror over the wood dresser, she slathered tinted moisturizer on her face. Her phone buzzed near her makeup bag with a video call. It was Nellie. After leaving Gable's house, she'd phoned her friend yesterday evening. Nellie had texted back that she was working and couldn't talk.

She tapped the screen and Nellie's face appeared.

"Hey!" Her friend smiled. "Sorry I didn't call you last night. I got home really late."

Brooke propped her phone on the dresser against the mirror. "I understand. How was work?"

"Cute and crazy. It was a forty-fifth anniversary party.

The couple celebrating was in their seventies, but they were like teenagers, holding hands and sneaking kisses. It was so sweet. After the bottles of champagne were popped, they and their friends turned into the party bunch and stayed until after midnight, but they tipped well so it was worth it." Nellie leaned forward, peering at her through the screen. "Why are you putting on makeup? Aren't you just hanging out with the bees?"

"I have a meeting. Long story. A lot's happened and I don't have time to explain." Brooke stepped back from the dresser. "What do you think of this outfit? I'm going for small-town business casual."

"Move further back. I can't see. Now I can. Add a jacket. Which shoes are you wearing?"

Brooke slipped off one of her sandals and held it up.

Nellie nodded. "You always look good in those. And don't forget jewelry."

"Perfect. Thanks."

As Brooke stepped back up to the dresser to apply mascara, the blonde asked, "So how are things at home with your sister?"

"Just as I expected." Back in Florida, during a cocktail-fueled girl chat, Brooke had told Nellie a little bit about her situation with Harper. "Hey, what's going on with my jack?"

"Jack? I thought you said he wasn't your type and that you weren't interested in him."

It took a beat for Brooke to catch on. "Not Jack the bartender. My *tire* jack. Months ago, you borrowed my Jeep to help a friend. Do you remember? My jack is missing."

"Oh…oh no." Nellie pressed her hands to her cheeks. "Please tell me you didn't get a flat driving to Maryland."

"I did." Brooke added berry coloring to her lips. Nellie

looked so regretful, she couldn't be upset with her. "Lucky for you, I was close to home. You need to check with your friend and get it back for me."

"I will. I'll send it to you. A flat is bad enough. I'm really sorry for making things worse."

That wasn't nearly the worse thing. If Nellie only knew the truth about what was going on with Harper and the farm, but it was too much to get into. An image of Gable flashed in Brooke's mind. "One good thing did come out of it. I met my neighbor…" She explained the falling off the horse incident but skipped over most of the details that happened at his house. Like her drooling over him.

"So from that smile on your face, I take it he's not too injured, and that he's probably cute?"

"I'm not smi…" Brooke looked at her reflection. She *was* smiling. "Yes, he's okay. At least he was when I left him. And yes, he's cute. Think actors Michael B. Jordan and Sterling K. Brown combined in a really good way. And he owns a cowboy hat and a guitar."

"Girl, stop before I pass out. Does this eighth wonder of the world have a name?"

"Gable Kincaid."

"Wait, did you say he's a singer?"

"No, I said he owned a guitar. I asked him if he played it, but he said he didn't."

A contemplative frown came over Nellie's face. "I swear I've heard his name before. Send me a picture of him."

"What am I supposed to do? Walk next door and say, 'Hey, neighbor, can I take a picture of you to send to my nosy friend?'" Brooke snorted a laugh. After the way she'd acted before leaving his house yesterday, plus causing him injury, Gable probably wanted to steer clear of her anyway.

"I'm just saying, if you do happen to take a picture of him…"

"Yeah, not happening. I really have to go. I can't be late for this meeting. Don't forget to find my jack. Not the bartender, the one that belongs to my Jeep. Wait, are you dating him?"

"Maybe." Nellie's grin supplied more of an answer. "Good luck with your meeting."

After hanging up the phone, Brooke unearthed some jewelry that complemented her outfit, then she snagged her tablet along with her small cross-body purse and hurried out the room.

Walking down the hall to the foyer, the house was eerily quiet and none of the homey smells she was used to were in the air.

In the past, on her first day home, Aunt Ivy would make breakfast, and they would spend most of the morning talking before going to the apiary to check the bees. The loss of that ritual magnified her aunt's absence. She knew how to take care of the bees, but inspecting the hives that afternoon wouldn't be the same without Ivy.

Brooke looked to the second floor. Was Harper still asleep in her bedroom? They hadn't spoken to each other since their blowup over the farm. Yesterday, after not being able to talk to Nellie, the rain finally let up, and Brooke had taken advantage of the break in the weather to fix her flat tire. By the time she'd gotten the Jeep and truck back home, it was late in the evening and she'd been starving. She'd sent Harper a text about the status of the leftover food in the refrigerator.

Harper had messaged back: Mac and cheese is good. I'm busy.

Brooke had taken the hint and stopped texting her. She'd

considered ignoring Harper's curtness and bringing her food, but her sister knew where the kitchen was. Instead of worrying about her, she'd accessed the cloud drive using her tablet and read through Aunt Ivy's notes about the honey month promotion as well as reports on the hives.

After that, she'd watched one of Nellie's movie picks— *Zombie Robot Soldier Beasts*, a film where robot scientists turned into zombies and so did the elite soldiers who blew up their lab after inhaling zombie dust.

Brooke gave an inner eye roll. She should have known better than to watch a movie Nellie had recommended, but she'd been bored. Forty-five minutes in, she'd hated the futuristic thriller but was too invested to stop watching it. Then exhaustion had gotten the best of her. She'd fallen asleep and missed the rest of the film. Now she'd either have to admit to Nellie she'd actually watched one of her recommendations or subject herself to more torture by watching the end of the movie.

Or she could do a deep dive online to find out what happened to the *one* character she actually did care about— Mitzi, the teacup Yorkie. She'd been the smartest one on the island. While everyone else stood by watching their friends and colleagues morph into killer zombies, she'd had the good sense to slide down the air conditioning duct. She'd even managed to keep the perky red bow on top of her head intact, and she'd taken a chew toy and a small bag of dog treats with her.

Moments later, driving her Jeep from the front of the house, she spotted Harper's car parked in the same spot where it had been last night at the cottage. Had her sister worked and slept in her office last night? Had she even bothered to eat anything? Annoyed and concerned, Brooke stepped on the gas.

As she drove out the farm's front gate, her gaze drifted next door. Imagining Gable sleeping on his thin mattress with all of his injuries raised empathy. After what he'd experienced yesterday, hopefully he'd gotten some rest.

Thrashing in his sleep, Gable awoke from a dream where he'd been drowning in the ocean. Heart racing, he shot up to a sitting position on the foam mattress situated on the floor in the bedroom. The air-conditioned room wicked sweat from his brow and bare torso. Chest heaving, he rubbed his hands back and forth over his head. Pain rippled through his left arm, and his heavy breaths buried his groan, but the discomfort of his arm didn't come close to what he'd felt after going through the agony of that dream. He hadn't experienced that nightmare in a while. He hated it. The dream always ended the same, with a hand reaching out to save him. In real life, he should have been the one doing the saving.

Sadness and regret pooled in Gable's chest. As it threatened to overtake him like the ocean in his dream, his phone chimed beside him with a familiar ringtone. Tamping down his emotions, he took a steadying breath then answered the call. "Mom…hey."

"Hey? Is that all you have to say to me?" A gentle admonishment laced her tone. "You were supposed to call me yesterday and tell me what happened with the house."

"I meant to, but things were a little hectic."

"You sound funny. Is everything okay?"

As always, Andrea Atkins's mom radar was on, but if he told her anything was wrong she'd be on a plane before the end of the day, headed his direction.

Gable cleared his throat. "I'm fine." Rising to his feet, he cataloged the stiffness and aches sounding off in his body. He rotated his shoulder. It was a little sore but using the ice pack Brooke had given him along with the pain pill he'd taken last night had helped. But today, his left wrist and part of his forearm looked swollen. He flexed his hand, ignoring the discomfort. "I just spent a little too much time in the saddle with Pep yesterday riding around the property." That wasn't a total lie.

"You did, huh?" She chuckled. "You just stopped riding a desk for a living. You're not used to spending hours on a horse. You have to ease into it. So, what happened? Is the place like Wes's farm? Did you decide to move in?"

The sun shining through the partially closed slats in the window blind illuminated the corner with his guitar and the boxes he hadn't opened. He glanced away from them. "It's not as large as Wes's place had been but it's more than I expected. I like it. I'm still unpacking, but once I'm settled in, I'll start getting some work done. I'm looking forward to it."

"Working on you or the house?"

"The house. It needs work. I don't."

"Well, I think you should fix both."

As usual, his mother was worrying about him. He'd just convinced her a few weeks ago that she didn't need to call or text him every other day to check on him. "Mom, I'm good."

"If there was a hole in one of the walls of the house you're in, would you just patch it up with sand and balled-up paper and say that was good?"

Accepting there was no avoiding the lecture to come, he dropped his head with a sigh and massaged the back of his neck. "No, I'd replaster it."

"Losing a friend is like a hole in the wall of your life. It leaves a space, and it's tempting to ignore it instead of facing grief. I know you have your reasons for moving to

Maryland, and I hope one of them is to fill that hole with forgiveness. You have to stop blaming yourself for Theo's death."

Hearing his friend's name opened up memories of last night's dream. It was always Theo's hand reaching out for him. Theo had been one of the most generous people he'd known, and he'd taken advantage of that quality instead of looking out for him.

He closed his eyes as the memories resurfaced of meeting Theo that night at Lou's along with all of the things Gable wished he'd done differently. *A heart attack?* A part of him still couldn't believe that's what had taken Theo. He was only thirty-three. Still, when he'd noticed something was off with Theo during their early breakfast, he should have questioned him more. If he had, maybe he could have done something to prevent the heart attack that had taken his friend not long after they'd parted at the restaurant. If he had, Theo would be smiling at home with his family today. Gable opened his eyes, dismissing the what-ifs, and faced the cold hard reality of truth. He'd been too focused on finishing his audition recording to think of anyone but himself.

He released a heavy exhale. "Mom, I have to go. I have an appointment in town."

"Alright. I won't hold you up." From her tone, she knew he didn't have anywhere to be and just wanted to get off the phone with her. "If you need anything, I'm here."

"Yep...thanks."

He ended the call. Frustration and remnants of unresolved grief tugged and pulled in his chest. He didn't have anywhere to go, but he had plenty of things to do, like sketching out his plan for adding a dedicated wash bay to the barn. He also needed to rent a farm tiller to prepare the field for planting a crop. There was also a half-built gazebo on the property he wanted to finish. But first, he wanted to unpack the few boxes he'd brought with him that had clothes, dishes and other items to tide him over until the moving van arrived.

His gaze strayed to the guitar. *Do you play?* He'd almost answered yes to Brooke's question, but he didn't play or sing anymore. How could he continue to chase success as a musician after his ambition had taken away something much more valuable from the world? Melonie had lost her husband. Theo Jr. lost his dad. Why had he brought the damn guitar with him to Maryland? He should have left it behind. It didn't have a place in his life.

Irritation and guilt drove his steps. He reached down and knocked one of the smaller boxes aside to get to the case with his guitar. With his phone still in his right hand, he picked it up with his left. Fire blazed through Gable's wrist. He dropped the guitar and a string of f-bomb variations flew past his lips. Yeah, he'd done more damage than he'd realized.

Chapter Eight

> Welcome to Bolan. Friends and Smiles for Miles Live
> Here.

Brooke zipped past the sign just outside of downtown proclaiming the declaration. Following the flow of traffic, she reached the intersection where Main Street split into two, bordering a center square.

The neatly cut grassy area had flowering bushes and old-fashioned-style streetlamps lining the paths. A few people sat on park benches surrounding a large stone fountain centerpiece, enjoying drinks and eating food undoubtedly purchased from the café.

The popular corner establishment on the left, a two-story, light-colored brick building with Brewed Haven Café stenciled on the large storefront window, stood on its own while the rest of the businesses were linked together in strip mall fashion.

Pedestrians darted in and out of familiar shops: the corner ice cream parlor, Wonderland Florist, Bolan Book Attic, the wine bar, Buttons & Lace Boutique, as well as other small businesses. But traffic seemed heavier than it had been last year when she'd popped into town to shop. Every parking spot on both sides of the thoroughfare were taken.

On her second loop around, as she squeezed between two waiting tour vans at the end of the square, she caught a glimpse of the clock in the tower at Bolan's town hall. Oh no! Her meeting with Rina was in less than fifteen minutes.

A block over from town center, she had better luck and nabbed a spot near a yoga studio. As she quickly strode toward Main Street, she glanced around. This older part of Bolan was being revitalized to match the center of town. The mayor's new growth initiative that Ivy mentioned in her notes seemed to be paying off with more tourists and new businesses to continue to attract them. Expansion could open up opportunities for the bee farm as well.

The gourmet food and gift shop she'd passed near the yoga studio could be a prime place to have a honey display. A spark of interest hit, and Brooke automatically started working out a strategy in her mind for contacting the owners and presenting the idea to them. She stopped herself. No. Connecting with new businesses wasn't on her radar. She was just helping organize the partnerships for the honey month promotion. Exploring other sales and marketing opportunities was Harper's responsibility, not hers.

Near the intersection at Main Street, she walked by the tinted glass entrance to Dr. Kyle's office. The door opened, and she looked twice at the attractive Black woman with a single long ebony braid down her back, dressed in a navy pantsuit, strolling toward the sidewalk. At first glance, she looked like Rina, but it was her older sister, Zurie.

Zurie was too engrossed in her phone conversation to notice her. "I'm leaving Dr. Kyle's office now," she said to the person on the phone. "I have good news…"

A doctor's visit that ended with good news was definitely something to be thrilled about. Another thought popped into Brooke's mind. Had Gable made an appointment to see the doctor like she'd suggested? Why was she so preoccupied with him? Brooke gave herself a mental shake. She'd mentioned him to Nellie, that's why he was on her mind. Taking a shortcut through center square, she arrived at Brewed Haven Café with just minutes to spare before her appointment.

As she waited at the host stand, she watched the baristas at a curved station up front preparing coffees and serving up baked goods from the glass showcase below the service counter.

Some of the patrons exited with their food and drinks. Others took what they'd ordered along with their laptops to a cozy alcove on the left with beige couches tucked under the windows.

Waitstaff in purple T-shirts with the café's coffee cup logo served customers at tables and the booths along the wall, as well as the long dining counter. From the wonderful smell of savory food and coffee hovering in the café, it was easy to understand why the place was full.

The hostess came to the podium and smiled. "Welcome to Brewed Haven."

"Hello, I have an appointment with Rina Tillbridge. My name is Brooke Bishop."

The young redhead tapped the screen on the tablet in front of her. "Yes, I see you on her schedule. Follow me." She seated Brooke at a four-top corner table. "I'll let Rina know you're here. Would you like something to drink?"

The advert on the table tent caught her eye. "I'll have a mocha cappuccino, please."

"My pleasure."

Moments later, instead of the hostess or a server delivering the coffee, it was Rina. The pretty Black woman wore a purple apron over a yellow T-shirt and jeans. Her black hair styled in micro twists was secured by a matching purple band. She also carried a plate of baked goods.

Having attended the local high school together, they'd remained friendly toward each other. This was their first time meeting to discuss business, and Brooke wasn't sure of how to approach their meeting, but Rina's cheery smile set the tone.

"Good morning." Rina put the mug in front of Brooke along with the baked goods and two smaller plates.

"Good morning." Returning the café owner's smile, Brooke pointed. "What's all of this?"

"A little something extra to go with your mocha cappuccino. Cinnamon rolls. I made them this morning especially for you."

"Wow. Thanks. They look amazing."

Rina sat down. "Would you like anything else? Or have you eaten breakfast already?"

"Actually, I didn't get a chance."

"Me, neither. I hit the ground running this morning. What about today's special? It's a skillet breakfast scramble with eggs, cheese, country ham, mushrooms and tomatoes."

Brooke's mouth watered. "I'll take it."

Rina flagged down a server and placed the order.

"So when did you get into town?" Rina asked, handing her a roll on a plate.

"Yesterday afternoon."

"You didn't even get a day to relax? Sounds like I'm not the only one who hit the ground running today."

Or scampering. Harper's verbal jab still irritated Brooke. "Yes, I've got a little more on my schedule than usual."

"I was surprised Ivy moved our meeting to today. We usually don't work out the details for the big honey promotion until midsummer."

Brooke chose her words carefully. She and Harper would have to discuss how they wanted to share the news of their aunt's departure. "She just wanted to get a jump on things. Did you get a chance to read through what we have in mind for this year?"

Aunt Ivy had scheduled a full lineup. Weekend tours at the apiary and honey harvesting demonstrations. Children's activities at the greenhouse designed to teach kids about the relationship between bees and the environment, and the collaboration with Brewed Haven Café, the Montecito Steakhouse bar, and Pasture Lane Restaurant at Tillbridge. The food and beverage establishments were each featuring a special menu with items made with the farm's honey.

"I did get a chance to look over the plan, and I love that the Montecito is a part of it this year. I can't wait to try their honey-themed cocktails, and speaking of honey-themed items, you have to taste my latest creation." Rina pointed to the rolls.

Eyeing the treats that were soft, gooey and dripping with glaze, Brooke took a bite from the one on her plate. She moaned, lost in a moment of food ecstasy as a blend of cinnamon, honey and a hint of berries practically melted in her mouth. "You have to move the rest of those rolls away from me or I'll eat the entire plate."

Rina laughed. "Then my work is done. I made them with the special reserve berry honey you're planning to feature during the celebration. Ivy gave me a jar in advance so I could play with a few recipes."

Along with the special reserve berry honey, Aunt Ivy had chosen to feature their lavender and hibiscus flower variations. The berry honey came from hives Bishop Honey Bee Farm maintained in a berry patch at a local fruit and vegetable farm. The other two were infused with flowers that came from the bee farm's greenhouses.

By the end of breakfast, Brooke and Rina were both excited about the ideas for the café's honey-themed menu. And they also brainstormed a new idea Brooke had in mind. A booklet featuring recipes from all three establishments along with information and fun facts about honey and bees. Rina was in on the new project, now Brooke just had to pitch it to the Montecito and Pasture Lane.

As their meeting ended, Rina swiped over the screen on her phone. "It's too bad you won't be around for the final menu tasting. When is Ivy coming back from her vacation? I asked her the other day, but she never said."

Brooke bought herself time with a sip of coffee. "Well… she's going to be gone longer than usual. I'm not sure of the date she plans to return."

"Good for her. Breaks are important. And we have plenty of time to schedule the tasting." Rina glanced to the front of the café and frowned. "My sister's here? That's odd. This time of the day is her busiest at the stable. She's normally chained to her desk."

Near the coffee counter, Zurie stood in line with her significant other, sheriff's sergeant Mace Calderone. He was dressed for work in a tan-and-brown uniform.

Lost in thought, Rina tapped her finger on the table. "There's something up with those two."

"Like what?"

"I'm not sure, but they've been a little secretive."

As Zurie stared up at Mace, he briefly rested his hand on her stomach and she laid her hand over his.

Rina's eyes widened. "Oh, my gosh. Is she pregnant? She *has* been glowing lately. But why hasn't she said anything? Zurie wouldn't keep something like that from me.

Would she?" Her expression grew concerned. "Unless everything's not okay."

Brooke recalled Zurie talking on the phone earlier. *I have great news...* But it wasn't her place to share what she'd overheard in her conversation. Zurie must have had her reasons for not sharing her great news with her sister.

"Maybe she's still adjusting to the news," Brooke offered. "I'm sure she'll tell you when she's ready."

"You're probably right. Becoming parents, I'm sure it's a lot for them to take in." Rina's excitement returned with a widening smile. She clapped her hands softly and said in a low voice, "Zurie's going to be a mom and I'm going to be an auntie. I can't wait."

As Brooke took in Rina's reaction, she tried to imagine Harper being happy over becoming an aunt. Not that she was planning on getting pregnant anytime soon. But someday, they both might fall in love with someone and start families of their own. Brooke tried to envision her and Harper sharing in happy moments like getting married or celebrating a pregnancy. She couldn't. When they were younger, they used to tease each other about boys they had crushes on, but these days, they didn't talk to each other about their personal lives. Harper was so devoted to work. Did she even date at all?

Mace left the café, and as Zurie picked up her coffee order, she noticed Brooke and Rina and gave them a small wave.

As she approached their table, Rina straightened in her seat. "I probably shouldn't let her know I suspect anything about her being pregnant, right? I don't want to ruin the surprise."

"I agree."

Zurie smiled when she reached them. "What's going on?

Fess up. From the looks on your faces, you two look like you're secretly plotting world domination."

"No, not us." Rina shook her head. "We're just talking about National Honey Month, nothing else. What about you? Are you planning anything big?"

Brooke hid a smile behind a sip of coffee. Rina was practically fidgeting in her seat, barely able to conceal her curiosity about her sister's possible pregnancy.

"Nope, just tackling the paperwork waiting on my desk." She smiled at Brooke. "It's good to see you, as always. I heard you have a new neighbor, Gable Kincaid. Have you met him yet?"

"Yes, I ran into him yesterday." Or more accurately, he'd practically fallen at her feet.

"Someone new moved into town?" Rina asked. "How did I not know that?"

"He's been keeping a low profile," Zurie said. "The funny thing is, a few people have said he looks familiar. Tristan swears he's run into him before, and a couple of the staff claim they saw him online somewhere, but who isn't on social media these days."

As Zurie raised her cup to take a sip, Rina pointed. "That isn't your usual black-eye coffee, is it?"

Zurie chuckled ruefully. "No, unfortunately, it's herbal tea. As much as I want it, I don't think my stomach can handle coffee with two shots of espresso. I woke up a little queasy this morning. Those cinnamon rolls look good, though. Can I have one?"

"Go ahead." Brooke slid the plate toward Zurie.

Rina pulled it back. "No. Too much sugar isn't good for you in your condition."

Zurie's expression grew puzzled. "What condition?"

Rina looked as if she wished she could have swallowed her words.

Brooke interjected. "If you have a queasy stomach, eating too much sugar could make you feel worse."

"She's right." Rina nodded. "Actually I put more sugar and honey in the recipe than I should have. I'll make you something healthy instead. What about that all-fruit smoothie you like?"

"No, I just wanted to say hello," Zurie said. "And you're in a meeting."

"I think we're done for now." Rina looked to Brooke.

"We are. And I need to get back to the farm and check on the bees. Thank you for your time, Rina."

"You're welcome and thank you." Rina's appreciation for helping her not ruin Zurie's secret showed in her eyes. She bent down to give Brooke a hug. "Put your money away. Breakfast is on me," she added in a whisper. "And take the rolls with you."

As the sisters walked away from the table, Rina looped her arm through Zurie's.

A pang of envy hit Brooke as they easily chatted, laughed and leaned on each other. Would she and Harper ever find their sisterly connection again or would it be lost forever because of their disagreement over the farm?

After leaving a tip, she left the café with the baked goods in a bag. While turning the corner from Main Street, she smacked into someone, squashing the rolls between them.

The guy sucked in a breath.

"Sorry." Her gaze traveled over a familiar-looking chest covered by a navy button-down shirt to the sling on his shoulder.

Brooke looked to Gable's face. "Are you alright?" What

a dumb question. Of course he wasn't. His arm was immobilized and she'd just slammed into him.

"I'll live." He followed her glance to his wrist in a brace nestled in the cradle of the arm strap. "It's just a mild sprain, and the sling is optional. Dr. Kyle wanted me to wear it so I wouldn't forget to give my arm a rest."

He gave her a lopsided smile that added even more interest to his face. Since she'd met him, he hadn't flashed a full-on smile. Maybe that was a good thing, considering the way her heart was jumping in her chest. If he did smile at her, she'd probably end up doing something embarrassing like staring at him with her mouth open.

Realizing she was staring now, Brooke focused on straightening the strap of her purse. "I feel like I owe you more than just an apology for causing you to get hurt."

"Yeah, you probably do owe me at least a conversation or ten." His mildly serious expression was softened considerably by the teasing in his eyes.

"Ten conversations? Is that all? About what?"

"Bees." Earnestness joined the humor in his eyes. "I know certain chemicals can hurt them. I'd like your recommendations on natural products I can use instead."

"I'm happy to share recommendations." His sincere interest in protecting the bees warmed a sense of appreciation inside of her.

"Maybe we could meet up?"

"Sure."

A small group of tourists came down the sidewalk.

Brooke and Gable stepped off to the side. As a woman involved in an animated conversation grazed against her, he cupped Brooke's elbow and brought her closer to him.

A pleasing scent with notes of musk and amber wafted up her nose. The way he smelled lured her in a little closer.

His collar slightly twisted underneath the sling almost became her reason to touch him. She shouldn't. Needing to keep her hands occupied, Brooke gripped the bag of cinnamon rolls a bit tighter, but her mind still wandered.

He was saying something, but she was having trouble separating her attention from his mouth. His firm-looking lips had just the right fullness to deliver deep toe-curling kisses.

"So about meeting up," he said, "when are you available?"

Brooke blinked up at him, trying to remember the thread of their conversation. Bees…that's what he wanted to meet up about. When was she free? Tomorrow? The day after? Next week? Those times seemed so far away.

Brooke thought of another option. "I'm free tonight."

Chapter Nine

Brooke parked her Jeep next to the garage at the farm. She was having dinner with Gable in a few hours. Why was she so excited? They were just meeting to talk about bees, and as far as having dinner together, that was a practical decision. They needed to eat, and what they were having wasn't fussy. She was bringing a chicken pot pie she'd spotted in the freezer last night from Pasture Lane Restaurant. Gable was providing the sides. It was a meeting, not a date, and bringing him a meal was more of a welcome to the neighborhood gesture on her part.

Call tonight what you want, but... Brooke couldn't help but laugh at herself. Yes, she liked Gable, and why shouldn't they spend time getting to know each other while talking about the bees? It was better than her hanging around the house not talking to Harper.

After changing into a T-shirt and trading her heels for boots, she hopped into the truck she'd used yesterday and drove the wide gravel path to the bee shed near the apiary. Although they called it a shed, the tan brick building consisted of a large storage area for beekeeping supplies as well as a fully equipped honey extraction room.

Bishop Honey Bee Farm had the capability to process its own honey, including bottling and labeling, in small batches. For larger batches, they utilized the services of a cooperative processing facility that served hobby beekeepers to larger bee farms in the area.

Brooke removed the bee suit she'd worn the day she'd met Gable from the bed of the truck. It still smelled like horse and needed to be washed. Memories of him telling her Pepper's name versus his as an introduction made her smile. Instead of being embarrassed by the mistake, he'd recovered without missing a beat. She liked that. And the way he'd put Pepper's well-being first showed he had the ability to think beyond himself. She liked that about him, too. He also seemed grounded and confident in his skin, but that part of him that seemed so troubled. Maybe he'd experienced a setback in his career instead of his personal life? When she'd been suddenly laid off from her marketing job, the news had blindsided her. It had taken over a month for her to find her way again. But why did people keep saying he looked familiar? She could search for him online. Details were bound to come up.

Brooke grabbed her phone from the front seat, started tapping in his name, but paused. Did she really want to read about his life versus learning more about him firsthand? He didn't seem cagey or dangerous, just guarded. She could relate to that. There were things about her life that she wasn't interested in discussing, either. Despite the possibility of information to satisfy her questions about him just a few taps away, she put her phone in her pocket and went inside the bee shed.

The smells of wood, beeswax and honey saturated the air. The process of beekeeping and honey making started in this building. All of the finished products—packaged honey, beeswax and propolis—were kept in a storeroom at the office cottage.

In the bee shed, she put the bee suit in the washer tucked in a small nook, then perused the freestanding metal shelving units lined up in the middle of the space.

Six-inch-high honey supers with empty frames sat stacked on one unit along with wood to assemble more frames. The unit next to it had shelves filled with basic hive inspection supplies: tools with a hook on one end and a scraper on the other to help pry apart the frames in the hive and scrape off excess wax, grippers to safely remove the frames and brushes useful for coaxing bees off of them and back into the boxes, and packages of pellets for the smoker.

The last unit had supplies needed to clean and sanitize the tools and honey extraction machine. The tools for today's inspection were already in the truck, but she needed hygiene supplies. After gathering the required items from the shelves, she made a solution of water and washing crystals in a large bucket at the sink in the nook. After that, she took a smoker from a hanger on the wall and added it to a second bucket she'd use for carrying her supplies. Instead of an all-in-one bee suit, she chose a beekeeper jacket, gauntlet-style gloves from a shelf and a veil from an assortment of beekeeping clothing hanging on pegs nearby. Ready for the afternoon, she went back out to the truck.

A short time later, Brooke parked a distance from the apiary, and after putting on her protective gear, she grabbed the two buckets along with a notebook and pen from inside the truck.

Aunt Ivy had completed a thorough inspection of all of the hives last week, including the ones they maintained away from the farm. She'd been slightly concerned about a hive they kept on a homeowner's property. The construction of a gated community in the area could potentially become disruptive. While growth in Bolan had its upside from a business perspective, one of the downsides was the loss of natural green space and waterways that supported wildlife and the environment, including the bees. Her aunt had made a notation to herself to keep a closer eye on the colony in case she needed to make some adjustments. Other than that, the hives were in good shape.

Starting with the first hive, she puffed a little smoke near the bottom entrance with the smoker to calm the bees or, more accurately, fool them. The smoke masked the smell of the alarm pheromones the guard bees would give off once she opened the hive. Believing there was a risk of fire, the bees were now busy eating their fill of honey in case they needed to abandon their home to survive. This feeding also made their abdomens stiffer, making it more difficult for them to bend and sting.

Years ago, when her mom had told her the reason for smoking the hives, it had concerned her.

I promise. They'll be okay, her mother had reassured her. *We're not hurting them. We just don't want to needlessly distress the hive, so we have to do it this way. If we could talk to the bees and let them know we're not going to harm them, we would, but unfortunately, they can't understand us...*

But the day Brooke had stood in the apiary and whispered, *Mom is gone,* it seemed like the bees *had* understood. For weeks after that, they'd been more docile, even without the smoke, as if they'd known everything was in flux. The only thing that had remained constant during that turbulent time was the bees working in their hives.

Finding comfort in their routine, she'd sat by the hives for hours, entranced by the forager bees leaving and returning with their stomachs filled with nectar and clumps of pollen attached to their hind legs. A part of her had wished she could go with them. She'd daydreamed about the bees flying her higher and higher, all the way to Heaven to see her parents again. But even if they had been able to take her there, she couldn't leave.

During that time, Aunt Ivy had been on a steep learning curve, trying to handle her parental role and educating herself about the bees. She'd also relied on Brooke's help at the apiary and at home as she became a quick study, completing classes and absorbing knowledge from experienced beekeepers who'd volunteered to assist until she felt confident on her own.

Once Aunt Ivy stepped into the role of the farm's sole beekeeper, Brooke had continued to work side by side with Ivy in the apiary. Often, there were huge moments of silence between them. In that gap were the memories they both held of their parents and the lack of words to express how much they'd both missed them.

Instead of working at the apiary, Harper had retreated into herself, staring out the window at the small garden of flowers their parents had planted together near the house. One of the reasons Aunt Ivy had pushed ahead with setting up the greenhouses was because of Harper. The responsibility of tending to the flowers and plants had slowly pulled her out of her shell. With time, and Aunt Ivy's endless love and patience, the three of them moved through their grief and their bond grew stronger. That bond had stretched and loosened when Brooke had left for college. She'd needed the room to grow, and now Ivy seemed to require the same, while Harper...

As the bees in the hive she was working on became a little more agitated, Brooke set aside her recollections. Bees could sense emotion. Her agitation disrupting their peaceful environment was the last thing she wanted. It wasn't fair to them.

Refocused on the tasks of beekeeping, she moved from hive to hive, inspecting the frames in each super on top of the hive while noting how much capped honey was stored in the frames. At least two supers needed to be filled on a hive before they took one away for harvest. None of them were at that point yet.

Setting aside the supers, she looked into the brood box, reading the rainbow-like structure of pollen, honey and brood toward the middle of the bee frame, revealing the health of the colony. Thankfully, she didn't see a risk of the apiary being overrun by mites or disease.

In a few of the hives, she spotted the queen's regal presence, with an entourage circled around her attending to her every need so she could concentrate on a single task. Laying up to two thousand eggs per day.

Brooke became lost in the rhythm of the task and the steady hum of the insects, unobtrusively observing the bee's interconnectedness and industriousness. This was the part she loved the most. Every time she witnessed them working seamlessly together, she felt a sense of awe. These tiny creatures helped feed the world. Were they aware they had such a big job? Was that why they were so tireless and persistent? Did they understand the cost if they failed?

Growing hot and sweaty underneath the jacket and veil, she came to a natural stopping point a third of the way through the hives. She'd check more of them tomorrow and the remainder the day after that. At the end of the week, she'd inspect the hives they had set up away from the farm.

Done with her inspection, she went back to the bee shed. After cleaning her tools and putting everything away, she drove to the office cottage to use Aunt Ivy's laptop.

Harper's car wasn't there, but that didn't mean her sister wasn't in the building. Steeling herself for a possible confrontation, Brooke went inside. What she saw made her stop in her tracks.

The modest retail plus office space she'd known in the past had gone through a major makeover. It no longer looked like a wood-paneled general store. The interior of the cottage was now a brightly lit, modern presentation of blond-wood floors, sunny yellow walls with white trim, and white shelving replicating a honeycomb pattern.

Jars of honey as well as T-shirts, mugs and other bee and honey-themed merchandise were displayed in the hexagonal shaped nooks on the side walls. Large framed photos of flowers, bees and honeycomb added to the decor.

Up front, a tall brunette with wavy hair walked out of a corner room behind the sales counter.

"Hello." She flashed a customer-friendly smile. "We're not open." Seconds later, recognition flashed in her eyes. "Oh, you're Brooke. My name is Leah. I'm the new property manager."

Brooke shook her hand. "Hi, Leah. It's nice to meet you. Is Harper here?"

"She's at the greenhouses handling an issue. Can I help you with something?"

The tension from anticipating a confrontation with her sister flooded away, and Brooke relaxed. "No, I just need to use Ivy's laptop." She glanced around. Both offices used to be behind the counter but now there was only one door. "I guess she and Harper are sharing an office now?"

Leah's brows rose with a surprised expression. "Oh, they didn't tell you? Ivy moved her office inside the house."

Masking her own surprise, Brooke said, "They probably mentioned it but I just forgot. Our meeting yesterday was

kind of rushed. Thanks, Leah. It was nice meeting you."
Feeling a little left out of the loop of information, she exited the cottage and went to the truck.

Yesterday, Ivy really had been in such a rush. She probably had forgotten to mention it or she'd expected Harper would tell her about the change.

At the house, she headed upstairs, pausing on the landing.

The alcove straight ahead had once been a play area for her and Harper when they were kids. When they'd entered school, it had become a study nook. By the time she'd left for college, it had been a sunny place for houseplants. Now it was a fitness area with an exercise bike, treadmill and a flat-screen television on the wall.

The only other place for an office upstairs was the sitting area in Aunt Ivy's bedroom, but her aunt had believed in work-life balance. She always insisted on keeping workspaces separate from family and areas to relax in the house. She even discouraged working for extended periods at the kitchen table.

Down the hall on the right, Brooke went past Harper's bedroom to Ivy's at the end. She peeked inside. No desk. No laptop. Just a neatly made queen-size bed and the sitting area with cozy furniture. The absence of family photos on the dresser highlighted Aunt Ivy's absence.

The only other place for a home office was... Brooke swallowed hard.

Downstairs, instead of going down the hall off the foyer toward the guest room, she walked across the living room to another adjoining hallway. Even though it was lit by windows overlooking the back lawn as she walked down the carpeted hallway, it felt a little like a tunnel closing in on her. As she got closer to the closed door at the end, memories seeped into her mind. She couldn't remember the last time she'd been to that part of the house. It was almost as if she could hear the murmurs of her parents' voices behind the door interspersed with her dad's chuckle and her mom's bubbly laughter.

As she laid her hand on the doorknob, she took in a deep breath. A part of her was surprised not to smell her father's citrusy aftershave. It was one of the things that kept him from coming too close to the apiary. Strong scents aggravated the bees, but for her, that smell had signified he was home and all was well. As a part-time financial consultant, sometimes he'd traveled to see his clients. He'd also been the farm's operations manager. He would spend most of his work day at his desk in the wood-paneled office, and when the store was open on weekends, he would be at the counter ringing up customer purchases while her mom helped customers find what they needed.

A longing to see him and her mom again swelled in Brooke's chest. She hadn't realized she'd shut her eyes until she opened them to another space that looked entirely different than she'd remembered. Her parents' king-size bed. The Queen Anne oval floor-length mirror. The matching dresser and side tables. They were gone. Only one piece of furniture that was somewhat familiar remained. The chaise lounge in the corner. A square table next to it held Aunt Ivy's family photos.

Irritation hit Brooke like a blow to her stomach. Aunt Ivy leaving all of a sudden. Remodeling the office cottage and now this. What else would she find out at the last minute? One thing was clear, she couldn't work in the new office. Going to the black desk near the wall, she grabbed the laptop and walked out.

In the kitchen, her heart pounded as a mix of emotions

swirled in her chest. She sat at the table, clutching the laptop in her hands until the risk of slamming it down had passed. Brooke took a deep breath and gently set it down. Updating the office cottage and Aunt Ivy turning her parents' bedroom into an office were sensible choices, but it still bothered her.

Hours later, Brooke's negative thoughts about the changes, as well as Aunt Ivy's sudden departure, were as unforgiving as the wooden kitchen chair had become for her backside. The more she tried to focus on adding notes to the hive journal, the more aggravated she grew. Aunt Ivy and Harper could have given her a heads-up about the redesigns, but instead they'd blindsided her. Sure, she wasn't home for most of the year, but something major like this should have been mentioned, maybe even discussed, with her first.

Releasing a frustrated huff, she shut the laptop. The feeling that something had been snatched away from her irritated Brooke even more. It was time for her to stop anyway. She needed to heat up the chicken pot pie for her meeting with Gable.

While the food heated in the oven, she took a shower. Getting dressed, it almost felt like déjà vu, rummaging through her backpack again to find something to wear. Blouse and jeans—she wasn't feeling it. Leggings and shirt—too casual. Jeans and a T-shirt—that was what she wore to work in the apiary. Her hand skimmed over soft fabric. Brooke pulled the red floral dress from her pack.

She'd purchased it at a consignment store for a casual night out with newfound friends at a restaurant by the beach in South Carolina and hadn't worn it since. It had been a fun moment filled with laughter, good food, some the best cocktails she'd ever had made by a mixologist, and even better company. Remembered happiness showered over Brooke as she slipped it over her head and the skirt of the dress settled at mid-thigh. It was comfortable, not too wrinkled, and it had pockets. Triple win. A matching headband, earrings and pair of cute white tennis shoes completed her outfit.

Moments later, carrying the food and a bottle of wine in a canvas grocery bag, she paused in the foyer, struck by the silence of the house and all that was missing from it. Wouldn't Harper feel lonely living there by herself? Concern for her sister pinged in Brooke's chest. But the desire to leave pinged louder, and Brooke walked out.

She wanted to laugh and enjoy herself just like the first time she'd worn the red dress. Gable was a newfound friend. Having dinner with him and forgetting her problems was exactly what she needed.

Chapter Ten

Gable stood in the middle of the empty living room and looked around. The place looked sparse but it was clean. He'd spent most of the afternoon wiping things down. Plates, silverware and glasses were set up on the counter for dinner. If he hadn't brought dishes with him, he would have gone out that afternoon and bought some. No, it wasn't a date, but he still wanted to make a good impression on Brooke.

A slight ache throbbed in his shoulder. He'd ditched the sling almost as soon as he'd gotten home. It kept getting in the way. Aside from the wrist sprain and being a little banged up, he felt fine. He'd even managed to make a salad to go with the entrée Brooke was preparing for dinner. While wrestling with cutting vegetables with a brace on his wrist, he'd kicked himself for not inviting her to use his kitchen. He could have helped her cook, and they could have talked, hopefully not just about the bees.

Yeah, he'd been the one to choose that topic. Shaking his head, Gable huffed a chuckle. Not that he wasn't concerned about bee friendly farming. The subject was just a lot more interesting with Brooke involved. So far, he'd enjoyed their conversations. She had an easy approach to life that enhanced her bright, carefree personality. Brooke also didn't come across as overly complicated. He wouldn't mind spending time with her on a casual basis. Since Brooke was in town for only a few weeks, maybe that would fit her agenda, too, if she was interested.

The doorbell chimed.

After one last glance around the room, he went to the door and opened it.

Brooke stood just outside the entryway holding up a green canvas bag in one hand and a bottle of wine in the other. "I come bearing gifts."

Whoa. Forget about what she'd brought. Brooke was the gift that he was more than happy to receive.

Remembering his manners he stepped back and opened the door wider. "Come in."

As she walked by, a fresh clean fragrance with a hint of berries followed her, along with the smell of savory food. He liked both, but her fragrance and the way she looked in that dress were what sped up his heart rate.

He shut the door. "Dinner smells delicious. What did you bring?"

"Pasture Lane Restaurant's signature chicken pot pie."

"Good choice. I had it one night at the restaurant when I was staying at the guesthouse."

"Hope you don't mind having it again."

"Not at all." He approached her, trying his best not to stare at her bare, silky-looking legs. "If I enjoy something, I don't mind having it again."

"I feel the same way. Not that I had time to make anything else. There was a lot going on this afternoon." The smile still curved up her lips but a hint of irritation flashed in her eyes. Instead of her carefree spirit, she emanated restless energy.

"Is everything okay?"

"Yes, why do you ask?"

He shrugged. "For a second, you seemed a little preoccupied about something."

"I do have a few things on my mind, but work is over and I'm ready for a break." Brooke's smile grew more genuine. "I'm also hungry."

"Then we should eat." He led the way to the counter. "Does anything need to be heated up?"

"Nope. The pot pie is fresh out the oven. Do you have something for me to put the dish on? It's hot."

He put a glass cutting board on the counter. "I made a salad. Would you like ranch or blue cheese dressing?"

"Ranch works for me. I should have asked if you like chardonnay." She used the opener she brought and popped the cork on the bottle. "It's the perfect wine to serve with chicken pot pie. The notes of vanilla and oak will complement the creamy filling and buttery crust."

"That's an impressive observation. So are you a wine enthusiast?" He set the salad and ranch dressing on the counter.

"I'm very enthusiastic about drinking it." Brooke softly chuckled as she poured glasses of chardonnay for them both. "I only know about the pairing because I read it on the label attached to the pie, so don't be too impressed."

"I still think you're impressive."

"Let me guess. It's the way I chased down plastic bags that amazed you."

Encouraged by the gleam in her eye, Gable said, "Hey, who wouldn't be amazed by that? Especially since you did it in a bee suit. The way you snatched one bag out of the air and then swan dived for another. I mean, wow, I can't even describe it. It was so…"

"Stop, you win the prize."

"What did I win, exactly?" He offered her a serving spoon.

"Honey, of course."

If she was delivering it to him, he'd gladly take it. As she accepted the utensil, their fingers brushed and something that felt like an invisible charge, wild and enticing, rippled through him. He'd felt the same thing when she'd handed him the hot-cold packs yesterday.

From the surprised, almost confused look on Brooke's face, she'd felt something, too. Or maybe she was just wondering why he hadn't let go of the utensil.

He surrendered the spoon. She quickly looked away and used the spoon to put a serving of food on her plate.

As he served himself, Gable said, "Don't wait for me. Eat it while it's hot."

She took a bite.

It was impossible not to watch her lips close around the fork. And what a lucky fork that was. The bold red color highlighting her lush-looking mouth reminded Gable of berries, just like the scent of her perfume.

Catching himself staring at her, he focused on his plate. If he wasn't careful, he might be tempted to get a taste of her.

Brooke did her best to ignore the awareness that had sparked inside of her just because Gable's hand had touched hers a minute ago. And now she had to calmly sit next to him and pretend she wasn't bothered by his closeness? Maybe the distraction of eating would help.

It didn't. Not even the chicken and vegetables in an addictive sauce and wrapped in a perfect flaky crust could steal her attention from him. His proximity alone wreaked havoc on her system and it didn't help that she'd seen him shirtless in the spot where they were sitting. That memory was even more delicious than dinner. She took a long sip of wine, hoping to drown out the spark. It didn't help. Searching for a safe place to land her thoughts, Brooke shifted her focus to the topic that had led to them having dinner together.

She turned to him and asked, "So, what do you want to know about the bees?"

Gable sat back in his seat. "Anything useful you want to tell me. I've been doing some research…"

Research? She'd met too many guys along the way who once they found out she was a beekeeper would only pretend to have an interest in bees. But Gable actually had dived into the subject and asked key questions. He was smart and hot. By the end of their meal, she couldn't deny she was in deep like with him.

He got up and cleared away their empty plates. "So it sounds like common sense is the important factor when it comes to using chemicals around bees."

"Definitely. Things like not applying chemicals on a windy day so they don't drift toward the apiary. Or letting us know when you plan to use them so we can take extra precautions. Those steps sound really simple, but they're crucial to protecting our hives."

"I'll be sure to do that, and I'll check out the products you recommended." He took a box from the refrigerator and set it on the counter. "I hope brownies are good with you for dessert. I picked up a dozen from Brewed Haven."

The café's brownies? He'd chosen one of her weaknesses. "Did you get the toppings that come with them? And are you warming up the brownies *and* the chocolate sauce?"

"Is there any other way to have them?"

Gable's smooth deep voice followed by his full-on smile

made Brooke's heart skip a few beats then flutter to recover
them. If she was in the market for a boyfriend, he would
have been perfect. *Damn*, he was hot. And smart. And he
had a sense of humor. He was also good to his horse, liked
ranch dressing, and he understood the value of toppings on
brownies. And she really needed to stop crushing on him
because she wasn't interested in becoming involved with
anyone in Bolan. She was leaving as soon as she could,
and proximity relationships, like getting involved with the
guy who literally lived next door, was a very bad idea.
Privacy—gone. Unless you were hiding out in a cave or
sneaking around, people always noticed or picked up on
what was going on. And if things went wrong in a hookup
situation, awkwardness was guaranteed. Still, thinking
about that kind of situation with Gable, it was hard not to
focus more on the upside of the hookup equation. The con-
venience of everything she could want being in walking
distance. No. It was a bad idea for so many reasons, and
she needed to remember that.

Moments later, vanilla ice cream, fresh whipped cream,
warm chocolate sauce, nuts and fresh berries sat in front of
them along with the brownies. Standing nearly shoulder to
shoulder, they built sundaes in their own bowls.

She caught him smiling at her as she put ice cream on
her brownie, then berries, then topped it with a heaping
spoonful of whipped cream.

"What?" she asked.

"You're topping building skills are…"

"A lot. I know." She made a well in the whipped cream
then filled it with chocolate. "But I learned how to do this
in a very special place."

Gable drizzled a moderate amount of chocolate on his

brownie before adding a scoop of ice cream. "You did, huh? And where was that?"

She plopped a few berries in the well of chocolate. "The mud and sand building training camp."

"Okay. That type of training sounds odd, but I guess you have to learn all types of things for your jobs." As she failed to stop a quiver in her bottom lip from held back laughter, he pointed at her. "And you're messing with me."

As she released a laugh, she held up her thumb and index finger close together. "Just a little. In a few of my positions, I've worked with kids, and trust me, they know their stuff. Indestructible mud pies. Sandcastles designed to swallow up toys forever and guarantee the biggest dust up you ever saw if they're not found. Making ice cream sundaes are actually a good distraction if things get really tough."

"And what about you? Who or what distracts you when things get really tough?"

Brooke recognized a fact-finding mission when she heard one. "By chance, are you asking me if I'm available?" While she waited for his answer, she sucked chocolate from her thumb.

His gaze fell to her mouth. The flash of heat passing through his gaze was like a jolt that made her lips tingle. When he looked back into her eyes, it was gone, buried in the depths of his gaze. "And if I am, will you give me an answer or will it remain a mystery?"

Intrigued by his fact-finding mission, she ended his quest. "No mystery there. I'm single, and I don't date, not in the relationship kind of way. I'm moving around all the time. And the whole long-distance thing. I'd rather not deal with the drama that comes with going all in."

"Not going all in—is that just with long-distance relationships?"

Any kind of a relationship... The confession almost slipped out. The last time she'd admitted that to a guy, he'd tried to psychoanalyze her, claiming it had to be tied to some deep-rooted family issue. It wasn't. She just didn't want to be tied that deeply to anyone at this point in her life.

Conjuring up a smile, she responded breezily, "In my opinion, going all-in usually messes up a good thing."

As he studied her face, a slightly quizzical expression passed over his as if he had a question. Instead he said, "I agree. I don't date, either. I've always had other priorities. I'm not a right fit for commitment...especially now." As he added that last part, a bit of humor left from his eyes.

Especially now? What did he mean by that? Brooke held back the question. Possibly for the same reason he'd held back his. Too many questions could open the door to ones she didn't want to answer and topics she didn't want to talk about. And tonight, she'd rather focus on all the fun things they had in common. Not that she was counting them for any particular reason.

Gable's gaze dropped to her mouth again. He pointed. "You have chocolate on your face."

That old trick? Was he really going to pretend she had chocolate on her face just so he could sneak in a kiss? She'd expected something more original for him, but why not play along if it answered the question of whether or not he was a good kisser.

Eager to find out, Brooke leaned in, making it easier for Gable to meet her halfway. "Do I? Where?"

He handed her a napkin. "Left cheek. Near your mouth."

She actually had food on her face? *Oh no.* She wiped her cheek and cringed at the large smudge. Brooke laughed sheepishly. "How embarrassing."

"No need to be embarrassed. Telling you was the only

way I could help you take care of it." A smug, playful smile tugged at his lips as if he'd known she'd expected him to make a move. "I've had food on my face before. It's nothing."

"Like now?"

"Uh-uh." He turned his attention to his dessert. "I know you're trying to play me."

"But you do. Right there." She dabbed her finger in the whipped cream and dotted it on his cheek.

"I can't believe you just did that."

"Did what?" As Brooke stuck a spoonful of dessert in her mouth, she met his playful, accusatory stare with an innocent look.

He wiped his face. "You're lucky I don't believe in wasting a perfectly good brownie sundae in a food fight. Otherwise, you would be in so much trouble right now." After taking a quick bite, he surreptitiously wiped his finger low on her cheek.

As warm chocolate dripped toward her chin. She calmly wiped it away and kept eating her sundae. Oh, he was good, but he'd met his match, and he didn't even realize it. She was the queen of stealth. "You know, I agree. Doing anything other than eating this dessert would be a crime."

"Glad we got that straight."

She made her next move, quickly dipping her finger in the whipped cream.

But to her surprise, in the next instant, they both had cream-tipped fingers pointed at each other.

How had he managed to move so fast?

Brooke feigned irritation over the standoff. "Wait a minute. I thought you said you weren't wasting a good sundae?"

Copying her expression, he leaned in. "I did, and the

funny thing is, you agreed. So how are we ending this? Fingers up or spoons back down in our bowls?"

"Fine. Truce." She laughed and sucked the whipped cream from her finger. Watching him do the same with his beautiful mouth made her breath hitch.

Captivated, she blew out a slow breath, and her greatest fantasy whispered past her lips. "I would really love to kiss you."

The words had escaped, and she couldn't take them back. Now he knew what was on her mind.

Gable leaned in. "I was thinking the exact same thing."

Chapter Eleven

Which one of them closed the distance? Gable had no idea. The soft sweetness of her lips made it impossible to care about anything. He drifted his tongue along the seam of her mouth, asking…hoping, and Brooke responded, welcoming him in for a deepening kiss. As he explored her luscious mouth, need rose inside him, and he craved more.

She wound her arms around his neck. He slid his free hand around her waist, damning the brace that prevented him from molding both hands to her curves.

Moaning softly, she slid her hands down his chest. Her fingers grazed over the top button of his shirt. She unfastened it then moved down to the next.

He kneaded her hip, tempted to inch up the fabric of her dress, but they needed to take a minute and make sure they were on the same page.

Reluctantly, Gable pulled a hairbreadth away. "Brooke… hold on."

"What's wrong?" As he lightly caressed up and down her back, the haze of desire started clearing from her eyes and she frowned.

"I just thought we should take a beat. We just went from zero to a hundred in less than a minute…"

"Oh, I understand." A look of disappointment and something akin to embarrassment crossed her face. She started backing away from him.

But he caught her by the waist before she slipped away. "No, I think you're *mis*understanding me." He connected with her gaze. "I'm willing to go as fast and far as you want, but I think we should be honest with each other before we do. You walked in here preoccupied over something you don't want to talk about. I think what's happening between us now is a diversion from that, and I get it." He gave her waist a reassuring squeeze. "There are things I'm dealing with I don't want to talk about, either. Because that's in my headspace, like I said earlier, it makes me a bad pick for anything beyond a physical relationship. I know you said you don't date in a relationship kind of way, but I just want to make sure we're talking about the same thing."

Brooke stared directly in his eyes. "What that means to me is that I'm not looking to start anything serious. I'm leaving in a few weeks, and when I do, I want to walk away on good terms. We get along. I've enjoyed being with you, and I'm hoping we're compatible in other ways. A distraction is all I'm looking for."

Honesty and no games. She was his type. A breath of happiness and relief glided out of him. Widening his stance, he cupped his hand to her hip and brought her flush against him. "Then we're definitely on the same page."

Brooke rested her hands on his chest, toying with the next unopened button near her fingertips. "I do have one really important question."

He cocked his brow. "What?"

"Can we get back to me taking your shirt off?"

"Do I get to do the same with your dress? You look pretty, by the way."

Smiling, she pressed her lips to his. "Thank you and yes."

"There is one thing, I should mention," he murmured. "I don't have a bed yet. I'm sleeping on a foam mattress."

"I saw it, but I'm not interested in your sleep number." She broke from his lips to press a kiss to his chest. The heat of her mouth and the feel of her palm against the front of his jeans fueled his rising need.

Yeah, they were definitely compatible.

Standing in his bedroom, Brooke slipped open one button and then another on his shirt. The reveal of his muscular chest made her giddy, as if she was unwrapping a present she couldn't wait to get open.

But the barely there brushes of his mouth along the side of her neck clouded her mind with anticipation. His lips found hers with a soft kiss. The tip of his tongue drifting lightly against her mouth prompted her to open to him. But he teased her, sucking lightly on her bottom lip before entering her mouth the smallest bit, driving her close to insanity as he increased the pressure so slowly her legs grew weak. Finally, he dove in, sweeping…searching, he explored her mouth and she explored his. The ever-deepening kiss made her feel she was rising higher and higher.

Moments later, nothing, including the mattress, got in the way of pleasure. The heat of his mouth washed over her skin as he kissed down her neck to her breasts that were full and heavy, and begging for his touch. He cupped one in his hand and the sensation of him closing his lips around her nipple and gently drawing her into his mouth unleased spirals of desire through her middle.

With every kiss and caress he delivered, she arched under him, grasping on to his back as his muscles bunched and released under her palm. She wanted him. Needed him inside of her. When the time came, she rolled a condom down his length, mesmerized by the weight of him in her hands and the way his abs tightened as he drew in a breath.

Urging her back on the mattress, he found her completely ready for him, and he glided inside of her. As she matched his rhythm, she slid her legs around his waist. Every. Single. Thrust of his hips took her closer to orgasm. She hovered on the precipice until one final roll of his hips took her over in a rush of ecstasy.

Afterward, snuggled close to Gable on the mattress, she actually did sleep, using him as her pillow.

The following morning, Brooke left Gable's bedroom, allowing her nose to lead the way. *Coffee.* She'd awakened alone, burrowed in the sheets on his mattress, but the wonderful aroma in the air made up for his absence. Almost.

As she walked out of the hallway, Gable was crossing the living room, shirtless, wearing a pair of black sweatpants, holding a mug.

She wore the matching shirt. The soft fabric grazing over her breasts and along the tops of her legs reminded her of his caresses. The replay of last night in her mind made her warm all over.

They met halfway.

The shadow of hair along his cheeks and jawline had grown a little heavier overnight. It framed his small sexy smile. "Morning."

"Good morning." She pointed at the mug in his hand. "Is that for me?"

"It is. Sorry, I don't have any milk or cream. Just sugar."

"I like sugar." She accepted the mug from him and took a sip. Blessed caffeine brought a rush of heat.

"How is it?" He studied her face. "Be honest."

"Good, but I usually like it a little sweeter. I take it with three teaspoons of sugar."

"I'll remember that and make it the way you like it next time." Gable took hold of her hips.

Her lower body gravitated toward his, melting them into a perfect fit. "Next time… I like the sound of that."

"I do, too." He pressed his mouth to hers. The steaminess of the kiss rivaled the steam wafting up from the mug.

Desire unfurled inside of Brooke. She was tempted to toss aside the coffee, peel off the T-shirt and relive last night all over again. But they hadn't covered everything during their "just checking if this is a hookup" conversation. They'd nailed down most of it, but that morning, something else had come to her mind.

Brooke flattened her hand on his bare chest and reluctantly eased back. "We really should talk about something."

Gable led her to the counter. He sat down. "I'm listening."

Preferring to stand, she naturally gravitated toward the space between his legs. Her hand itched to run her fingers along his wide shoulders and hard chest.

She took a sip of coffee to keep desire in check and to give herself a moment to order her thoughts. "Expecting people to mind their own business in this town is impossible. It's one of the reasons I don't miss living here. They always exaggerate things. Some of the locals actually call me the psychic beekeeper just because I have good instincts about the bees. One time, a few tourists caught wind of the rumor, and they asked me to read their fortune in honey."

"You're joking."

"I'm not. The whole psychic beekeeper thing is annoying, and it's a prime example of small-town weird not having boundaries. Honestly, I wouldn't be surprised if someone made up some dumb story about us hooking up so quickly because I supposedly used my mental powers to persuade you or something."

He smiled. "Definitely something."

"I'm serious." She rested her hand on his shoulder and drew a random pattern on his skin. "Someone is bound to notice how much time we're spending together. If you don't want people wondering or talking about you, the two of us being together is going to lead to the opposite. So if you're looking for privacy…"

"I appreciate the concern." Gable fit his hands to her waist as he looked into her eyes. "But I'm not completely naive to small-town talk. I have a confession to make. I've been to Bolan before. I visited my great-uncle one summer a little over sixteen years ago. He was the local farrier."

"You're related to Wes Brunson?"

"So you knew him?"

"I knew *of* him. Everyone around here did, but since we didn't have horses, he didn't come to our farm." She chuckled. "How funny. We might have passed each other walking down the street or something."

"Maybe, but I didn't go out much, especially at first. I didn't want to be here." Gable told her about how he'd ended up at Wes's farm and how the older man helped turn his attitude around.

"It sounds like he had a major influence on your life."

"Yep. He helped turn me into who I am today. I'll always be grateful to him."

"So why haven't you told anyone Wes was your great-uncle?"

Gable offered up a slight shrug. "It didn't come up, and

Peggy was just a little too curious. The way she talked about the Rosses made me not want to tell her anything."

A brick in the invisible wall Brooke had imagined he'd built around sharing information about himself came down. He'd returned to a place that was fairly familiar to him. Why? That was still a mystery, and she didn't need to know the answer. During dinner last night, neither one of them had been eager to talk about themselves, their families or their past entanglements, and she was good with that. She didn't need to know the details if he didn't want to explain, but some people...

"So you got a dose of Peggy, huh." Brooke huffed a breath. "She's good at making up rumors. After I leave, she'll be the main one spreading them about your clandestine relationship with Brooke the Wanderer."

He gave her a light squeeze. "I really like you, Brooke, and if we only have a few weeks together, I'd rather not waste it worrying about what other people think now or when we go our separate ways. I'd rather focus on our time together."

Happiness turned her worry into a smile. Three weeks with a guy who wanted to focus on being with her—could she ask for more? A funny thought came to mind. "Well, the good news is, we're not famous enough for the *Bolan Town Talk.*"

"The what?"

"The weekly online paper. Actually, it's more like a gossip blog than a source for real news. It's written by the mayor's sister-in-law. But I heard she's being a lot more cautious after the mayor's wife threatened to take her poison pen away. Apparently, a story she reported almost caused some major backlash."

A slightly pensive look crossed his face. "That's... interesting."

I swear I've heard his name before.... A couple of the staff claim they saw him online somewhere... Nellie's and Zurie's comments floated through Brooke's mind. Was he well-known for something? But Zurie was right about social media. Almost everyone was online. Anyone could have stumbled across a name or picture or someone with a similar name or photo. Anything was possible, and her comment about the online paper could have been interesting to him for no big reason.

He leaned in. "So, are we done talking?"

He nipped the side of her neck then gently sucked the spot. Tingles radiated over Brooke's skin. Closing her eyes, she tilted her head, giving him better access. "I think we've covered it." He cupped her breast, and as he feathered his thumb over her nipple, she swayed in his arms, nearly dropping the mug she held out of the way.

As Gable stood, he slipped the mug from her hand and put it on the counter. "Do you have to leave right away?" Before she could answer, he kissed her.

In between light teasing kisses she responded, "No." She went willingly as he started backing her toward the couch. "I've definitely got time."

Much later in the morning, Brooke rushed from her Jeep to the front door of her house. Once again, she was running late for a meeting. But the delay had been worth it. Remembering the last couple of hours with Gable raised shivers of delight. She only left him because she had somewhere to be, but they'd made plans to see each other that night.

She opened the door.

Harper, dressed in blue pajamas and a sweater, paced

in the living room near the foyer. She looked at Brooke. "Where have you been?"

She hadn't been home two seconds and Harper was already on her for no reason. Brooke closed the door. Harper actually sounded more like a parent than a sister. Since when did she think she reported to her? "I was at Gable's house."

"You were at our neighbor's all night? Why?"

She and Gable being together wasn't a secret. Might as well start with Harper in delivering the news. "Yes, all night. We're seeing each other. Anything else?"

"Well, you could have answered your messages. I sent you a text and left a voicemail."

"You did?" Brooke glanced at her phone. She'd changed her setting to Do Not Disturb last night. When she'd rushed out of Gable's house earlier, she hadn't changed the setting back or checked the screen for notifications. "Sorry. My phone was on silent."

Harper crossed her arms over her chest. "Next time, you should pay attention and not ignore your phone."

"Seriously?" Brooke choked out a laugh. "You've been ignoring me for almost two days."

"At least you knew where to find me. I had no idea where you were. You could have been hurt…or something." A hint of worry and vulnerability came and went from Harper's face. She wrapped her arms around herself and studied her bare feet on the floor.

As Brooke thought of Harper imagining the worst while she'd been enjoying a pleasurable night with Gable, guilt pinged in her chest. "I'm sorry. I should have let you know I was next door. No matter how we feel about our situation, right now, we should at least let each other know our plans, especially if we're not coming home. And at some point, we have to start talking."

"About what?" Harper's glance held shades of her usual judgment and accusation. "You've already made your position clear. You're bailing on me."

"Not necessarily." Her sister only saw a door closing, but what about the one that opened to opportunity? Brooke reasoned, "I know you love this place, and, yes, we inherited the farm from Mom and Dad, but it's not mandated that we have to stay. Think about it. If we sell you can move away from Bolan and start a new life."

"I don't want a new life. I want this one. Do what you want, but I'm not selling."

Accepting the certainty in her sister's eyes, Brooke said, "If that's what you want that's fine with me, but I'm sure you'd rather own this place outright and not have to partner with anyone. I can give you time to raise the money. Or you can pay me in installments."

"I'm not worried about the money. I already checked. I can take out a loan."

"Good." Accepting the conversation was over, Brooke turned to walk away. "Then you don't need me. I can leave for my next job assignment on time."

"Actually, I do need you. The farm is in the running for a business grant. But we have to meet certain conditions, like having the needed personnel. We could lose our chance at the money if the committee found out Aunt Ivy left and we don't have a full-time beekeeper. It would help if you stayed until they've made their decision."

Brooke faced her. "How long?"

"Four or five weeks. When you thought Aunt Ivy was just going on vacation, you said you could stay that long."

No, she'd said a week or ten days longer than her normal three weeks.

Harper swallowed hard. "Please."

Brooke released an exhale. If she stayed five weeks, she would have to drive straight to California and not take her time. But her sister had actually said please. And she did want to help. "I'll stay for five weeks. But what about after that? Who'll take care of the bees when I'm gone?"

"I will, with Leah's help, until I find someone to do it permanently."

Leah the groundskeeper? Brooke almost asked the question, but choosing the next beekeeper wasn't in her hands, along with any other future decisions about the farm. But was Harper making the right choice? Did Leah even have experience?

During the uncomfortable silence, Brooke tamped down her concerns. Now what? Did they give each other a hug? A handshake? Neither of them seemed to know what to do.

Brooke pointed down the hall. "I have to go or I'm going to be seriously late for my meeting."

"Should we message Aunt Ivy?"

Their aunt had left the decision of what to do with the farm in their hands, and they'd made it. Why bother her with the result? Aunt Ivy hadn't asked them to keep her informed. They could tell their aunt about the legal transfer of ownership when she got back from the cruise. She'd be happy for them. They were making the right decisions. A hint of uncertainty needled Brooke about that last part. "No. Let Aunt Ivy enjoy her vacation."

Chapter Twelve

"The plan for the celebration looks great." Executive Chef Philippa Gale Crawford nodded in agreement over the details she and Brooke had just discussed.

Her restaurant, recently renamed Pasture Lane Restaurant at Tillbridge, was located at Tillbridge Horse Stable and Guesthouse. The lull between breakfast and lunch was the perfect time for Brooke to meet with the busy chef with almost no interruptions.

The Black woman in her late twenties sitting across from Brooke at the four-top table exuded authority and poise. An apple green and black headband secured her dark locs. Her uniform—an ensemble of an apple green chef's jacket with black buttons, black pants and green Crocs—added to her crisp, polished look. Her restaurant reflected the same sense of modernness mixed with sensibility.

In the dining room, natural light shone through a wall of glass overlooking a courtyard with trees. Light wood tables with a centerpiece of white flowers in a bud vase along with green potted plants situated throughout the dining room gave the pale wood-floored space an open, airy feel.

"I'm glad you approve." Brooke nudged her nearly full coffee cup farther away. She was afraid to drink it, concerned she'd make a bad impression by spilling a drop on her cream-colored blouse. She wouldn't have worn it, but the blouse was the only clean top she had that could elevate her jeans, heels and beige sweater to a professional level. Continuing, she added, "And I'm excited about the cooking demo your husband is adding to the celebration and that you're willing to provide a couple of recipes for the booklet."

Celebrity chef and bestselling author Dominic Crawford was the founder of the celebrated LA and Atlanta Frost & Flame restaurants and hosted the popular television show *Farm to Fork with Dominic Crawford*. Many of the episodes for the series were filmed in Bolan.

"Anything for the bees. Dominic and I both believe in sustainability and supporting the environment. And I love the idea of a booklet." A contemplative look came over Philippa's face. "As far as the budget for the booklet, I agree that all three establishments could help with the cost, but what if you had a sponsor?"

"Like who?"

"Tillbridge Horse Stable and Guesthouse. Zurie is always willing to connect the stable to a worthy cause. In fact, she just walked in with Chloe."

The co-owner of the stable and guesthouse looked all business, dressed in a navy and white wrap dress. Chloe Daniels, an actress who was married to Tristan Tillbridge, was more casual in jeans, a light sweater and boots, and her curly dark hair was in a messy bun.

Philippa added, "The three of us were planning to have a quick chat this morning. Why don't you join us? You can pitch the idea of the booklet to Zurie."

"Like now? I don't want to intrude."

"You know what they say, 'Strike while the fire is hot.' She's free, you're here, and you'll have her undivided attention. Just tell her what you told me." Before Brooke could object further, Philippa waved Zurie and Chloe over to the table.

As the two women approached, Brooke's palms started to sweat and she wiped them on her jeans. Years ago, as a marketing representative, she'd made several presentations to clients, but that was after weeks of preparation and strategizing about how to meet a company's needs. She'd understood their strengths as well as weaknesses and how to turn both into advantages. But not having time to study all of the details about Tillbridge Horse Stable and Guesthouse wasn't her biggest problem. She hadn't made a marketing pitch or business presentation in years. Could she still do it?

Zurie and Chloe reached the table. Heart pounding, Brooke smiled through the hellos. She'd met Chloe once before, and the actress remembered her.

"Take a seat," Philippa said. "Brooke and I are talking about the plans for this year's honey celebration. She has an idea I think the two of you should hear, especially you, Zurie. I'll get us more coffee."

"Actually, I'll have orange juice," Zurie and Chloe said at the same time. They looked at each other and laughed.

"I'm cutting back on caffeine," Zurie confessed to Chloe. "What's your excuse?"

"I've got a new role coming up. My nutritionist has me on a plan. I can only have a cup of coffee a day and I've already met my limit." She looked to Philippa. "Could I have a waffle with fruit and some fudge poured over it, too? Oh, and put a couple of scoops of whipped cream on it please." She shrugged at the questioning looks. "It's kind of a cheat day."

Philippa stood. "Two orange juices and a loaded waffle. Got it. I'll be right back. But go ahead and start, Brooke."

Zurie and Chloe looked to Brooke expectantly.

Suddenly, Brooke's mouth felt dry. She risked a sip of coffee. *Let's do this...* Taking a deep breath, she smiled. "I have an idea to support the bees that I would love for you to be a part of..."

In the larger kitchen at his house, Gable put the dishes he'd just unpacked into the dishwasher.

The moving company had shown up a day earlier than anticipated, and he'd spent most of the day unpacking. The containers for the kitchen were some of the smallest and easiest to unbox with his wrapped wrist.

The house was already coming together. He now had a fully furnished living room. The black leather sectional, wood furniture, rug and flat-screen television above the fireplace made the house look like a home.

Although it wasn't in the contract, the guys from the moving company had taken a look at his injury, empathized with his situation and hung the television for him.

One of the things he had managed to set up on his own was the mattress railing for his bed. Installing the headboard would have to wait until his wrist was less sore, but it was a relief to roll up the foam mattress and put it away. Tonight, he would sleep comfortably off the floor on his plush king-size mattress. And maybe Brooke would share in the moment with him. He couldn't wait to see her again. How was her day going?

Ever since she'd left that morning, he couldn't stop thinking about her. Starting a relationship, temporary or otherwise, hadn't been on his agenda, but he had no regrets. He'd meant it when he'd told Brooke he wanted to focus on their short-term thing. They could do that more easily since they'd been honest about being each other's distraction. No strings. No expectations. No complications. No plans for something more. Remaining exclusive was a gray area in a situationship, but they'd only agreed to keep it that way because they wanted to enjoy what little time they had together.

The doorbell rang.

Brooke. His heart sped up by a beat or two as he went to the door and opened it.

She looked pretty in her casual yet professional outfit. But that didn't grab his attention the most. The sun was dropping on the horizon, but she beamed a radiant smile brighter than a sunrise.

"Hello." Brooke walked in.

He wrapped an arm around her. "You look happy."

"I am. I received some great news." She pressed her lips to his.

During their lingering kiss, Gable pushed the door shut so he could wrap both arms around her.

His mom had been worried about him having a missing hole in his life. He was filling it by getting to know the most interesting woman, no, possibly the sexiest, most interesting woman he'd ever met.

As they eased away, she glanced at the living room and her face brightened a bit more. "Your furniture came. That's great."

"It is, but I'm sure it's not as great as your news." He held her hand and led her into the living room. "Tell me."

"It's work related. I don't want to bore you."

"You can't leave me hanging. From the way you're smiling, you look like you won the lottery."

Laughing, Brooke set her keys and phone on the glass-topped coffee table before sitting next to him on the sectional. "Close but not quite. I had another idea to help promote National Honey Month—a booklet featuring honey-based recipes from the Brewed Haven Café, Pasture Lane Restaurant and the Montecito Steakhouse bar..."

As he listened to what Brooke said, he was captivated by the graceful way she talked with her hands and how her face lit up with an exuberant smile. The peachy color on her lips also distracted him. When she was done talking, he was definitely kissing her.

"So," Brooke said, "I got to the end of my pitch, and I went for it. I asked Zurie if Tillbridge Stable and Guesthouse would sponsor the printing of the booklet, and she said yes."

"Congrats, but I'm not surprised. You're very convincing. I'm convinced."

"About what?"

The corny line he was about to say was worth delivering because she was already smiling as he leaned in. "That I should really kiss you right now."

Her smile faded and she shook her head. "No, I don't think so."

"You don't?" He'd been wrong about the corny line.

"Nope." Brooke's serious expression lightened with a teasing smile. "I should really kiss you." Closing the distance, she laid one on him.

The feel of her pillowy soft lips on his went straight to his head. She opened to him, and his senses were overcome by his new favorite pastime, maybe his only hobby. Hell, he'd make exploring the lush warmth of her mouth his sole profession and gladly do it for free.

As he reached to lift her up, she was already moving to straddle him, but then she stopped.

Breaking away from the kiss, Brooke said, "Hold that thought. I need to make a note to add the cooking demo to our social media schedule." As she reached for her phone, she glanced at the growing bulge at the front of his jeans. "And hold that, too."

Was she seriously putting him on hold? Of course she was. The look of concentration and enthusiasm on her face as she made a note on her phone made it impossible for him not to chuckle. Expect the unexpected. That was one thing he was learning about Brooke, and also that she was worth waiting for.

"Can I get on your social media schedule?" he teased.

"That depends on if you're following Bishop Honey Bee Farm." Brooke shot him a mock glare. "You *are* following us?"

He reached for his phone on the side table next to him. "Guess I should fix that." After a few quick swipes and taps, he'd followed Bishop Honey Bee Farm on their platforms. "Done." As he went to close the last app, a notification about a post caught his eye.

Theo Jr.'s birthday... His hand involuntarily tightened around the phone. He couldn't just ignore it.

Heart drumming in his chest, he clicked on the notification and the post opened up on the screen. It was a close-up picture of Melonie holding Theo Jr. The laughing toddler wore a crown birthday hat and had a smear of frosting on his face. Melonie had tears on hers.

Gable silently read her post:

To the love of my life… Our little prince turned two today, but how can I smile? All I can see is you holding our son on your lap singing "Happy Birthday" to him. But it's only a dream. You're not here. You'll miss the rest of our son's birthdays. I miss you so much…

A swell of sorrow pushed the air out of Gable's chest.

"Aww. What a cute little boy. Is it his birthday?" Brooke leaning against his arm to look at his phone reminded him to breathe. "Is that his mother holding him? She looks so sad."

Gable swallowed against a raw feeling in his throat. "She's sad because the one person who should be there isn't." He felt the need to speak the truth aloud. He never had. "Theo, my friend, isn't there because of me."

Brooke looked at him. She opened her mouth as if to speak but then she paused.

What happened? What had he done? Gable could almost see the questions running through her mind. He was glad she didn't ask them because he might not be able to stomach the disappointment that would come into her eyes if he told her the truth. The compassion in her eyes now, he didn't deserve it.

Leaving his phone behind on the couch, he got up and walked to the sliding door. Head down, arms straight, he put his hands on the glass. His left wrist throbbed as he tried to make a fist but couldn't. Not that he cared about the discomfort. He almost wished the glass would shatter from the pressure he was putting on it, but not even the deepest cut could compare to the pain Melonie felt over Theo not being there for her and their son.

The stress of working two jobs, not getting enough sleep plus living on caffeine had all had a part in Theo's heart attack. If only he'd questioned him more about the chest discomfort he was feeling that night at the bar. If only he hadn't kept Theo out late that night. If only he hadn't persuaded Theo to start working at Lou's in the first place. If he hadn't, Theo might still be with his family.

Brooke came over to him and gently laid her hand on

his shoulder. "Do you want me to leave? If you do, I understand."

He didn't want her to go. He also didn't want to burden her with his problems. She'd been happy when she'd walked in and now he'd dampened the joy of her success. His wrist throbbed but not enough to mask the pain of sorrow and regret. "You don't have to leave, but you should be celebrating your big achievement with your sister."

Brooke ducked under his arm and stood in front of him. Even greater compassion was in her eyes. "I can celebrate tomorrow. I'm right where I want to be, and I'll stay for as long as you want me to be here. Losing someone close to you, I understand how that hurts." She laid a hand on his chest. "Do you want to tell me more about him or about your friendship? It sounds like you were close."

For a second, Gable thought he'd imagined what she'd said. Since the accident, no one had ever asked him to share memories of his friend, only what had taken him. He hadn't known her long, but just Brooke asking the question made him want to open up to her, but should he cross that boundary? The one separating a no-strings, short-term hookup from reality?

Chapter Thirteen

As Brooke waited for his answer, her heart hurt for him. He'd lost a friend. Now the glimpses of emotional pain in his eyes along with his times of stillness made sense. In those moments, he was caught up in his memories, maybe even paralyzed by them. When she'd lost her parents, she'd felt that, too.

He stared into her eyes then shook his head. "Dealing with my baggage isn't what you signed up for."

"I signed up because I like you. Period." She rested both of her hands on his chest. "I think talking about it will help. I'm here to listen if you do."

Gable closed his eyes. Tension emanated from him.

All she wanted to do was make him take his hands down from the glass and hold him. Explaining how Theo died, she could see it was a raw subject for him. That's why she hadn't asked how it happened, but maybe he could find the emotional release he needed by telling her about his friendship with Theo. Still, it made sense that Gable was hesitant. Memories of Theo were probably some of the most painful of his life. Not to mention, they'd only known each other a minute, and what they had agreed to was to be each other's distraction from the things they didn't want to dwell on.

But he needed to let go of what was building inside of him. The memories were obviously tearing him apart.

Brooke weighed the value of sharing from her own life as the gateway to helping him open up about Theo. She rarely told people about her own loss, but maybe he'd feel less apprehensive sharing about his personal life if she revealed something more intimate about hers.

Briefly closing her eyes, she released a breath. "I can't know everything you're feeling about Theo, but I know what it's like to lose people you care about. I lost both of my parents in a car accident years ago."

"Both of them?" A small frown furrowed his brow. "I'm sorry. I didn't know." He took his hands from the glass and laid one of them over hers on his chest. "That must have been rough."

"It was." Brooke fiddled with a button on his shirt, refusing to recall the full memory of all she'd felt when it happened. "But right now, it's not about what I've lost. Tell me about Theo. How did you meet?"

"Well…" Gable cleared his throat. "Theo and I were both musicians in Atlanta. We sang at some of the same clubs."

"Did Theo play the guitar?" That would explain the instrument in Gable's room. Perhaps he'd kept it for sentimental reasons?

"No, the guitar you saw belongs to me. Theo played the piano, and as a singer…" As a hint of a smile ghosted over his lips, Gable looked as if he was searching for the right words. "He was a cut above most performers. He had the ability to make every song his own. It was as if the lyrics came from a place inside of him. You didn't just hear the words, you felt them."

As Brooke adjusted her stance, they rocked a little. "It sounds like he was an amazing talent."

"He was very talented, but Theo was an even better person. Solid and always optimistic." Gable paused and a faraway look came into his eyes. "He was an encourager. There were so many times when I or someone else wanted to give up on something, and he would chime in, pointing out all of the possibilities we'd miss if we did. He was the one who put me on the path to singing country music."

The guitar. The cowboy hat. The richness of his voice singing a country song. It all snapped into place for Brooke as she imagined Gable the performer. "So he was wise about a lot of things."

"A lot of the time, but not always." Gable chuckled as he rested his hands on her hips. They swayed again and kept swaying to the silent song of good memories. "Theo never used an instruction manual to put things together. He'd just wing it. He put together a dining room set once. When he was done, the chairs wobbled, one of the legs on the table was too short and he had screws left over."

"Oh, that is bad." Brooke chuckled with him.

"Not as bad as his sports picks. He couldn't pick a winning team to save his life, not even in fantasy football. And he had no skills in the kitchen. He could mess up microwaving a cup of water."

"I can relate to that. The stove has been my enemy on more than a few occasions, but no one can be good at everything, right?"

His ghost of a smile surfaced a bit more as he studied her face. "But being good where it counts, that's important."

The intensity of his gaze drove hers down to his chest. "Theo sounds like someone I would have liked. Tell me more about him."

As Gable told her a couple more stories, it was easy to visualize the two of them having fun and backing each other up in the midst of shenanigans and looking out for each other's best interests. They'd had a tight friendship.

Gable paused and she said, "It's wonderful that you have a lot of great memories of Theo."

"I do. And I understand what you're trying to tell me without saying it." Gable stopped them from swaying. "I should hold on to all of the best memories about Theo, but none of them can erase what happened. Theo walked away from music. He moved to Jacksonville with his family for a fresh start, but I talked him into performing again. I even got him a job at a club. And then, a little over six months ago, I paid him a visit one night. He seemed a little off, but instead of being concerned about his welfare, I took advantage of his talent instead and took him to breakfast. Shortly after I left him, he had a heart attack." The shadows of anguish and hurt grew in Gable's eyes, and his heart thumped heavily against her palm. "His wife blames me for taking him away from her, and she has every right to be upset. And I don't have the right to forget that or what I did to him."

Brooke hadn't known Gable very long, but he was considerate and thoughtful. She couldn't imagine him intentionally causing harm to anyone, especially a friend he cared about. If he would have known Theo was in trouble, he would have done something, but he couldn't have predicted what happened to his friend.

Just as she started to point that out, Gable lifted her hand and kissed her palm. "Now that you know the story, I would really like to stop talking about it."

Based on what he'd told her about his and Theo's friendship, she couldn't imagine Theo wanting him to shoulder the responsibility of his death. That's what she wanted to say, but Gable was buried under too much guilt to even entertain that possibility, especially from her, someone he'd just met.

Her deep breath coincided with his. "No more talking about it then. What would you rather do?"

"The TV's hooked up. Let's watch a movie. There's a frozen pizza in the refrigerator. Or if you want something else for dinner, I can thaw out chicken or steak."

"Pizza is fine. Why don't I take care of the food while you find a movie."

He gave her hand a squeeze. "Sounds perfect to me."

Later on, shoes off, she sat curled up next to Gable watching an action-comedy film. Eating pizza and watching the film had succeeded in lightening the mood. They laughed in all the right places, but underneath the light-heartedness an undercurrent flowed between them filled with a new understanding. She knew where the glimpses of sadness in his eyes came from, and he appreciated that she wasn't going to coddle him. Still, it was hard for her to know Gable was beating himself up in a losing fight with guilt.

The movie ended and he clicked on the sequel. Before the opening scene finished, she fell asleep on his shoulder. She woke up with no clue about the plot, and Gable couldn't tell her about it, either. He'd fallen asleep, too.

Carefully slipping from his arm around her shoulder, she sat up and studied his face. With his head resting on the back of the sectional, he looked boyish, innocent and peaceful. Through her travels, she'd learned to read people. Yes, Gable was flawed. Who wasn't? And he'd probably made huge mistakes. She definitely had. But having met her share of bad people, she innately knew he was one of the good ones.

Brooke slipped on her shoes. It was time to go home. Rule

number one of a temporary fling: don't make things weird by hanging around too long. She glanced over at Gable and met his hooded stare. He had that just-woken-up sexiness down to a science.

Her heart skipped beats. "You shouldn't look at me like that."

He reached over and took her hand in his. "I'm not sure what 'like that' means, but when it comes to staring at you, I can't help it, Sun Angel."

That was the second time he'd called her that. The first time, he'd been a little out of it from falling off of his horse. "What does sun angel mean?"

"It means you're beautiful."

Brooke let him tug her back to him. "When you say things like that, you make it really hard for me to leave."

"Then don't."

His invitation wrapped in his sexy voice followed by a soft, deep kiss she didn't want to end made leaving impossible. It also obliterated her copy of the temporary relationship rule book. Who'd written that dumb thing anyway?

Brooke indulged in a longer kiss that quickly led to what they'd promised when they'd agreed to start seeing each other. Passion. Titillation. When he brought her to orgasm, the rise to ecstasy was so powerful, her cries of pleasure momentarily stole her voice. The perfect diversion.

Later that night, Brooke awoke in bed with Gable, lying on his chest. Moonlight shone in her eyes and rain splattered hard against the window.

The night she lost her parents, a moon just like it had shone in the sky. She shivered, stopping her imagination before it could fully unfold.

"You okay?" Half asleep, Gable glided his hand down her bare arm and up again.

"I'm fine. Just a little cold."

He brought the sheet up higher, covering them both, and held her closer. "Better?"

"Yes." His steady heartbeat soothed her. Her breathing naturally synched with his. In and out, as if they were... connected.

That's actually how she felt after telling Gable about losing her parents and hearing his story about losing Theo. She'd tried opening up to someone she'd been seeing once, but their dynamic changed afterward. It was as if he saw her as different, fragile.

With Gable she'd felt safe, seen, understood. Was that why she suddenly felt so connected to him? Shifting her head more toward his shoulder, she looked at his face. He'd called her an angel, but in the moonlight, he actually looked like one. Strong, noble and undeniably sexy, and he was hers...for the moment.

As Brooke snuggled back into position on his chest, Gable held her closer in his sleep. Feeling as if she was co-cooned in a wonderful space meant only for her, she started to drift off. Even though what she had with Gable was only for the short-term, she had to admit, experiencing a real, human connection to him that went beyond liking brownie sundaes and sharing passionate moments felt wonderful.

Chapter Fourteen

Brooke stood at the closed door of Ivy's office with her hand on the doorknob. Two days of trying to work at the kitchen table was killing her backside, and it wasn't practical. Important files. Office supplies. A printer. They were all in the office.

You have lots of good memories to cherish... That's what she'd told Gable. She should take that approach with the office. She couldn't get caught up in what had changed. The memories of her parents would always be there regardless.

Turning the knob, Brooke entered the room. Knowing what to expect made it easier to view it for what it was now. It was an office. A place for work. That's all.

The dove gray and black color scheme was modern, but the office had a coziness to it. The black desk was adjustable. The large leather chair behind it looked comfortable. The small pots of African violets on the credenza behind the desk added pops of color. The couch along the wall signaled family and friends were welcome for a visit, but this wasn't a space for business meetings with strangers.

Her gaze drifted to the oak-wood-framed chaise lounge tucked in the corner by the picture window. Framed photos were arranged on a round table next to it.

The color of the upholstery on the chaise was different.

Instead of intertwined pink roses on a beige background, the striped fabric matched the decor and so did a gray throw folded on the seat.

As she approached the chair, a vision of her mom resting against the high curved back with her feet up came into her mind. Almost every morning, she stretched out on the lounge to drink her first cup of coffee before sunrise.

Brooke's gaze moved to the picture frames. Aunt Ivy had moved her collection of family photos from her bedroom to here. Two photos hinged together in a gold frame caught her attention. The picture on the right was of Brooke and Harper when they were kids. The one on the left was of their mom and Aunt Ivy around the same age. It was slightly bubbled up in the middle of the frame as well as a little lopsided.

As Brooke reached down to fix it, her hand bumped against a large oval frame with a picture of her dad carrying her mom across the threshold of the house at the farm. Waves of emotion filled with love and loss swelled in Brooke's chest. She looked away from the table, refusing to allow herself to fully take in the rest of the photos and the recollections that came with them. She didn't have time for a trip down memory lane. She had work to do. Quickly turning away, Brooke went to the desk and became absorbed in work on the laptop.

She'd finished inspecting the hives on the farm. Tomorrow she'd inspect the ones off property, and Gable was coming with her. Maybe they should pack something for lunch. One of their stops was a fruit and vegetable farm. The owners of the farm wouldn't mind if they took a break there to enjoy the view. And while they would have a chance to relax, visiting the hives away from the farm would allow him to see how they naturally fit into those environments. Or could face potential harm if those environments changed.

Aunt Ivy's notes about the hives located at other farms and private residences reflected valid concerns. Developers had purchased farmland outside of town, including a small orchard, and planned to build housing subdivisions. The loss of natural pollen sources and clean water in those areas could affect the bees—something the investors and contractors didn't care about.

A soft tap on the door made her look up.

Harper came in. She was dressed for work in a T-shirt, jeans and a pair of purple work boots that Brooke immediately coveted. Back in the day, they'd practically lived in each other's closets. "Hey, I heard you in here. Am I interrupting?"

The lack of bite in her sister's voice almost made Brooke uncomfortable. "No. It's a good time for me to take a break. What's up?" She sat back in the office chair as Harper approached the desk.

"I wanted to let you know the farm's prospects look good for the grant. They're doing a deep dive into our financials now. Speaking of financials, staying on track for this year's honey harvest is important. After you leave, I'm shifting most of the greenhouse responsibilities to my new supervisor so I can focus on the apiary. Since Leah and I will be handling the hives together, I think it would be good for her to shadow you when she can while you're here."

"How much beekeeping experience does she have?"

"Aunt Ivy taught her a lot, so she has a good foundation. When Aunt Ivy was in the hospital, Leah was actually the one who held things down then, and the week after, until she fully recovered."

Hospital? Brooke sat up in her seat. Their aunt never got sick. "Wait—Aunt Ivy was sick? When?"

"Last year, just after Thanksgiving. It was just a bad case of the flu. She ran herself down and passed out one day. She was just a little dehydrated, but Dr. Kyle insisted on admitting her overnight for observation."

Working herself to the point of dehydration. How had that happened? Why hadn't Harper stopped her from working when she was sick? Their aunt was the main relative in their life. They couldn't lose her.

Brooke held back those questions and asked the even bigger ones on her mind. "Why didn't you call me? Don't you think I should have known she was sick?"

Harper looked baffled. "She was only in the hospital for a couple of days."

"But what if she'd gotten worse?" Brooke couldn't stop the tone of her voice from rising higher. "Seriously, Harper, you should have called me."

Irritation flickered across Harper's face. "As if you cared. It wasn't like you were coming home. You bailed on Thanksgiving."

The accusation hit Brooke like a slap, leaving her momentarily stunned. But Harper coming after her hard shouldn't have been a total surprise. "Yes, I chose to spend my holidays elsewhere, but that has nothing to do with Aunt Ivy being in the hospital. If she needed me, of course I would have dropped everything and come home."

As Harper released a long breath, her expression softened a little. "I'm sorry. I shouldn't have said that." The genuineness of her apology reflected in her tone. "The truth is—Aunt Ivy made me promise not to call. She didn't want to bother you."

Aunt Ivy had stopped Harper from calling her and chosen to rely on Leah instead? Brooke digested the revelation and the disappointment that came with it. "Well, I'm glad she recovered and that it didn't turn into anything more serious."

"She was fine once she got some rest, and even after that, Leah pitched in to make sure she didn't overdo it."

Leah, again. Apparently, the new groundskeeper had become important to Aunt Ivy and Harper. Something akin to feeling territorial of her family, maybe even a little jealousy, rose in Brooke. But Harper needed Leah now since she wouldn't be around.

Forcing herself to brush her feelings aside, Brooke said, "Can you send me Leah's number? I'll text her so we can work out a plan."

Harper nodded. "Sure, and thank you. I appreciate you making time for her."

But shouldn't Harper spend time with the bees, too? Sure, her sister knew the functions of beekeeping better than Leah, but as a team looking after the hives, they would have to learn to work together. Capitalize on each other's strengths and make up the differences. Otherwise, the bees could suffer. The farm would, too.

Brooke held in her thoughts. The future of the farm was Harper's territory, not hers.

"Well." Harper sighed. "I'll let you get back to work. I better head over to the greenhouse."

As Harper turned to leave, Brooke noticed her sister looked troubled.

"How is everything going over there? Leah mentioned you were taking care of an issue at the greenhouses the other day."

"It's fine…for the most part."

For the most part? That didn't sound good. She probably couldn't help her sister with any major issues at the greenhouse, but she could always listen. Maybe talking about whatever it was could give Harper some insight. On an impulse, Brooke said, "I'll be home tonight in case you want to have dinner together and catch up on anything."

"Oh…" Harper's brow rose a fraction. "Well, actually, I've got plans, and I think we're caught up on the farm."

Her sister had plans? She'd just assumed Harper was a homebody. "Well, good. Have a nice time."

"Thanks, I will."

As Brooke stared after her sister, a hint of worry started to rear up. The apiary, the greenhouse, the upcoming honey promotion, the running of the retail space—Harper had a lot on her shoulders. Would she be able to handle it all on her own? What if she couldn't?

Scenarios of how Harper could fail started spinning up in Brooke's mind, creating a cloud of concern. Should she stay in town longer to help? Maybe ask Gable if he could pitch in, too? An image of her and Gable spending more time together, working to help Harper, started forming in her mind. It looked like the perfect, happy plan. But it wasn't. If she stayed in Bolan for too long instead of leaving, she wouldn't be happy.

But what if…

Brooke silenced the small voice in her head. There were no buts or what-ifs. She had to stick to the plan of cutting all unnecessary ties to Bolan and the bee farm, and that included him.

The only thing she could do now was make sure Harper was in the best position possible before she left town and enjoy the time she did have with Gable.

Chapter Fifteen

Brooke pulled into the front driveway at Gable's house. She couldn't wait to spend the day with the two things that had made her smile as soon as she'd thought about them that morning. Him and the bees.

She got out of the farm's truck. Before she got to the walkway, he came out of the house and shut the door behind him. He reached her, and she didn't hesitate to step into his arms for a kiss that made her heart flutter from the intensity of it.

A long moment later, they eased apart and Gable smiled. "Good morning."

"Good morning."

They'd spoken on the phone a couple of times since he'd spotted the post about Theo Jr. and Melonie the day before yesterday. Something about him seemed lighter. As if part of a burden had been lifted. It was good to hear that in his voice and see it in his demeanor now.

He stepped away and held his arms out from his sides. "Is what I'm wearing okay for today?"

Dressed in a light tan button-down shirt with the sleeves rolled up to his forearms, jeans and work boots, he looked hot enough to melt butter.

She warred with the urge that made her want to go inside of his house and forget the agenda for the day, checking the hives away from the farm.

"You're fine. I brought a bee suit for you to wear. We keep them on hand in various sizes. You'll be protected from head to toe." Brooke stepped out of his loose embrace. "We should get going."

She got in on the driver's side, and he sat in the front passenger seat. Leaving his house, she headed north down the two-lane road. They passed houses set back from the road with cows and horses grazing in pastures. Stretches of just trees dappled with afternoon sunlight were interspersed with farmland. A few miles later, the two-lane road turned into four lanes. Traffic was nonexistent to light.

As Gable stared out the side window, he put on a pair of sunglasses. "So what's our first stop?"

"A fruit and vegetable farm just outside of town."

"So how does it work? Do you approach people about putting hives on their property or do they approach you?"

"A little of both." Brooke changed lanes, accelerated past two slow-moving cars then glided back in. "Once Aunt Ivy put the word out that we were interested in forming partnerships, there was a lot of interest. It's a symbiotic relationship with perks. We set up and maintain the hives on their property, and in exchange they have the benefit of the bees pollinating their crops or garden. And of course, they also receive some of the honey."

He settled back in the seat. "I'm assuming they also have to agree not to use anything on their crops or in their garden that could harm the bees."

"Correct. And there's also an exclusivity clause—no other hives except ours will be kept on the property. Years ago, Aunt Ivy set up hives on a property. The owners allowed another beekeeper to have a colony there as well, but they didn't do a good job of maintaining their bees and our hives suffered."

"You're really passionate about protecting the bees."

"Yeah, I get that from my mom, but when it comes to beekeeping, my skills don't even compare to hers. I'll never forget the day I saw her handle wild bees in a hive near a day care center in a hollow of a tree. She did it without a bee suit. It was beyond amazing."

"She sounds amazing. I can understand why you admire her."

"My mom was—" Brooke cut herself off. Why was she going on about her mom? He wasn't interested in hearing about her family.

Gable laid his hand over Brooke's, resting them both on her thigh. "What were you going to say about your mom?"

"Nothing."

The other night, her telling him about her parents, and him sharing about Theo, was a one-off. If they kept diving into intimate details about their lives it could ruin the whole point of why they were together—to be a distraction from their complicated realities.

"What are we looking for during the inspection?" Gable asked.

Dressed in a bee suit with a veil, he looked like a professional, but Brooke was still distracted. Was it the way he filled out the bee suit? As loose fitting as the canvas material was, it couldn't hide his broad shoulders. She easily envisioned the rest of him.

Brooke forced her mind back to the question and the bee frame in her hand. "Since this frame is from the brood chamber, we're looking for honey, pollen and brood." She held it more toward him so he could see. "No two frames are alike, but there is a standard pattern. We describe it as a rainbow. The brood patch toward the middle. A ring of pollen around that and honey on the outside of the frame. The nurse bees use the pollen and honey to provide nutrients to the brood during their early stages of development."

"What are those capped-off areas?" As he slowly raised his hand to point, she smiled. He'd remembered one of the rules she'd given him: no sudden moves around the bees.

"Those darker areas are worker bees to come in the final pupa stage."

"And the queen?"

"She's not here. If she was, we would see a circle of bees and her in the middle of them."

"How can you tell with so many bees on the frame?"

"You can with practice." She carefully slid the frame back in the deep body brood box with the other nine. "But we might not see her today. We don't have to inspect every frame in the box. The brood pattern we just saw points to a thriving, healthy queen, and we don't want to interrupt her progress."

As they moved on to the next hives, Gable asked well-thought-out questions. And he didn't wince too much when she mentioned how male drone bees literally gave everything, including their lives, to impregnate the queen.

They continued their conversation about bees sitting on the grass under the trees eating turkey sandwiches and drinking the lemonade she'd made that morning. Their vantage point on a small hill gave them a prime view of a berry patch, and beyond that, fields of vegetable plants and a small apple orchard. Gable legitimately wanting to learn and paying attention to what she shared about the hives made dating him even more attractive. Wait. No, they were not dating. She and Gable were just spending time together for a few short weeks.

Gable reached over and smoothed a curl from her cheek. "Thank you for making lunch. This is nice. It would be even nicer if you were closer to me."

"It would, huh?" Lured in by his smile and her own need to be next to him, she sat between his legs and rested back on his chest. Glancing over her shoulder, she said, "Better?"

"Much better." He kissed her.

The salt from the chips, the sweetness of lemonade, desire—they all created a delicious headiness.

He pointed to a structure in the distance. "Is that a gazebo?"

"Yes. That part of the farm is often used for weddings. The fields make a perfect backdrop, and they've planted a small garden next to it. I wish we had something similar at the bee farm. When I was in Colorado, I fell in love with this gazebo that had bench seats along the wall and a firepit in the middle of it. It was square instead of round. The only thing I would have incorporated is what they did with this one. Make it an addition that blends with the landscape."

"I like that idea. The Rosses started building a square gazebo but never finished it. I thought it looked awkward, but what you're describing could work." As Gable held Brooke's hand, he intertwined his fingers with hers. "So what are some other things you really like or enjoy?"

She really liked how good it felt being close to him. Lying, sitting, standing—she always seemed to gravitate toward just the right spot against him. But that wasn't the answer he was looking for. "What do you mean by things? Tell me more."

"Well…like what's your favorite comfort drink?"

"Ooh, comfort drink instead of comfort food. I like this

question." Brooke weighed her choices. Hot versus cold drinks. Alcoholic versus nonalcoholic. Finally, she settled on one. "Watermelon schnapps mixed with cherry cola."

Gable chuckled. "As a comfort drink? How… No, tell me why. No one just randomly chooses that combination for comfort."

"But it can be comforting under the right circumstances. For me, it was while working as a temporary admin assistant for a guided cycling tour company in Oregon. There were five of us helping with a week-long tour, and apparently none of us had read the fine print in the job description close enough. It covered everything from picking up people at the airport to picking up the riders' garbage at every stop after we'd hauled everything they needed for comfort around in a van. And we were responsible for cooking all of their meals."

"Geez, I hope they paid you."

"Not nearly enough. On the third night, all five of us were moping around in the single room they'd crammed us into at the lodge. We didn't know each other well, but from the looks on our faces, we all felt the same. Miserable. Then someone pulled out a bottle of watermelon schnapps. Someone else pulled out a couple of bottles of cherry cola, and we all let loose." As Brooke recalled the happy memory, she smiled. "By the time we finished the bottle, we were friends, and after that, our horrible jobs felt a little easier."

Where her and Gable's fingers were intertwined, he lightly stroked his thumb over the back of her hand. "So it's not the drink that brings you comfort, it's the memory of how you and your coworkers comforted each other."

As she looked up at him, she couldn't help but smile wider. "I think you get me, Gable Kincaid."

He leaned in for an all too brief kiss. "I'm glad."

Having someone get you was like shorthand. You didn't have to spell everything out. Another type of a connection... or even a bond. Brooke swept the thought aside. "You get me" was a common expression. She was getting too hung up on it. "Now it's your turn to answer the question, but I've got a twist."

"Uh-oh," he said. "Sounds like trouble."

"It's not. I promise. Since you know about music, what's the best recent live performance you've been to and enjoyed at a music festival."

"Wow, that's a hard one."

"No overthinking it. First thought that popped into your mind when I asked the question."

"A couple of years ago. Austin. South by Southwest music festival, Thee Sacred Souls."

A jolt of recognition made her sit up and turn more toward him. "You were there that year? I was, too, and I went to *that* performance."

His brow shot up. "You did?"

She nodded. "A friend had an extra badge. Her friend, Nellie, who I know now but didn't back then, couldn't make it so I went with her." Brooke knew she was babbling, but the chance of them being in that exact place at the same time... She needed to share the entire story, maybe just to convince herself it was true. "I'd never heard of the group before, but once they started, I was glad I went to their performance. I loved how their music had a relaxed old-school vibe, but their lyrics were..."

"So now and relatable." She and Gable said it at the same time.

"Exactly." Her excited smile matched his. "And the lyrics in some of their songs, they have so much spiritual truth in them."

"Right," he added. "But not in a religious kind of way."

"Yes, because they're just about how connected we all are on so many levels."

Wait? Had they just had a conversation finishing each other's sentences?

Gable's baffled expression reflected her thoughts. Finally, he said, "I think you get me, Brooke Bishop."

"I'm glad." Brooke parroted what he'd told her, but she meant it, just like Gable did.

He traced his finger over her cheek. "It's so strange to think that sixteen years ago, we were both in this area, maybe even passed each other, but didn't meet. And now just a few years ago, it happened again. And now, here we are."

It was strange. What was that saying about luck? "The third time is the charm."

"It definitely is." Gable kissed her again, this time lingering long enough to leave her breathless. She was so caught up in him, she almost didn't hear her phone buzzing near the cooler.

She reached for it and checked the screen. "It's Etta Davies. We have a hive on her property. She's probably wondering when we'll be there."

If it were anyone else, she would have let it go to voicemail, but the older woman was a worrier. She really cared about her bees but tended to get overly excited about the little things when it came to her hive.

Brooke pressed her lips briefly back to his then answered the call. "Hi, Mrs. Davies. What can I do—"

"Oh, Brooke…something terrible has happened." Mrs. Davies sounded distraught. "Something is wrong with my bees."

Brooke sat up straight, moving away from Gable. "Mrs.

Davies. Calm down. Are you alright? That's what's important."

"I'm fine, but when I went to check the bees, they weren't moving in and out of the hive like they usually do. I called Mace Calderone to help me open the hive and take a look, but he said I should call you about what to do first."

Mrs. Davies knew some of the basics about bees but not enough to assess what could be wrong. Aunt Ivy had strongly discouraged the older woman from opening the hive without their supervision.

"No. Don't open the hive. I'll do it. We're on our way to you now." Behind her, Gable had already started packing the cooler. "Whatever is going on, we'll figure it out. Don't worry. Everything will be fine." After exchanging a quick goodbye with Mrs. Davies, she ended the call.

Aunt Ivy had mentioned worries about the colonies of bees outside the farm but nothing eminent. Had the bees swarmed?

As Gable closed the cooler, he gave her a concerned look as they stood. "I take it something bad has happened?"

Despite a sinking feeling in the pit of her stomach, Brooke kept her voice light as she picked up the tarp they'd been sitting on and hastily folded it. "I'm not sure. Apparently, Mrs. Davies is having a problem with her hive and she wants me to come by now. Could be something or it's probably nothing. She takes a little more interest in the bees than our other partners. She's a widow, lives alone. I think worrying about the bees gives her something to do. We love her enthusiasm."

Probably nothing... What Brooke had just said echoed in her mind, but the sinking pit in her stomach deepened.

Chapter Sixteen

Gable glanced at Brooke in the driver's seat. She'd mentioned what was happening with the hive at Mrs. Davies's house could be something or probably nothing. From the look on her face, he was eliminating the latter. She was clearly more concerned than she was letting on.

What could he do to help? Gable looked at his left wrist. He hadn't been able to wear the glove that went with the bee suit. He'd had to slip a large work glove over his hand and the brace and then wrap a band around it. It had felt bulky and awkward.

While inspecting the hives, Brooke had managed to intervene whenever he'd started to lift parts of the hive or carry equipment, but she didn't need to baby him. As good as his wrist felt, he probably could have left the removable brace off and worn a regular glove. Brace or not, he would definitely help lift and carry whatever Brooke needed once they arrived at Mrs. Davies's house. He'd just have to stress that he could.

On the four-lane road, older-looking white clapboard homes were intermixed with modern two-story houses. Less acreage separated them and there were fewer barns, open fields and crops.

Miles later, the countryside changed with entrances to a

couple of private subdivisions, plus others under construction. Neighborhoods with nearly identical houses and neat lawns were considered progress, but they looked out of place, especially as the landscape switched back to older homes.

"We're almost there." Brooke's tone had a professional distance, and she'd put on what Gable suspected was her game face, but she tightly gripped the steering wheel with both hands.

He briefly laid a comforting hand on her shoulder. "When we get there, just let me know what you need me to do."

"I will."

Moments later, they turned down a two-lane road into a wooded area, and then made a left into an established neighborhood. One- and two-story homes, built in different styles, were spread out down the street.

Brooke made a right into the driveway of a one-story gray house with white trim and black shutters.

A sheriff's cruiser sat parked in front of the two-door garage, and she pulled in next to it.

A petite older woman with short gray hair, who he assumed was Mrs. Davies, was dressed in a light pink bee suit without the hood. A bronzed-skin man with dark hair wearing a brown and tan uniform stood next to her.

The sheriff's department was on the scene. Maybe it was a lot more serious than Brooke was letting on.

As if reading his mind, Brooke said, "That's Mace Calderone. He looks out for Mrs. Davies. If anything's bothering her, large or small, she calls him. He goes out of his way to be here for her whenever she needs him."

"That's good. Especially since she's out here alone." Mace looked familiar to Gable. Hadn't he seen him at

Tillbridge Horse Stable and Guesthouse chatting with the owners?

As soon as they got out of the truck, Mrs. Davies hurried over to Brooke and Mace followed. Her gently lined face was flushed. "I'm so sorry. I don't know what I did to make the bees leave."

Brooke reassuringly patted Mrs. Davies on the back. "It's not your fault. If the bees decided to swarm, that's on us. We missed the signs. I'll take a look at the hive and then look around. Maybe they're close by."

"I'll help you look." Mrs. Davies started turning toward the house. "Just let me get my helmet."

Mace interjected. "Why don't you let Brooke and…?"

"Gable Kincaid." Brooke made the introduction. "But he's just observing me today. He's not handling the hives. Gable, this is Sergeant Calderone and Mrs. Davies."

Gable exchanged hellos with them.

Mace amended, "Brooke can take a look at the hive, and in the meantime, Mrs. Davies, maybe you could get us all something cold to drink?"

"Oh, of course. Where are my manners? As warm as this afternoon has been, I should have offered you something. What about iced tea? I just brewed it early this morning. It should be cool enough now. I just need to add water to it."

"Sounds good." Mace smiled. "Thank you."

As the woman walked toward the house, Mace said, "I didn't want to say this in front of her, but I don't think the bees swarmed."

"Why? What happened?" Brooke asked.

"The new subdivision that's being built down the road… Apparently yesterday, the landscapers taking care of the green spaces used a product in a higher concentration than they should have. As windy as it was yesterday afternoon…"

Brooke finished his sentence. "The product drifted."

Mace's face looked grim as he nodded. "We received complaints from people a mile or more from the subdivision about watery eyes and asthma attacks being triggered. The company said there won't be any lasting effects for anyone, but for the bees, I think the damage has already been done."

Gable translated what he was saying. The bees were dead.

From Brooke's disheartened expression, she'd heard it that way, too. "What about the landscaper or the contractor that hired them? Are they being held accountable for what happened?"

Brooke's response was exactly what Gable was wondering.

"They've received a warning," Mace said.

"That's it? But they were careless."

"I agree." Mace nodded. "I wish the department could do more, but as far as the mayor and everyone else is concerned, it's been classified as an accident instead of negligence." He looked as frustrated as Brooke did over the outcome. "Trust me, I get it. Protections need to be in place for the environment."

As Brooke sighed, her professional game face slipped back into place, but it didn't erase all of the irritation or concern in her eyes. "Well, what might have happened to the bees is abundantly clear, but how is Mrs. Davies? Was she physically affected?"

"Luckily, no. She'd been out of town visiting a friend when the incident happened. The chemical fog had dissipated by the time she got home. I didn't tell her what I think occurred. I didn't want to upset her."

"I'm glad she wasn't here." Brooke's relief was genuine. "And it's a good call not to tell her. She's already blaming herself and it's not her fault." She released a breath. "I'd better take a look at the hive now."

"Anything I can do to help?" Mace asked. "I'm off duty so I've got the time."

"Maybe you and Gable could keep Mrs. Davies busy while I check on things?"

"Will do." Mace walked toward the house.

Gable followed her to the back of the truck. "Why don't you let me help you instead?" He reached toward the bin. "Which tools are you taking? I'll get them out."

"No." Her voice had a slight snap to it as she grabbed her bee suit. "If you want to help, please don't start an argument with me. Just let me do what I need to do."

Starting an argument? He wasn't doing that. Why would she see it that way? As he took a moment before he responded, situations that had gone wrong for him came to mind. When it had happened at a club or another venue before one of his performances, sometimes he'd struggled with dialing back his frustration. No, it wasn't exactly the same as what she was dealing with now, but he could empathize with how she felt.

Keeping his own tone level, he said, "I'm not arguing with you. I just want to make sure you're good. You told me it was important to be calm around the bees. Right now, you're upset and I'm concerned about you."

"Sorry." Brooke closed her eyes, hung her head and released a deep breath. "I shouldn't have bitten your head off like that, and you're right. I do have to be calm around the bees, but I also need to go in alone." She met his gaze. "I'm not sure what I'm walking into. The bees could be gone or I could be facing a really pissed-off colony. You can help by helping Mace keep Mrs. Davies busy. She can be a handful."

"Okay, if that's where you want me, that's where I'll be." The thought of her facing angry bees was still unnerving, but Brooke knew what she was doing. He trusted that.

As she stepped into her bee suit, Brooke added, "I actually could use a hand getting the tools out."

He quickly went to the open bin. "What do you need?"

"Just the smoker and a hive tool, for now. I'll come back for the nuc box if I need it. We also have a few supplies in Mrs. Davies's shed."

She'd explained to him earlier that the nuc box could be used to house captured swarms or to transport bees in general for a short distance if necessary.

Gable took the items she'd mentioned out of the bin. He set up the smoker with pellets like she'd taught him and got it going.

"Thanks." She collected the tools then gave him a small smile through the veil. "See you in a bit." Fully geared up, she left him, trekking across the grass on the side of the house to the back.

As he walked into the house, Mace stood in the archway to the left. "Let me guess. You offered, but she wouldn't let you help?"

"Nope. Brooke said she needed to do it."

"I've been there. My—" He cleared his throat. "Zurie is independent like that, too. Don't take it personally." He pointed to the brace on Gable's wrist. "What happened?"

"My horse. He bucked me out of the saddle."

Mace grimaced. "That had to hurt."

"Who's hurt?" Mrs. Davies called from inside the kitchen. "Is it Brooke?"

Mace turned and assured her. "No, Brooke's fine. Her friend Gable was just telling me how he hurt his wrist."

Gable followed him into the tiled, homey space filled

with the sweet smells of baking. They sat with Mrs. Davies at a table in the kitchen alcove where she'd set up a pitcher of iced tea and a plate of banana nut muffins.

Behind her, a window framed with light blue curtains provided a view of the backyard bordered by trees. He didn't see Brooke or the beehive.

After accepting a glass of iced tea, he answered questions about his wrist and shared the humorous account of falling off Pepper and meeting Brooke. His story did as he'd intended. It wiped the worry from Mrs. Davies's face.

She smiled. "My husband, Joe, and I met when we smacked into each other at the beach. Or actually, he ran into me trying to catch a football. He wanted to take me out as an apology. We ended up having a whirlwind weekend together, but we didn't make plans to see each other again. He was in the army stationed in Georgia. I was going to college in Baltimore. But neither one of us could forget each other. He managed to get another weekend pass two weeks later and found me on campus." A dreamy look of nostalgia took over her face. "He proposed and of course I said yes. We were married a month later. When two people are meant to be, nothing will stand in their way."

Gable asked, "How long were you and your husband married?"

"Fifty-two years," she said proudly. "How long have you and Brooke been dating?"

Confessing a no-strings relationship with Brooke to Mrs. Davies would be like telling his own grandmother. He couldn't. "We just met. I'm her neighbor. We're not dating."

From the slight smile on Mace's face, he wasn't buying his answer.

Mrs. Davies said, "You make a cute couple. If you want my advice, if you like each other, be honest and spell it out. Young people today waste too much time." She cast a look at Mace. "This one took forever to figure that out with Zurie, but he finally did and popped the question. Now we just have to get them down the aisle. When are you two getting married? I have a dress picked out for the ceremony and a hat. And what about babies? You need to get started on a family."

Mace's smile disappeared as he cleared his throat again. "Uh, well, we're working on it." He shifted his attention to Gable. "You stayed at the guesthouse, didn't you? You must have met Zurie and her cousin Tristan?"

Mace needed a lifeline and maybe a lozenge for his dry throat. Hiding a smile, Gable gave him the save he was subtly asking for. "I didn't get a chance to meet them, but I did see Tristan around the stable. I boarded my horse there. It's a great place."

"It is." Mace sat back in the chair. "Tristan remembered seeing you. He swears you look familiar. He used to ride bulls back in the day. Were you ever on the circuit?"

The truth was bound to come out, and it wasn't like Gable had intended on hiding his connection to the town forever. "No, but I was here for a summer about sixteen years ago. I was visiting my great-uncle, Wes Brunson. I went with him to Tillbridge Horse Stable a few times. I didn't meet Tristan, but maybe he saw me and that's why I look familiar to him."

Mrs. Davies perked up. "You're related to Wes? He was an excellent farrier. My Joe was a groom at Tillbridge. He would mention how skillful your great-uncle was with the horses."

Mace nodded. "Wes was definitely a good man. Small world. What brought you back here?"

Movement in the backyard caught Gable's attention. "Brooke's back from the hive." He stood.

Mrs. Davies wrung her hands. "I'm afraid to hear what she has to say."

Mace patted her arm. "Whatever it is, we'll work it out."

While Mace consoled the older woman, Gable went outside to meet Brooke. She'd taken off the hood.

As she got closer, she met his gaze. Hints of gloom were in her eyes.

"So Mace was right about the bees."

"Yes. Whatever was sprayed in the air decimated the hive. I usually see butterflies or ladybugs around. I didn't see any of them, either."

He reached out to hug her, but she took a step out of range, her game face back in place. "I should tell Mrs. Davies what happened." She met Mace and Mrs. Davies in front of the house. Turning to the older woman, she gave her an empathetic smile. "I'm afraid most of the bees are gone and so is the queen."

"Oh no." Mrs. Davies's shoulders slumped. "So they did swarm. I wish I would have called you sooner."

Brooke wrapped an arm around the older woman. "You couldn't have known. I'm going to take the remaining bees back to the farm and start another colony."

"And then you'll bring them back?" Mrs. Davies asked hopefully.

Brooke's smile looked a little forced. "I'll work on it."

"Oh, thank you. You're such a dear."

"And so are you." Brooke gave her a hug.

At the back of the truck, she reached for the hand truck and dragged it toward her.

Gable laid his hand on her arm, stalling her movements. "Are you okay?"

Frustration and despair filled her face like a fully charged thundercloud. She shook her head. "Please, don't ask me that right now. I have to stay focused on Mrs. Davies and the hive."

Her feelings were valid as well. Still, he understood why she wanted to hold them in, but she didn't have to carry the burden of the situation alone. "I'm coming with you." He grabbed his bee suit.

"No, your wrist—"

"Is fine." He cupped her cheek. "Brooke, let me help you. Please."

For a brief moment, she rested her hand against his palm, then moved away. "You still need to put on the bee suit, just in case. The super isn't heavy. It's mostly empty frames, but the brood box has some weight to it. We just need to get the hand truck under it. No heavy lifting is required."

"Got it." Wearing the bee suit, he wheeled the hand truck as they walked to the backyard.

Past a break in the trees, they entered a haven with raised plant beds filled with small purple flowers. Pots of various sizes with other colorful flowers were arranged around a small water fountain with water flowing down a natural staircase of stones. The beehive sat just off to the side.

Brooke ran her hand gently over the small purple flowers.

He recognized them but didn't know their name. "What type of plants are those?"

"Lavender. Mrs. Davies carried sprigs of it in her bouquet on her wedding day. She likes coming back here to the watch the bees and remember her husband."

"Will you be able to give her another hive?"

Brooke offered up a small shrug. "I hope we can but not until we know the bees will be safe."

They loaded the hive on to the hand truck and wheeled it to the back of Brooke's vehicle. As they loaded it in the bed of the truck, a few of the dead bees spilled out. She remained stoic.

Mrs. Davies wasn't around. It was just them. She didn't have to keep hiding how upset she really was about the devastated colony. She could let it all out. He was there for her. She could lean on him completely, but there didn't seem to be anything he could say or do to make her pick up on that.

While they covered the hive with a tarp, Mace came out of the house. "Mrs. Davies is a little worn-out from everything, especially the bad news. I made her sit down and rest, but she's insisting on saying goodbye."

Gable looked to Brooke. "Go ahead. I'll put everything away. Tell her goodbye for me."

Brooke and Mace went to the house.

A moment later, Brooke returned to the truck. "She wants to see you."

"She does? Why?"

"She wants to thank you, too."

"Thank me? For what? You did most of the work."

"You still helped. You were kind to her, and you kept her from worrying about what might have happened until we found out the truth." Brooke gave him a small smile as she briefly laid her hand on his arm. "That means a lot to her and to me."

"I appreciate you letting me know that." He wanted to hold her, but he could tell by her rigid body language that she wasn't ready for hugs yet.

He went inside the house.

Mace met him near the entry. "She's in the living room."

Gable walked down a short hallway with various pictures on the wall of Mrs. Davies and her husband, Joe, through the years. The older woman had mentioned that when two people were meant to be, nothing would stand in their way. From the smiles in the photo, nothing had gotten in the way of the couple's happiness during their years together.

Mrs. Davies sat with her feet up in a beige recliner. She reached out to him. "Did you think you were going to get away without saying goodbye to me?"

"I thought you just wanted Brooke."

"You helped, too." Her thin hands were full of strength as she guided him to sit on the padded ottoman next to her. She leaned toward him. "Can I tell you a secret?"

"Sure."

"I know Brooke and Mace aren't being completely honest with me about the bees. Don't worry. I'm not going to ask you to spill the beans. Those two are going out of their way to protect me so I'll let it be for now. It's in Mace's nature to guard people from harm. And Brooke, she's a natural caretaker at heart. And she's a real firecracker." Mrs. Davies chuckled. "But I suspect you know that."

Not sure where the conversation was going, he smiled back at her. "Brooke's definitely got spirit."

"That she does." Mrs. Davies's smile sobered. "But right now, that spirit is a little broken. When she was in here a few minutes ago, I could see that losing my bees has affected her more than she's letting on. She's always been one to hide her feelings. I remember when she and Harper lost their parents." The older woman shook her head. "They were teenagers still trying to find their way. It was hard on both of them, but Harper was the one who visibly struggled. Brooke buried her hurt by trying to take care of everyone but herself, until she couldn't."

Couldn't? It was hard for Gable to imagine Brooke not being able to do whatever she set her mind to.

Mrs. Davies filled in the blank. "She had to leave this town and grow into herself. Ivy understood that but Harper didn't. She took it hard and felt Brooke abandoned her, and since then, they've grown apart. Hopefully they'll find their way back to each other as sisters. That's why Ivy decided she had to—" Mrs. Davies patted his hand and looked him in the eye. "That part doesn't matter, but this does. Brooke is going to pretend she doesn't need you right now, but she does. Don't let her fool you. Don't let her push you away."

"I'll remember that."

"Good." She released his hand, and as he stood up, she studied him. "I see the resemblance now. You look like him a little, and you have a way about you, like Wes did. He was a good man. It was nice meeting you, Gable. Feel free to stop by for tea and muffins anytime."

"Thank you." Maybe he would drop by to see her. Mrs. Davies seemed really nice. Not someone trying to mine gossip like Peggy. She also genuinely cared about Brooke and her family. That part she'd mentioned didn't matter about something Ivy decided she had to do—what was that about?

During the drive home, Gable mulled over everything that Mrs. Davies told him. Look after Brooke and live up to his great-uncle's reputation? Yeah, no pressure in doing that. But he and Brooke didn't have the type of relationship Mrs. Davies thought they did. He was just a physical distraction for Brooke, not a significant other. And just because he'd disclosed things about his own life, that didn't mean she was obligated to share more than she already had about hers.

Brooke punctuated that understanding as she pulled up to his house to drop him off.

"Are you sure I can't help you with the hive?"

"No, but I appreciate it." Her quick smile went away with her shuttered expression. "It won't take long and it'll be faster if I do the cleanup on my own. I'll call you later, alright?"

Effectively dismissed, he gave her a kiss on the cheek before he got out. "I'm around if you need me."

But as he took a shower, he still couldn't shake what Mrs. Davies said or what he'd spotted in Brooke's eyes before she'd driven off. She was hurting. He couldn't just go on with his day and pretend he hadn't seen it.

After getting dressed, he gave into his concerns and decided to text her. He'd keep it simple. The equivalent of a knock on the door. Maybe she'd let him in. Gable messaged the question he'd asked her at Mrs. Davies's house that she'd refused to answer.

Chapter Seventeen

Brooke sat on the floor in her T-shirt and underwear leaning back against the bed with her legs in a crisscross position. She read Gable's message for the second time.

Are you okay?

A full minute or more had passed since the question had shown up on her phone, but she didn't know how to answer it. Her gaze traveled to the bee just past her foot on the rug. Its wings didn't flutter. It didn't make a sound. It would never find its way home again.

How could she explain to Gable that she'd encountered dead bees and lost them to swarms, but she'd never lost an entire hive like this? It felt as if her whole heart was with that bee, and now it was breaking. She'd failed. She should have done a better job of taking care of them. As she took a shaky breath, her chest burned from the raw emotions jumbled inside of her. Her eyes stung with the tears she refused to shed. But what was the point of crying? Tears didn't have the power to bring back the things or the people you cared about.

The doorbell rang.

Harper wasn't home, but she also had a key.

Rising to her feet, Brooke peeked out the window. Gable's truck sat out front.

She hadn't answered his text. She should have. Or she could just pretend she never saw it. She could tell him that she'd left her phone in the truck or that she'd fallen asleep. He'd never know.

Another text pinged in on her phone.

I'm at the door. Let me in. Please. I just want to know that you're alright.

After taking a fortifying breath, she went to answer the door. She would tell him she was fine. The excuse of needing a shower or having to spend the rest of the day working would nudge him away.

Brooke opened the door, planning to alleviate his concerns, but as soon as she saw the compassion in his eyes, her resolve gave out. She couldn't stop him from walking through the door. Her weak attempts to push him away quickly ended with her balling her hands in his T-shirt and burrowing her face in his chest as he held her in his strong embrace.

A sob almost escaped, but she clamped her lips shut. Emotional pain heaved in her chest and a pitiful squeak came out with a gasp. Tears stung in her eyes. "This is so stupid. Why am I crying?"

"Because you've been holding your feelings in the entire afternoon." His arms tightened around her. "It's alright to be upset. Let it out."

She meant to say no, but a cry she couldn't contain came out of her instead. She wept for the bees, Mrs. Davies and herself. And also for something else she couldn't define that was wrapped in bottomless sorrow. But Gable being there was the comfort she needed. The warmth of his body removed the chill that remained after her emotion had stripped so much away.

Long minutes later, Gable put his arm under her legs and swept her up in his arms.

"No...your wrist."

"I'm not putting a lot of pressure on it. It's behind you."

She looped her hands around his neck. "I can walk."

"I know you can. Where's your room? Upstairs?"

"Down the hall. You would seriously carry me up a flight of stairs?"

"Yep." He strode toward the bedroom.

"Why? Because I'm weak and in distress?" She hated the idea of him seeing her as weak.

"No. And you're not even close to being that." He stopped walking and looked her in the eyes. The sincerity in his gaze almost made her start crying all over again. "I'm carrying you because you've been running around taking care of everyone today. It's time someone took care of you."

Brooke's heart swelled in her chest. During her travels, she'd been the one who found soup for her friends when they were sick or empathized with them after their lives had gone sideways with an unexpected kick in the gut. She'd danced with them, drank with them until the wee hours of the morning as they'd tried to erase disappointment, and then rubbed their back as they'd prayed to the porcelain god, promising to never drown their sorrows in alcohol again. She'd never thought twice about being a shoulder to cry on...or ever considered she'd need a shoulder of her own to cry on.

Gable's presence felt like the refuge she needed, but was she asking too much from the man who was just supposed to be in her life for a few weeks?

* * *

Gable waited for the denial, the pushback, one of her joking, self-deprecating comments.

She blinked at him and said, "Okay."

Not expecting that answer, he was momentarily stunned. "Good." Now what? He'd been so focused on just physically getting to her, he hadn't figured out a next step.

Gable walked into the bedroom with Brooke still in his arms.

She glanced at her jeans and socks on the floor. "I was just about to take a shower when you texted."

Through the open door of the bathroom, he spotted a claw-foot tub. "What about a bath, instead?" He set her down. "You get undressed and I'll run it for you."

Gable went into the bathroom and turned on the faucet over the tub.

Brooke, dressed in a silk robe, poked her head through the doorway. "I'm going to put my clothes in the laundry room."

He glanced over the bath products on a built-in corner shelf. Part of what made a bath relaxing was what you put in it, right? Which one should he choose? Probably not the ones with honey or lavender on the label. He didn't want to remind Brooke about her day. He wanted to help her escape from it. He chose the container marked lemon balm and poured some in.

Bubbles foamed in the water and a pleasant citrus sent wafted in the air.

Brooke entered the bathroom. Some of the tension drained from her face as she took a deep breath. She wrapped her arms around him. "Thank you."

His own pent-up breath eased out. He'd made the right choice with the bath balm and coming to her house. Gable pressed his lips to her forehead. "You're welcome. Can I get you anything?"

"Some lemonade, maybe? There should be some left over in the refrigerator."

After finding what she'd asked for, he returned to the bathroom with the glass of lemonade and handed it to her as she lay in the tub. She took a long sip then set it on an empty space on the corner shelf.

As Brooke lay back in the tub, she looked up at him. A few of her curls clung to her forehead and cheeks. Drops of water dotted and trailed down her delicate shoulders. The top curves of her breasts crested above the surface of the bubbles. She was enticing and beautiful, but her puffy eyes provided a reminder of her ordeal.

He pointed to the bedroom. "I'll hang out in there."

"Will you hold me? The tub is big enough for both of us."

Want leaped inside of him. He couldn't help that he was attracted to her. Brooke was a beautiful woman, and yes, they were in a mainly sexual relationship, but this moment wasn't about his physical needs.

He took off his clothes and the brace. She made room for him in the tub and he settled in behind her. As Brooke rested back on his bare chest, she shifted positions and her luscious backside pressed firmly against him.

Gable closed his eyes, trying to think of anything but wanting her. He conjured up images of foods he hated— cottage cheese, lima beans, liver. He made a mental list of items he needed to pick up from the hardware store to start working on projects at his place. He envisioned mucking Pep's stall in infinite detail. After that, when he couldn't find anywhere else to focus on, lyrics floated through his mind. He let his palm drift over her shoulder. Her skin was silky smooth. She felt soft, warm and wonderful in his arms.

"What song is that?" Brooke asked sleepily. "It's nice."

"What song?"

"The one you're humming." She took a slow deep breath. "It's comforting."

Humming? Gable opened his eyes. He hadn't realized he'd been doing that. "It's not a song. It's just something that I came up with on the fly."

"What are the lyrics?"

"I haven't written anything. It's just a few words."

"Can I hear them?"

He didn't sing anymore, but this wasn't a stage. It was just him and Brooke. Comforting her was what he'd set out to do. If singing to Brooke would make her feel better, why not do that? And it was only a couple of lines.

He took a breath and let the words flow out of him.

"I was trapped in the shadows of my deepest fears. But then the sky turned blue, and I found you…"

As Gable sang the final words, contentment settled over him. Hearing his singing voice again was like connecting with an old friend.

"You have an amazing voice," Brooke said.

"That's only because we're in the bathroom. The acoustics in here are nearly perfect."

"What's the rest of the song?" She looked up at him. "I want to hear more."

With that sleepy look on her face, he wanted to kiss her, and do a whole lot more. But she was tired. "There is no rest of the song. We should get out. The water's nearly cold." Gable gently nudged her away from him.

They got out and dried off with thick towels he found in the closet.

After wrapping his around his waist, he put his brace back on.

Brooke yawned. "I feel so relaxed right now. I can barely keep my eyes open."

"Then don't." Bending down he swept her up in his arms.

She looped her hands around his neck. "Again, I can walk."

"And again, I know you can." As he carried her out of the bathroom, Gable met her gaze and lost himself in her eyes. "But right now, you don't have to. I got you."

Moments later, he tucked her in bed alone.

"Are you sure you won't lie down with me a minute?"

Getting under the covers with Brooke would be tempting fate. He gave her a brief kiss. "I need to check on Pep and handle some things. You get some rest."

Gable got dressed, and before he left the bedroom, she was asleep.

As he reached the entryway of the house, the front door opened.

A woman who resembled Brooke walked in.

They both paused, surprised to see each other.

He broke the silence. "Hello, I'm Gable, your new neighbor. You must be Brooke's sister."

"Yes, I'm Harper. It's nice to meet you." As she shook his hand, she glanced toward the living room then down the hall. "Where's Brooke?"

"She's in her bedroom."

"Oh." From Harper's raised brow look, she had the wrong impression about him coming down the hall from her sister's room.

A debate in his head about whether or not he should clarify the situation ended quickly. "There was a problem with one of your hives, and Brooke had to take care of it."

"What kind of problem?"

"I think she should be the one to explain it to you but give her a minute. The situation was a little rough on her. She's sleeping now."

"Thanks for looking after her." As Harper came inside, she glanced down the hall. "I would have come home sooner if I'd known she had a problem."

What Harper had just said sounded a little harsh. Like judgment. Or was he just recalling what Mrs. Davies had said about Harper and Brooke not getting along? "The hive had a problem. Brooke will be fine once she gets some rest. And you don't have to thank me. I just care about what happens to your sister."

"I see…" Harper looked surprised by his response.

Walking out the door, he gave her a polite nod and said, "Have a good evening."

On the drive back to his house, Gable contemplated what he'd told Harper about how he felt about Brooke. He did care. They might not have known each other very long, but it was true, and really caring about someone wasn't dependent on time. Mrs. Davies and her husband were proof of that. What the older woman had mentioned about when things were meant to be came into his mind, along with how he and Brooke had maybe just missed meeting each other a few short years ago in Texas.

A daydream of a different scenario of what could have happened rose into his thoughts. One where he'd spotted her vibing to the beat near the stage. But instead of the song from the group that had played that day, the tune he'd sang for her played in his mind along with Brooke's question. *What's the rest of the song?*

Chapter Eighteen

Brooke walked toward the lighted office cottage. Harper hadn't been in the house, so most likely she was there. Her sister needed to know about what happened to Mrs. Davies's bees.

Each step jarred her slightly aching head. She'd awakened with it a little over an hour ago that morning. The result of an emotional hangover. Or was it from hunger? Yesterday afternoon, she'd awakened with the same headache, taken something for it, slept all night and skipped dinner.

Gable had sent her a text earlier, asking her how she was feeling. She'd told him she was good for the most part and maybe she would catch up with him later that day. The other part of her was a little embarrassed about falling apart like that in front of him. Yesterday, he'd said he didn't view her as weak, but maybe he'd just said that to comfort her. Maybe he really saw her as needy or emotional. She'd never been that emotional before, and for some reason, the feelings were still there hovering inside of her. Uncertainty, frustration, sadness, despair—they threatened to surface at any moment, and she didn't want him to witness her falling apart again.

She reached the cottage and went inside. Just like she'd hoped, her sister was there.

Harper looked at her from where she stocked mugs in a section of the honeycomb shelf on the wall. "Good morning."

"Morning." As Brooke walked over to her, she ran through the order of her thoughts. She should get to the point. No need for throat-clearing conversation starters. "I have some bad news about the bees at Mrs. Davies's house. We lost the entire colony."

Harper paused in shelving merchandise. "Did they swarm?"

"No." Brooke handed her a mug. "From what I learned, a landscaper working at one of the new subdivisions near Mrs. Davies's neighborhood over-applied some sort of chemical. The wind caused it to drift."

"So Aunt Ivy was right to be concerned." Harper shook her head.

"I'm sure this incident will come up at the next town or business council meeting. If it doesn't, I'll definitely bring it up."

As Brooke thought of the damage that was done to the bees and how it had impacted people, her irritation sparked. "They have to do something, otherwise it could happen again. Next time the consequences might be even more serious."

"I know. Honestly, with all of the expansion projects going on, something else is bound to happen. That's what makes the prospect of Bolan growing into a larger town a double-edged sword."

"But those of us who have lived here for years shouldn't have to suffer." *Us.* No, Brooke wouldn't suffer, but other people would. That's what she meant to say. As Harper held out her hand for another mug, Brooke waited for her sister to point out the mistake in what she'd just said.

Instead Harper said, "It's never good for us to lose bees, but what happened may have an upside to it. Me and another business owner had mentioned the lack of a detailed environmental plan, but no one was interested in hearing it. This could be the right time to bring it up again."

Brooke had a thought. "I'm putting together a booklet for National Honey Month with tips on how to protect and support the bees, as well as recipes. During my research for what to include in the booklet, I've come across some really great graphics illustrating bees and biodiversity. I can send you the links."

"A booklet? Aunt Ivy didn't mention plans for a booklet to me."

"No, it's something I came up with. All of the participating establishments liked the idea and they're coming up with the recipes." Brooke added, "And don't worry about the cost. I pitched the booklet to Zurie Tillbridge. The stable is going to pay for the printing costs. I can write the copy and format it myself."

"You're doing it?" Harper looked stunned. "But I thought you weren't interested in the farm?"

"I'm not" didn't feel like the right answer. Brooke hesitated. "Aunt Ivy left me with the task of organizing the event. I just want everything to be right."

"I appreciate that, and the links you mentioned would be helpful. With all of the things happening at the greenhouse, it's a relief not to have to worry about National Honey Month."

"Leah had mentioned something was going on."

Harper looked away. "Yeah, we've had a few problems." Brooke expected her to leave it at that, but then she said, "A couple of weeks ago, the mayor had a VIP reception. His wife wanted braided hibiscus trees as part of the decorations. The florist downtown ordered pots of them, but they didn't have a place to store them so we did. Unfortunately, they came with luggage."

"They were infested? That's never good." Brooke set the empty carton aside.

"It was my fault. I should have made sure they were quarantined away from our flowers. Luckily, the part-time greenhouse supervisor I recently hired is a plant wizard..." Harper shared about how her new employee had helped save the day.

Brooke had assumed she hadn't seen much of Harper because her sister was avoiding her. She hadn't considered Harper had her own fires to put out.

When Harper opened boxes with Save the Bees T-shirts inside of them, the conversation shifted to the new bee-themed merchandise the farm was now stocking. Her sister's face lit up as she talked about her plans for expanding the retail space.

Brooke could see it all in her mind, and she felt an excitement for her sister.

As Harper put the last stack of T-shirts on the shelf, their conversation came to a lull. "You know," she said, "while you're here, maybe we should plan to meet at least once a week to talk...about the farm. We should stay caught up with what we're both doing."

"We should," Brooke replied, happy to accept the olive branch her sister extended. "Are mornings good for you?"

Checking their calendars, they settled on Wednesday mornings.

"Okay, good." Harper also seemed pleased as she tapped the details into her phone. "I'll understand if you're running a little late because of all you have going on with Gable. I'm sure your mornings with him are really…busy."

Brooke thought she heard a hint of playfulness in her sister's tone. No, she must have imagined it. "I'm not that busy with him."

Harper gave her a raised brow look. "Why not? You're not planning on being here forever. If I were in your shoes with him… No, that doesn't sound right. If I were in your shoes with a guy *like* him, I'd be late for every meeting, *and* I wouldn't feel bad about it. In fact, I would walk around with a big ole grin on my face for the entire day."

As Harper showed off a dazzling smile, Brooke had to laugh. "Oh really? And when people asked why you were smiling that way, what would you tell them?"

"Depends on who's asking. If it's someone I don't like, I'd tell them the reason behind it was for me to know and take advantage of as much as humanly possible, and that they should mind their own business."

"Dang, sis. Just tell them how you really feel."

Harper laid her hand on her chest and gave an exaggerated look of concern. "Well, no, I couldn't do that. I wouldn't want to be impolite." When her gaze met Brooke's, humor and mischief twinkled in her eyes.

Laughter bubbled out of Brooke. It was good to see this fun side of Harper again instead of the reserved side she usually showed the world. "Maybe I will take your advice about being late for our meetings." Memories of her meltdown yesterday crossed her mind. "Or maybe I don't have a reason to do that anymore."

"What do you mean? You two haven't broken up, have you?"

"No, and technically, there isn't anything *to* break up. We're not in a relationship. But he might not want to spend a lot of time with me anymore." Brooke's phone buzzed in with a text. It was Gable letting her know he was working in the barn instead of the house.

"If that's him, I think that text clears up your worries."

"Maybe." Brooke hesitated in sharing her own messy details from yesterday. "It's just, I took him along on my emotional roller coaster ride yesterday when I was dealing with Mrs. Davies's hive situation." Turning, she leaned back and slumped against the open wall next to the shelves. "He probably has whiplash from all of my twists and turns."

Harper's phone rang and she looked at the screen. "I'm sorry. It's the greenhouse. I have to take this."

"That's okay. You need to get back to work, and I should do the same. I'll see you later." Brooke headed for the exit. It had actually felt good to unload some of her baggage about what happened yesterday, but they couldn't spend all day chatting about her problems.

Harper answered her cell. "Hello—Reggie. Can you hold on a minute? I'm putting you on mute so don't panic when you don't hear anything. Hey, Brooke," she called out. "Gable—I met him yesterday when he was leaving our house. You know, he really cares about you."

Brooke faced Harper and shook her head. "I wouldn't read too much into him checking up on me. He's just naturally a good guy."

"I'm not reading into anything. That's what he told me. If you want my opinion, you should answer that text he just sent you, in person."

The revelation filled Brooke with a mix of hope and doubt. "And then say what to him? That he doesn't have to worry about taking another ride on the emotional roller coaster with me again?"

"You could lead with that."

"Based on your expression, you don't think I should. What do you think I should do?"

Harper shrugged. "It doesn't matter what I think. You have to do what feels right, but since you're asking, you could start by letting him know you're okay, and then explain why you two ended up on that ride in the first place."

Brooke walked from her Jeep parked at Gable's barn. A cool morning breeze was in the air, filled with the sweet smell of hay and fresh-cut grass.

Pepper grazed contentedly in the pasture.

The echo of hammering sounds came from the barn.

Brooke walked to the open sliding doors then paused.

Gable stood on one end of a portable worktable, measuring a piece of wood.

Promise he'd never have to take a ride on the emotional roller coaster with her again or explain to him what caused it to happen in the first place. On the drive over, she'd debated which direction to take their conversation, but she still wasn't sure. Especially since she didn't entirely understand why her emotions had gotten away from her so easily.

He glanced up, stopped what he was doing and took off his work gloves. "Hey, I wasn't expecting to see you. I assumed you were busy since you didn't answer my last text."

She walked down the aisle of the barn. "I thought I should just stop by instead of replying to it."

"I'm glad you did." He strode to meet her, his booted footsteps muffled by the rubber flooring.

Concern was in his eyes but so was his smile. His happiness matched her own in seeing him, too. By the time he reached her, all she wanted to do was wrap her arms around him and sink into the strength of his embrace. That's exactly what she did.

Gable leaned away and held her loosely in his arms. "You look rested."

"I pretty much slept from the moment you left until this morning."

"Good, you needed it."

"Thanks again for being there yesterday." Brooke dropped her gaze to the open top buttons on his blue Henley-style shirt. "I know seeing me like that was a lot, considering our situation."

"It wasn't a lot. You were having a normal reaction to a difficult situation. It happens to all of us. It was nothing."

Wanting to roll back in time to a more lighthearted moment and forget what happened yesterday, she looked up at him and forced a laugh. "Nothing like me having food on my face that first night we had dinner together? You know, I honestly thought you were lying and just wanted a reason to kiss me."

"I'd actually considered it, but then that's what you expected."

"Oh, so you were trying to be unpredictable."

"No, I was just waiting for the right time."

Brooke had anticipated the memory making him laugh, but only a faint smile tipped up his mouth. Had she been right about him not wanting to spend as much time with her? Was he going to tell her he needed more space after what happened yesterday? If he was, it was best to face that conversation head-on.

"Is something wrong?" she asked.

"Not with me, but something is bothering you. What is it?"

Was she that transparent to him that he could read her mood so easily? That was a little daunting, but it also paved the way for an answer she hadn't expected to tumble out.

"I'm upset because I've never lost bees like that before, but I honestly don't understand why it affected me like that. And not knowing why bothers me."

"Maybe you do know."

The lingering mix of emotions she'd been feeling all morning threatened to seep out in tears. She closed her eyes. "I just feel like I should have read the signs…followed my instincts and done something. I could have stopped the car accident…" As Brooke heard the verbal slip her eyes flew open. "That wasn't what I meant to say."

Gable looked directly in her eyes. "Or is it possible that is what you meant to say because your reaction yesterday wasn't just about the bees?"

Brooke wanted to deny it, but there it was. The answer, intimately intertwined with the remnants of grief that had almost devastated her as a teen. Raw, jagged and ugly, the two weighed heavily in her chest, digging into her heart, reopening the scars from the wounds grief had made there when she'd lost her parents.

Brooke laid her cheek to his chest, and Gable wrapped his arms around her.

She waited for him to ask questions. He didn't. He just held her. The strength of his arms. The steady thump of his heart. Without using words, he coaxed it out of her. Fighting to push her voice past a whisper, she said, "The Saturday my parents died, Harper and I were supposed to go to Pennsylvania for the entire weekend with them to sell honey at a festival. But there was a basketball tournament, and the teams from our schools were in it and my sister and I wanted to go. Our parents made arrangements with one of our friend's parents to take us, and instead of spending the night in Pennsylvania, our parents had planned to return that night and pick us up at our friend's. But when I woke up that morning, I wanted to go with them, but they said no."

Have fun... The memory of her mom shouting those words out the window from the driver's seat of their parents' van grew vivid in Brooke's mind. Tears welled. "The only reason they drove back was to pick us up. If I would have gone with them, we probably would have stayed the night, and they wouldn't have been in an accident. They would..." The words evaporated in her throat. *Still be alive.*

"Brooke, sweetheart." Gable spoke softly to her as he held her tighter. "They still might have come back that night, and you might have been in the car. You can run a different scenario than what happened over and over in your mind, but the truth is we can never know if our actions could have made a difference. Blaming yourself... your parents wouldn't want that for you."

Something he'd said caught her attention. She looked up at him. "You said *we* can never know."

He nodded slowly. "Yeah, I did. I understand where you're coming from. I need to remember that, too."

Gable didn't have to explain. She could see it in his face. He was referring to his own struggles about Theo.

Brooke laid her cheek back to his chest. Deep down she knew he was right about her parents, but it was hard not to wish for a different outcome. Telling him how she felt had lightened some of her burden, but... "So much for being a good distraction. All I'm doing is digging stuff up for you."

"And don't forget you made me fall off of my horse."

She looked up at him, and the hint of humor in his eyes made her smile a little. "I'll never forget that."

Gable reached up and cupped her face. "We might not be the best at being each other's distractions, but maybe we're something better."

"Like what?"

He glided his thumbs over her cheeks. "We're reminding each other that when it comes to facing hard things, we're not alone."

Chapter Nineteen

Gable walked with Brooke from the parking lot toward the steps of the porch to the entrance of the Montecito Steakhouse. She had a meeting there, and he'd come with her. Once she was done, they'd planned on having a late lunch.

With each step, they gravitated toward each other. His hand brushed hers, and they instinctively intertwined their fingers.

Over a week had passed since that day in his barn after the bee incident at Mrs. Davies. Since then their connection to each other had grown stronger as they'd come to realize understanding each other's baggage wasn't a hindrance. With that acceptance came a greater ease and honesty that really allowed them to enjoy each other on every level, not just in bed.

And Brooke learning to deal with the guilt she still felt over her parents' accident seemed to have also helped her relationship with Harper. According to Brooke, their meetings and general conversations about the farm were really productive, but those conversations with her sister seemed to always happen way too early, and they took her away from him, and he knew that complaint was purely from his selfish point of view. He'd just gotten used to him and

Brooke waking up together, just holding each other for a while, talking about random things or making love.

But he needed to get used to her not being there. How much time did they have left? The topic of her leaving hadn't come up in their random morning conversations. Not wanting to think about it, he'd pushed the exact date from his mind.

Inside the restaurant, the light clinking of plates reverberated from the dining room to the right of the lobby. In between the lunch and dinner rush, the dark leather booths and wood tables in the brick-walled space were mostly unoccupied.

Down the short hall to the left in the bar, there were even fewer patrons.

A lone bartender served three customers at the U-shaped wood counter with stools off to the side. All of the wood tables in the center of the bar were empty.

A small group occupied one of the dark green upholstered booths lining the walls. They playfully harassed a couple playing darts in a corner area that also had pool tables.

Broadcasts from golf to gymnastics to a highlight reel from last night's ball game played on wide flat-screen TVs above the bar and high on the walls of the main space.

Brooke looked to Gable. Her demeanor matched her casual business attire, relaxed but professional. "I don't think this meeting will even be an hour. We worked out most of the details in an email. Maybe thirty to forty minutes, tops."

"I'm not in a hurry. Do your thing. I'll wait at the bar."

She checked in with the bartender about where the manager's office was located then walked down a nearby hall.

Gable took a seat on one of the stools and ordered a bottled beer. As he watched the sports highlight reel, he and the bartender made small talk about the broadcast.

Customers walked in and the bartender had to get back to work. Two couples went to a booth while a younger dark-haired guy stood a few seats away from Gable.

After serving the guy a beer, the bartender left to wait on the couples.

A moment later, the dark-haired guy answered his phone. He smiled. "Hey, I'm already at the Montecito. Where are you? We need to practice. I want to make sure we nail the song for tonight." As he listened to the person on the phone, his smile disappeared and his brow rose. "You missed your flight? You overslept? Are you kidding me?"

The conversation sounded like a disagreement between musicians. Gable took a pull from his bottle. Trying not to listen, he focused on the golfer on the flat-screen TV above the bar lining up his next shot.

The guy snorted in frustration. "No, I can't change things up for you. You know how important tonight is for me. You shouldn't have gone out last night and gotten wasted. This isn't a game. This is about the rest of my life. Hell yeah, I'm pissed at you. Look, I've got to go. I have stuff to figure out." He ended the call and tossed his phone on the counter. It slid near Gable.

As the guy retrieved it, he said to Gable, "Sorry about that. It's the most important night of my life and the friend I was counting on to help me just screwed me over."

Gable understood the guy's pain. He'd been in the position more than once where a musician he was counting on bailed at the last minute. "Were you two supposed to perform here tonight?"

"Sort of." The guy's shoulders slumped with a heavy sigh. "I'm proposing to my girlfriend. It's all set up. Her friends are bringing her here for a girl's night out, and I already arranged things with Pat, the bar manager." He looked to the front of the bar as if visualizing a scene. "My buddy was going to perform my and Jill's favorite song on his guitar, and I was going to propose. Now it's ruined."

Gable felt sorry for him. "That's rough."

"Yeah, it is. Tonight really was important to me." The guy took a ring box from his front jeans pocket and opened it. A diamond ring flickered in the light. "I wanted everything to be right for Jill."

"Which song were you planning to sing?"

The guy gave the name of a song. "Have you ever heard it? The lyrics describe Jill to a T."

"Yes, I've heard that song. It's a nice one." Actually, Gable wasn't just familiar with the country ballad. He'd sung it during his own shows a few times. Lifting his beer, he took a drink, swallowing that confession.

"It's on the karaoke machine. I guess I could do it that way." The guy sighed. "But it's not going to be the same, is it?"

"No, probably not." Gable silently went through a list of excuses about why he couldn't get involved. As he flexed his left hand that was now free of the brace, all of his reasons fell apart. "I play guitar and sing. I can probably fill in for your friend."

"Really?" The young guy sat up straighter with a hopeful look on his face. "If you could, that would be great. I can pay you. It won't be a lot."

Gable waved him off. "You don't have to pay me. What time is the big moment happening tonight?"

"Jill and her friends will be here at seven thirty. I was thinking around eight. Can you make it?"

"I can. That gives us enough time to practice, if you're

free. My guitar is at my house. I can go home and get it, but I have to wait until my girlfriend finishes her meeting with the bar manager." *Girlfriend?* He'd meant to say Brooke.

The guy grinned. "No problem. I'll wait here until you get back. I'm Lucas, by the way."

"I'm D—" Gable caught himself before he said Dell. Why was he having so much trouble keeping his details straight? "Gable." They shook hands.

Just then, Brooke walked down the hall with an auburn-haired woman.

Lucas pushed away from the bar. "I should let Pat know about the change. Is that your girlfriend?"

Gable found himself a little tongue-tied. Hopefully, Brooke hadn't overheard Lucas's last sentence. If she had, that would open the door to an awkward explanation that he hadn't come up with, other than it just slipped out. "Uh, yeah, that's Brooke."

As Lucas went over to the women, Gable prayed he wouldn't drop the *G* word on Brooke. When they came over to him at the bar, from the way she smiled as Lucas introduced him to Pat, he was spared from having to explain the mix-up in his words.

Gable gave Lucas his phone number and assured him he would be back for a quick rehearsal. Unfortunately, that meant Gable and Brooke had to skip having lunch at the restaurant.

Lucas, who was grateful and more than a little nervous about proposing in general, ordered a drink at the bar.

Outside, Gable and Brooke walked down the steps of the raised porch in front of the Montecito. She glanced at him a few times.

When they reached her truck in the parking lot, she

faced him and smiled. "What you're doing for him is really sweet."

"It's nothing."

"It is." Earnestness was in her eyes as she laid her hand on his chest. "I know this performance is a big step for you. You didn't have to volunteer to help him. Why did you?"

"I could see how important it was to him. Proposing is a big step. He wanted to do it right." As he contemplated all of the reasons, Gable laid his hand over hers resting on his chest. "And, it's what Theo would have done. He believed music was something that needed to be shared."

Her eyes grew soft. "Those are all perfect reasons." Rising on her toes, she kissed him.

Taking her by the waist, he brought her close. Girlfriend. That's what he mistakenly called her. But the way Brooke kissed him, soft and inviting. The way she fit so perfectly in his arms. The way she wasn't afraid to express herself. If he was looking for a girlfriend, it would be her.

Brooke eased out of the kiss but stayed in his arms. "I need to get you home. You don't want to be late for practice."

Practice. The reality of the word hit him. Sure, he'd sung to Brooke in the bathroom that day, but he hadn't played or sung an entire song in months.

She looked up at him. "Are you okay?"

Gable sidestepped the real question. "I was just wondering, since we're missing having lunch together, will you come back with me tonight? After I'm done helping Lucas with his proposal, we can have a drink. Grab some dinner. I could use a friendly face in the audience."

Brooke gave him a widening smile. "Of course I'll be there."

Chapter Twenty

I'm ready... Brooke checked her makeup in the mirror one last time. She had on the same red dress she'd worn the first night she'd had dinner with Gable, but this time she'd paired it with her chunky-heeled sandals. It worked for the most part.

She walked down the hall.

Harper sat on the couch eating dinner and watching television. She'd stopped hiding out in her office and started having breakfast at the house in the morning and eating dinner there as well. A couple of times Brooke had joined her in passing when she wasn't at Gable's. Having a bit of normalcy together made the house feel a lot less isolating.

Harper glanced at Brooke. "You look nice for your date. Where are you and Gable going?"

Brooke hesitated to call it a date. Technically, she was supporting Gable, but she had dressed up, and he was picking her up. On the surface, it did look like a date. "We're going to the Montecito." She glanced into her cross-body bag. "I forgot my keys." Hurrying back to the bedroom, she retrieved them from the dresser.

When she returned to the front, Harper was peering out the narrow side window next to the door. "I hope you have a strong 'he's all mine' stare prepared because a lot of women are going to be looking at him tonight."

"Let me see." Brooke peeked over her sister's shoulder. Gable was on the phone near his truck. *Whoa.* Black cowboy boots, jeans, a black button-down shirt...and he wore the hat. Even from a distance, he was nothing short of jaw-droppingly gorgeous.

Harper looked Brooke over from head to toe. "You can't wear that."

"Why? A minute ago you said I looked nice."

"That was before I saw Gable. He's got the whole sexy cowboy vibe going on and you look...a little average."

"Thanks a lot. Well, I'll just have to be average because this is all I have to wear. And now that you mentioned it, I'm going to feel self-conscious all night."

Her sister shook her head. "No, we have to fix this." Harper opened the front door. She smiled and waved. "Hi, Gable. Brooke will be out in a minute." She slammed the door shut, grabbed Brooke's hand and pulled her along.

"Harper, what are you doing?" Brooke tried not to trip as her sister rushed her up the stairs. "Gable and I really need to leave. We're meeting someone."

"This will only take a minute. No, maybe five minutes."

"I don't have time to change. I'll mess up my hair."

At the landing, Harper dragged Brooke into her bedroom. "The dress is fine. You just need accessories." She hurried to her closet, organized by color. Diving into the back of it, she pulled something out and tossed it to Brooke. "Put this on."

A fashionable short black suede jacket with just the right amount of fringe. Brooke slipped into it, buttery soft, the garment glided over her arms. Harper lived in jeans and

T-shirts. This was the last thing Brooke expected her sister to own.

Seconds later, Harper emerged with her second find. A pair of black cowboy boots. Brooke took off her heels. "Ooh, those are perfect, but I need socks."

Already on it, Harper threw her a pair.

Brooke put them on along with the boots. They fit perfectly. When they were younger, they used to steal each other's shoes. She was tempted to slip them into her backpack when she left.

Harper pointed at her. "Don't even think about it. I'm loaning them to you. I want them back." She turned Brooke toward the floor-length mirror next to the closet. "Now, you're ready."

Brooke stared at herself and her sister's reflection. She looked good. Touched by Harper's generosity, she gave her sister a kiss on the cheek. "Thanks. You didn't have to do this."

Smiling, Harper waved her off. "I couldn't let you go out to the Montecito looking all boring with Gable. And seriously, I want my stuff back."

Moments later, Brooke hurried down the steps of the porch. "Sorry to keep you waiting."

Gable stood near the truck with his back to her. He turned around. "That's..." As she approached him, he took her in from head to boots and back up again. "You are worth the wait. You look amazing." He took her hand and tugged her closer. "And I'd really love to kiss you."

Hearing him repeat the line she'd said the first time they'd had dinner together made her smile. She rested her hand on his chest. "You can kiss me all you want later tonight."

His gaze heated with desire. "I'm holding you to that."

Moments later, driving to the steakhouse, Gable's mood sobered. He looked preoccupied.

Brooke asked, "Did you and Lucas get a chance to practice this afternoon?"

"We did. It's a simple setup. I'll be on stage singing and playing the song. Lucas will join in and then he'll propose. Can't get any simpler than that."

It sounded like he was trying to convince himself about what he'd just said. She laid her hand on his thigh. "Don't worry. It's going to turn out wonderful."

He picked up her hand. After kissing the back of it, he intertwined their fingers and rested both their hands back on his thigh. "I hope so. I want to give Lucas and his fiancée a memorable night for all the right reasons."

Less than a half hour later, they parked into the almost full lot of the Montecito Steakhouse.

Lucas had told Gable to enter through the side door and meet him in the manager's office. They were going over everything again, and Lucas didn't want anyone to see Gable with his guitar.

On the other hand, Brooke couldn't take her eyes off of him. As she gave him a kiss on the cheek, she breathed in his cologne. She couldn't wait until they indulged in those kisses they talked about before they left the farm. "See you inside."

She went in the restaurant through the front and went to the bar. It was busy for a weekday night. Craning her neck, she looked for an empty table or a couple of available seats.

Across the room, she saw a familiar face.

Rina waved her over to where she and a few other people were sitting at tables that had been pushed together.

The café owner stood and gave her a hug. "Hi, Brooke."

"Hey."

"Are you here by yourself?"

Not wanting to risk ruining Lucas's plan, she offered the simplest answer. "No, Gable will be here in a minute."

"Why don't you sit with us?" Rina gestured to the table where members of her family were seated.

"Are you sure? I don't want to intrude."

"You're not intruding. We have plenty of room." She turned to everyone at the table. "Hey, guys, Brooke and Gable are joining us."

Brooke said hello. All of the faces were familiar. Tristan and his wife, Chloe. Zurie and Mace. Rina and Scott.

As the conversation flowed freely between the family, Brooke felt out of place. From the way they bantered across the table, they clearly loved and liked each other. But hadn't there been a time when Tristan, Zurie and Rina hadn't gotten along over issues involving the stable? They were clearly past whatever had put a wedge between them.

She and Harper were getting along better, but whenever they talked about the legal transfer of ownership, Brooke sensed that Harper was still disappointed in her for not wanting to stay and run the farm. If Harper really needed her, especially during the first few months of running things on her own, she could swing by for a few days. And maybe she would be able to catch up with Gable, too. Would he want that?

Pat walked to the mic at the front of the room. "Hello, everyone." A hint of a southern lilt flowed through her words. "We have some special entertainment tonight that I think you'll like. Help me welcome singer Gable Kincaid to the stage."

Everyone at the table, including Brooke, joined in the polite applause as Gable took a seat on a stool behind the microphone in front of him.

Pat positioned another mic in front of his guitar.

From the looks of puzzlement on people's faces, they were wondering who Gable was.

Rina nudged Brooke and whispered, "I didn't know he was a singer."

Brooke nodded. "He is." Unable to resist, she added, "And he's really good."

"Hey, everyone." Gable's voice reverberated through the bar. "I'm here because I agreed to help a friend by singing a song for him. You might recognize it." He flashed a smile that made Brooke's heart jump and probably the hearts of a few other people in the bar. "I hope you like it."

Gable strummed his guitar.

From the way people smiled and nodded, they recognized the opening chords to the popular ballad.

As he played, Gable sang, wrapping his voice around the song about being in love. Goose bumps rose on Brooke's arms as he graced the high notes, true and clear, and when his voice dropped closer to bass.

Soon everyone in the bar was mesmerized.

Then Lucas appeared in the bar. Dressed in his cowboy finest, he strode over to Jill, who was sitting with her friends at a front table.

She was clearly surprised to see him and was even more shocked when he dropped to one knee.

Gable lowered his voice and strummed his guitar a little softer as Lucas held up a ring and proposed to Jill.

"Oh, look at them." Rina sighed. "That's so sweet."

Jill nodded emphatically, and Lucas slipped the engagement ring on her finger. She jumped to her feet, and as she wrapped her arms around Lucas, he picked her straight up. Everyone in the bar whistled and cheered.

Gable sang and played louder.

Jill and Lucas swayed to the music, wrapped in their own little bubble, clearly in love with each other.

Gable brought the song to a close, and the final notes of his guitar echoed.

More claps and cheers erupted for him as well.

Lucas went over to Gable and they chatted for a moment.

Gable nodded then spoke into the microphone. "It looks like I'm playing one more song. This one is a song I wrote. It's called 'Chances.'"

The lyrics about doing everything not to lose love resonated with the crowd. Couples got up to dance while others swayed in their seats.

"What I'm feelin' for you I just can't hide. I'm standing here for as long as it takes...for a chance at something real...my love."

Rina elbowed her again. "He's fantastic. A man that can sing. You are so lucky."

As Brooke watched Gable light up the stage and reach the crowd, she actually felt lucky. Yes, that was her man. At least he was for the next few weeks.

Gable ended the song with a flourish to resounding applause. "Thank you." A server handed him a bottled beer and he lifted it in a toast. "And why don't we all send our best to Lucas and Jill."

The crowd applauded and lifted their glasses to toast the beaming couple.

A server brought glasses of wine to the table.

Zurie, who sat next to Rina, was about to take a drink when Rina slipped the glass from her fingers. "I'll take that."

"Hey." Zurie reached for the pilfered wine. "You already have a glass. Don't be so greedy."

"I'm not being greedy," Rina said. "You just shouldn't have alcohol."

Zurie's brow rose. "Since when?"

"Since…" Rina glanced down at her sister's stomach.

"Seriously?" Zurie shot Rina a slightly annoyed look and shrugged. "Yes, I've gained a few pounds because I've been baking bread and eating it, but not that much."

"I'm not commenting on your weight," Rina insisted. "Putting on weight is necessary in your situation."

"My situation. What…" Zurie's eyes widened. "Oh my gosh." Her voice rose higher. "You think I'm pregnant?"

Mace nearly spit out a sip of beer.

Zurie patted his arm. "No, relax, honey, I'm not."

"You're not?" Rina looked crushed.

"No." Zurie stole back her glass. "What made you think I was?"

"You said you've been feeling queasy, and you were cutting way back on caffeine. And since you got back from your trip, you've been glowing. And you've had…cravings." Rina's gaze moved to Chloe's along with everyone else's.

Chloe paused in shaking more parmesan on the chicken wing in her hand. She blushed.

Chuckling, Tristan wrapped an arm around Chloe's shoulders. "I think we just got our answer to when would be a good time to tell everyone."

"I guess so." Chloe smiled at her husband then looked at the table. "Yes, I'm pregnant."

Rina and Zurie both got up to give Chloe and Tristan hugs.

As they sat back down, Tristan's eyes narrowed as he studied Zurie and Mace. "But I can't blame Rina for thinking something was up with you two. I've been wondering the same. Actually, both of you have been all lovey-dovey and glowing lately."

Mace shrugged with an all too innocent look. "Nothing's going on." He averted his eyes from Tristan as he took a sip of beer.

Zurie quietly cleared her throat and suddenly became absorbed in her glass of wine.

Scott crossed his arms over his chest. "Yeah, I'm with Tristan on this one. Something's up. You two have been acting like love-struck teenagers."

"Acting?" Chloe snorted a laugh. "The other evening, I spotted them sneaking out of one of the guest cottages."

Brooke laughed. "Well, that doesn't sound like nothing to me."

Chloe glanced over at Brooke. "Oh, it most definitely wasn't. From the looks on their faces, they'd been doing a lot more than inspecting the premises."

Zurie objected, "No, we weren't acting like love-struck teenagers. Were we?" She looked to Mace.

In silent communication, he returned her smile. "No, we were acting like husband and wife. We got married in Vegas."

"What?" Everyone at the table except for Mace, Zurie and Brooke asked the question.

Near pandemonium erupted as the two slipped wedding rings from their pockets and slipped them on. Hugs were exchanged, along with back-and-forth conversations.

"So when are we having the real wedding?" Chloe demanded.

More banter erupted.

It must have been nice to be part of a big loving family. Just as Brooke was starting to feel like she didn't belong at the table, Gable dropped down in the chair beside her. He glanced at the Tillbridges. "What are they celebrating?"

"Mace and Zurie eloped."

A laugh shot out of Gable. "That explains Mace's dry cough at Mrs. Davies's."

"What?"

"I'll tell you later. Just know that Mrs. Davies is going to be put out. She already bought a hat and a dress anticipating their wedding."

On the bar's small stage, two couples were completely messing up the Bon Jovi song "Livin' On a Prayer." But Lucas and his fiancée were oblivious as they swayed slowly together on the dance floor.

This was one of the happiest moments of their lives. One they'd never forget, and Gable had helped make it happen.

Pride swelled up inside of her. Needing an outlet for it, she gave him a lingering kiss.

Gable smiled. "What was that for?"

There were too many reasons to count. Helping out Lucas. Being kind to Mrs. Davies. Being good to his horse. Being the best distraction she'd ever had in her life. She summed it up. "For being you."

Later that night, they fulfilled the promise of more kisses, and those kisses led them to pure ecstasy. As they fit as one, moving to a rhythm that took her higher and higher, Brooke felt as if she soared through the sky on the wave of a shooting star.

After making love, they held each other, and she floated with him in pure contentment.

Their legs were intertwined. As he absently glided his hand along her hip, he kissed her temple. "It meant a lot to see you in the audience at the Montecito. Thanks for being there for me tonight."

"Of course." *I'll always be here for you.* For some reason, a part of her longed to say those words and mean it. But she couldn't. Sure, she might come back to help Harper, but she couldn't ask him to wait for her. When she left in a few weeks, that's when it would end for them. That was the best plan. A hint of bittersweetness broke through her haze of contentment.

Brooke snuggled closer to Gable, finding her right spot against him, and pressed a kiss to his chest where his heart beat near her cheek. One thing was for sure, Gable would always have a place in her heart.

Chapter Twenty-One

"Hexagonal or round?" Brooke asked the question as she stared at the empty six-ounce jars with gold tops she held in each hand. Standing alone in the office cottage at the checkout counter, no one was around to give an answer.

The company creating the packaging for the honey they were featuring during the celebration in September had sent the jars for her approval. They both had the same floral graphic label with the bee farm's logo. The round one had Lavender Honey written on it. The other had Special Reserve Berry written in the same bold script, and they both had a honey dipper attached by a gold band circling below the lid.

They were well made. Cute. And not all that different from their standard packaging. She just wasn't wowed by it. Shouldn't the products they featured for National Honey Month have a bit more pizzazz?

Needing a little inspiration, she dipped a mini sample spoon into an open jar of berry reserved honey from the personal stash they kept in the office. It was from the farm's last honey harvest. A tart, clean sweetness with a hint of berries floated across her taste buds.

The door opened.

A welcome sight as well as a possible objective opinion walked in.

Gable paused, cocked his head and gave her a questioning look. "If I didn't know any better, I would think you were plotting something."

"I am." Brooke let her gaze travel from his head to his boots and back again. He made a T-shirt and a pair of jeans look absolutely sinful. "I'm hatching a scheme of how to take advantage of you."

"That's easy." Gable joined her behind the counter and took her in his arms. "What are you waiting for?"

Since his appearance at the Montecito two nights ago, his smiles came easier. His laughter was richer. His moments of stillness where he just stared into space were fewer. She could feel happiness emanating from him.

A video of Lucas's proposal along with Gable singing had been posted on a few people's social media timelines and was gaining popularity. Gable's talent manager had even gotten wind of it and had reached out to him. But despite the popularity, Gable viewed the performance as a good deed that had made Lucas and Jill's engagement special, not an opening to revive his music career.

She wasn't sure if she agreed with that. Gable was so talented. From the comments on the posts she'd read, his song "Chances" had touched people. But either way, music as a part of his life again or not, it was good to see him this way.

Brooke wound her arms around his neck. "I'm trying to be really good right now because we're out in public, but when I get you home, cowboy…"

"Promises, promises." Smiling, he leaned in.

They indulged in a lingering kiss and a couple of short ones where he gently sucked on her bottom lip. "You taste good," he said. "What is that?"

"Berry honey." She picked up a clean sample spoon, dipped it in the jar and fed him some of the liquid sweetness.

"Hmm," he said. "I like it, but it tastes even better on you. Any chance you can bring that jar to my place later on for some taste testing?"

"There's a strong possibility that can happen, but first I have to figure out my jar problem."

He followed her gaze to the containers on the counter. "What's the issue?"

Brooke disentangled herself from his arms. She gestured to the two empty jars. "I have to decide which one of these to use for our featured honey selections in September."

He faced the counter with her. "The one shaped like a hexagon is nice. It looks like the inside of a honeycomb."

She shook her head. "Nice. I was hoping for more. I want our product to be mouthwatering. Enticing. It should make you want it because it exudes that it's special, and you can't possibly walk away without having a jar and buying a few extras for your friends."

"Okay. Pretend I'm not already a loyal customer. What makes your honey special?"

Brooke considered the question. "Well, Aunt Ivy chose lavender, hibiscus and berry because they're different from our main offerings. They're also interesting on their own, but they fit together in a special way."

"So kind of like musical notes in a song or members of a band."

As an idea percolated in her thoughts, she picked up the hexagonal jar. "You're on to something. Songs have names. Bands have names. Maybe this trio needs *its* own name. Something that reflects how they stand on their own but blend together. Soft, smooth, sensual, but with moments that stand out."

He stared away from her with a contemplative look on his face. "Like a symphony?"

"That's it!" All at once, Brooke saw the entire concept in her mind. "We can call it the symphony collection. These labels. They have to change. Maybe musical notes or a sheet music type of a concept. You are brilliant." She cupped his face and kissed him hard on the mouth.

He grinned. "I'll take that. So, does this mean I will or won't see you later tonight because you'll be working on this?"

"No, you'll see me. Aside from indulging in berry honey, didn't you say you wanted to watch a movie?"

"That was the plan. What type of movies do you like to watch?"

"Good ones. And definitely not any of the ones my friend Nellie recommends. I'm still kicking myself for falling down the trap of watching *Zombie Robot Soldier Beasts*, and I still don't know the ending."

His brows shot up with interest. "*Zombie Robot Soldier Beasts*. That one's on its way to being a classic."

All Brooke could do was just blink at him and wonder at the odds. "Are you related to Nellie Harris? She's a blonde, sometimes a redhead, about yea high?"

"I don't think so. Why?"

"Because she has the absolute worst taste in movies."

"Wow. In less than a minute I've gone from brilliant to the one who picks really bad movies?"

"I didn't say that…exactly." She laughed at the cute hurt expression on his face. "I'm sure all of your tastes in movies can't be as tacky as Nellie's. And on second thought, I'm loving that you watched *Zombie Robot Soldier Beasts*.

You can tell me how Mitzi the industrious teacup Yorkie escaped."

His mischievous grin was kind of similar to ones she'd viewed on Nellie's face. "Nope. You should see it for yourself."

Hours later, sitting next to Gable on his sectional with her fingers clutching popcorn in a bowl on her lap, Brooke stared at the television in disbelief. Just a few minutes ago, Mitzi had jumped from the island, zombies literally snapping at her hind legs, and landed on a log floating toward the open water, red bow still intact. She'd had to leave her chew toy behind, but at least she'd escaped. A kind couple in a sailboat had found her and all was good. Or so Brooke thought. Now at the end of the film, the Yorkie had a feral look in her eyes and she was lunging at the throat of the woman who'd saved her. And of course her husband was standing there doing nothing, just waiting to be next.

Beside her, Gable's shoulders shook as he tried to contain his laughter.

She pointed at him. "I hate you so much right now. I can't believe you tricked me into watching the end of this movie."

"But you said you wanted to know."

She threw popcorn at him. "Only because I thought Mitzi got away. You told me she escaped."

"No I didn't. I said you needed to see the ending for yourself." He shrugged innocently. "I didn't want to spoil the ending."

"I'll give you an ending." Brooke put the bowl on the side table next to her then jumped on him.

Laughing, Gable caught her around the waistband of her leggings. Slipping his hand under the hem of her T-shirt, he tickled her, finding all the sensitive spots that made her shriek.

"No…wait! I'll stop."

"Oh no. I have to protect myself." He doubled down on tickling her. "You have the same look Mitzi had in her eyes in the movie."

"No, I don't." She tried to tickle him back, but in one swift move he had her on her back on the couch.

As he lay on top of her, he delivered a different kind of torture. A sensual one, involving him kissing her neck and his palm skimming along her belly and up her shirt.

Unfortunately, she had to stop him. "Gable…"

He swept a kiss along her mouth. "Yes."

"I have to move. There's a popcorn kernel jabbing me, and I need to take a pause for the cause."

Gable let her up. As she stood, he smacked her on the butt. "You had some popcorn there. Just dusting it off."

The playful gleam in his eyes made her laugh. "You are being so wicked tonight."

"Wait until you get back."

A couple of minutes later, before she left the bathroom, Brooke pulled a piece of popcorn from her hair and smiled. She still didn't like the movie, but she honestly had fun watching the ending of the film with Gable.

As she walked into the living room, she said, "So since Mitzi is a zombie dog, is there *Zombie Robot Soldier Beasts 2* on the horizon? 'Cause if there is, I'll have to…"

Gable wasn't paying attention. He stared at his phone with a stricken look on his face.

Alarmed, she hurried and sat beside him. "Did something happen? What's wrong?"

"Keith called." Gable swallowed hard. "He sent me a link to a social media post."

"About what?"

"Take a look."

Brooke accepted his phone. She tapped play on the paused video of a young woman on screen.

Remember the hot cowboy country singer who helped with a marriage proposal?

Well, turns out he wasn't such a nice guy. The song he claimed was his was actually written by his deceased best friend. His widow has the receipts. Music written in her husband's handwriting. According to the post she made this morning, she'll reveal all of the details soon...

Brooke shook her head. "Oh no, we have to put a stop to this. They're spreading lies."

Bent over his elbows to his knees, Gable held his head in his hands. "It doesn't matter."

"It does."

"The receipts Melonie claims to possess are most likely notes about 'Chances' Theo had written for me on some napkins." He lifted his head and looked at her. Stoic bleakness was in his eyes. "It's my word against hers. Who do you think everyone will believe?"

More comments popped up, adding to the ones that had already been posted under the video with a steadily climbing number of views and likes.

The commenters' opinions were all basically the same. Gable was a thief.

Chapter Twenty-Two

Sitting at the counter of his galley kitchen the next morning, Gable felt as if he'd been struck by a load of bricks. He hadn't slept well last night, and the current strategy session he was in with Keith on speakerphone wasn't sinking into his brain. Most of what his talent manager was telling him was skipping over the surface.

"So, everyone here agrees," Keith said. "The song is resonating with people, so the faster you put up an apology video, the faster people will forgive you. I know it sucks that you're going to have to say you misspoke about writing the song, but just focus on the light at the end of the tunnel. You have a shot at a record contract that can help make it all go away. Even Theo's wife will get what she wants. A fat check if she stops making claims against you. It'll come with an NDA, of course."

A headache started to pound, and Gable massaged his temple. "What Melonie wants is her husband back. I tried to give her money for the fund that was set up for her and her son but she refused to take it." She'd sent it back with a note that made it perfectly clear how she felt and what she wanted.

I want nothing from you. You took Theo away from us...

She also asked that he not attend the funeral. He'd said his goodbyes to his friend at the cemetery days later.

Keith released a long exhale. "Unfortunately, no one can give her that, but it's been over six months. Strangely, as unfair as it is, her shaming you publicly and you showing remorse could be the thing that gives her closure so she can move on and you can, too."

Movement drew Gable's attention.

Brooke had come downstairs. She walked into the living room.

Gable spoke to Keith. "I need to think about this."

"Remember, the faster we address this, the faster you can get back to what you should be doing. Pursuing your career. I know you said you weren't interested in performing again for a living, but you have talent, Gable. You shouldn't let it go to waste."

"Give me the rest of the day to think about it. I'll talk to you tomorrow."

Gable ended the call.

As Brooke came over to him, he turned toward her in the chair. She immediately walked between his widened legs and wrapped her arms around him. He hugged her back, resting his forehead near her throat, and breathed her in. She smelled like his soap, her own light scent of berries, and she was pure warmth.

Brooke cupped his face, raised it up and looked into his eyes. "Did you sleep at all last night?"

They'd gone to bed together, but, too restless to sleep, he'd come downstairs and stretched out on the sectional.

"A little. I was just dozing off when Keith called."

As he rested his hands on her waist, Brooke rested hers on his shoulders. She glanced at his phone on the counter. "So, are you making the video?"

She'd heard that part of the conversation. It was a relief not to have to explain. "I'm not sure. Possibly."

Her frown reflected her opinion.

"You don't think I should? Keith said it could make this entire nightmare go away."

"Or maybe it won't. One minute you were the cowboy that saved a marriage proposal and everybody loved you, and now, just two days later, you're being vilified. Everyone is happy to jump all over Melonie's accusations, and she hasn't even posted her so-called receipts as proof. Even the *Bolan Town Talk* has jumped on the bandwagon."

"What are they saying?"

"Their usual brand of speculation. It's more of a blind item. An anonymous quote from the acquaintance of a friend, of a friend of a relative of the newly engaged woman, meaning Jill. Supposedly, she's upset that her engagement is linked to you and she's threatening to call it off." Brooke sunk her teeth into her bottom lip as if she was censoring herself and looked away.

He lightly grasped her chin and made her look at him. "What else did they say?"

She closed her eyes a moment. "They said a certain farrier is turning in his grave over being linked to...a fraud."

"They're calling me a fraud? That's not even accurate to the situation." And worse, they were bringing Wes into it.

"It illustrates the point I'm trying to make. Once you take the blame, people will spin whatever outcome they want based on more salacious untrue accusations just because it gives them more likes and views. No matter how many more songs you write and perform, this will be the thing that social media highlights about you and your career."

"But if I'm not pursuing a career in music, it won't matter. Honestly, I couldn't care less what the world thinks of me. I'm good being here in my home and spending time with you."

Brooke's slight wince as she looked away from him was a glaring reminder. She wouldn't be there for long. "Bolan is a whole different world, Gable. Walking around town, you'll receive looks, stares. People like Peggy will talk behind your back. You'll probably never be comfortable in the Montecito again. Is that the kind of life you really want?"

The picture she painted was bleak, but the fierceness in her eyes... The way she was fighting for his best interests, he would do the same for her if she was in his shoes. It was easy to imagine them supporting each other, no matter what, side by side.

He pressed his lips to hers. "Thanks for not doubting me and for believing in me."

She pressed her finger to his chest and leaned a little away from him. "You need to believe in yourself. Are you sure there isn't someone who can corroborate your side of the story?"

As Gable looked away and pondered her question, he blew out a breath. "No. The only person I showed the song to was Theo when we were at the club. I sang it for him. But when he performed 'Chances,' it sounded like a different song. People applauded for him."

"People? There was an audience?"

"No, just the staff cleaning up. The club was closed."

She gripped his shoulders. "So one of them might have seen Theo making notes for you on a napkin."

"How does that make a difference?"

"It opens the possibility that you cowrote the song and you have rights to it. It also takes something away from the claim Melonie is making that you stole something from her."

"But didn't I?" She blamed him for taking Theo away from her, and in a way, he did.

Exasperation and caring filled Brooke's face. "Gable Dell Kincaid, the one thing I know about you with all of my heart is that you are not a thief." She sighed. "You mentioned how Wes was a major influence on your life. What do you think he would tell you to do?"

After she left for the apiary, Gable pondered the question. His great-uncle would tell him to do what was right. But what was right? Giving Melonie what she wanted and maybe closure by taking the hit for an unfair accusation, or standing up for himself?

Walking to the counter, Gable picked up his phone and called Keith.

His talent manager said, "You're calling me back already? That was quick. So I guess you've come up with an answer?"

Gable went to the glass sliding door. As he stared out at the field he remembered all of the possibilities he'd envisioned for himself when he'd first arrived at the house. And meeting Brooke. She was right. He'd always face undue speculation in Bolan if he gave in to the accusations, and his actions would be tied to Wes. His great-uncle had been nothing but good to him and a good man. Wes's reputation didn't deserve to be associated with anything less.

Breaking his contemplative silence, Gable responded, "I need your help with something."

Brooke walked hand in hand with Gable into Lou's Uptown Lounge.

Outside, it was a mild sunny day, made for lounging near the beach and touring the local spots, but their visit to Jacksonville wasn't a vacation.

Keith had reached out to Lou on Gable's behalf about checking in with the staff who'd been there the night Gable and Theo had been on stage practicing music. Lou had agreed to assemble who he could, though some of the staff members no longer worked at the club. But instead of having Lou or anyone else talk to them, Gable had wanted to do it, and she'd come with him to lend support. Their plane had arrived that morning, and after checking into their hotel, they'd driven straight to the bar.

Inside the empty establishment, the smells of beer and fried food intermingled with the sterile scent of industrial cleaning products. Stools sat lined up at the bar. Padded chairs rested seat-down on the tables. Lights in the ceiling and windows facing the street fully illuminated the space, including the stage where a microphone and speaker sat near the back wall. A piano was off to the side.

Gable gravitated forward and Brooke went with him as they walked past the bar counter on the right. Her heels clicked and his booted footfalls thudded on the wood floor. The light rustle of their jeans-clad legs interrupted the silence. They stopped in front of the raised platform. His face reflected a mix of emotions, suggesting he saw more than just an empty stage.

As she moved closer to his side, his warmth seeped through the light fabric of her blouse. Gable wrapped an arm around her back and rested his hand on her hip. He released a heavy breath. "Standing here, it almost feels unreal. Like I only imagined being here that night with Theo."

Brooke laid her head on his shoulder a moment and rested her hand on his chest, feeling his heart beat through his long-sleeved shirt. There wasn't anything she could say to comfort him, because that night had actually happened, and the ripple effect of occurrences and actions since then was all too real.

A blond-haired man walked out from a door off the side of the stage. He strode over to them. "Hi, Gable, I'm Lou Bingham."

For some reason, she'd envisioned someone older as the bar owner, instead of the fit, fortyish guy in front of them wearing a white button-down, olive green shorts and tennis shoes. His deep tan and sunglasses perched on top of his head implied he spent most of his time near or on the water.

Gable shook hands with him. "Hello, this is my friend Brooke."

She shook hands with Lou as well. "Hi."

Gable said, "Thanks for setting this up today."

"No, problem. I was able to contact most of the staff who were here that night. Two of them moved away. They're gathered in my office. I'll take you back there, but I'll leave you with them. I thought you should talk with them alone. They might volunteer more information if I'm not in the room."

"Okay, let's do it."

"Good luck." Brooke reached for Gable's hand and gave it a quick squeeze.

He squeezed back and gave her a small smile. "Thanks."

Gable left with Lou and walked through the door the bar owner had come out of moments earlier. A short time later, Lou came back out to the bar.

He took two chairs down from a center table and put them upright on the floor next to it. "Please have a seat. Can I get you something to drink? Water? A soda, or maybe some coffee?"

Brooke sat in a chair. "No, thank you."

Lou sat down with her at the table. He set his phone and

sunglasses in front of him. "I really hope Gable is able to find out what he needs. Having what happened come up again all these months later, I can't imagine what he's been going through."

"It hasn't been easy on him."

Lou shook his head. "I still can't believe Theo had a heart attack. He was so young, but apparently his family had a history when it came to heart-related issues. I don't think I'll ever shake the memory of finding him here that morning."

Brooke had always assumed Theo had been elsewhere when he died. "You found him?"

Lou pointed. "Right next to the stage. As far as we could piece together, he left with Gable, they went to the restaurant, and afterward, instead of going home he came back here, and that's when it happened. He had napkins in his hand with a song written on it. I thought maybe it was something he'd been working on. That's why I gave them to his wife. I didn't know the song wasn't his."

"So you believe Gable?"

"Absolutely. My goddaughter is Keith Carson's admin assistant. I've known her since she was born. If she says the song belongs to Gable, and it's all a mistake, I believe her."

The door near the stage opened and Gable walked out. From the look on his face as he came toward the table, she already knew the results of the meeting.

"Any luck?" Lou stood.

Gable shook his head. "None of them heard or saw anything that might make a difference. I gave them Keith's number and told them to call him if they remember anything."

"I'm sorry to hear that." Lou's expression reflected his disappointment. "I'd really hoped one of them could clear up your situation. And like I told Keith when he called, I'm sorry. I feel like I'm to blame for this mix-up. If I would have known it was your song, I would have given everything to you instead of Theo's wife."

Gable waved him off. "You made a logical assumption. I appreciate you bringing your staff together and giving me the opportunity to talk to them."

"Well, if there's anything else I can do, please don't hesitate to reach out."

After exchanging goodbyes, Lou answered a call and went behind the bar.

Brooke stood beside Gable as he stared at the stage. She took his hand. "You still know what happened to Theo wasn't your fault, don't you? You couldn't have known he was going to have a heart attack."

"But I did know that he wasn't feeling well. If I would have questioned him about what was going on with him, I might have recognized the signs. I could have insisted that we go to the hospital."

"You could have insisted and he could have refused." She stood in front of him. "Theo had a family history when it came to heart problems. Did you know that? It's possible he could have had a heart attack at any time. Driving to work. At home with his wife and son." As stubbornness started to shadow his eyes, she pulled out her ace. "What did you say in the barn that day when I was telling you what happened to my parents? You can run a different scenario than what happened over and over in your mind, but the truth is *we* can never know if our actions could have made a difference. You said *we*, Gable, so what you said applies to you and not just me. And so does blaming yourself. Theo wouldn't want that for you, either."

Gable blinked at her for a long moment, and then his

shoulders dropped with an expression of resignation. "I know you're right. Maybe I couldn't have prevented it, but Melonie blaming me for it, that will never go away."

"She's grieving, and I'm sure she has her own list of what-ifs. Blaming you. Calling you out for the song. It could be a way to mask her own guilt, but it's not up to you to carry that for her."

He laid his forehead to hers and breathed.

"What are you going to do?" she asked.

Gable took both her hands in his and threaded their fingers together. "Right now, I want to go back to our hotel and just hold you. And in the morning, I'm going back to my farm." He lifted his head. "After that, I don't know yet."

They turned and walked toward the entrance.

Just as they reached the door someone shouted, "Wait, Mr. Kincaid."

A young redhead hurried over to them. She held up her phone. "About your song. I think I can help."

Chapter Twenty-Three

A video from that night? Sitting at the bar counter, Gable still couldn't believe what he was seeing on the phone in front of him.

Kendra, the barback who'd stopped him—her boyfriend had been in the bar that night when he and Theo had been on stage. She'd been hesitant to mention it during the meeting earlier. One, her boyfriend shouldn't have been in the bar drinking a beer after closing, and two, she hadn't been sure if he still had the video or what all had been captured until she'd reached out to him.

Rusty pipes? Gable's voice came through clearly on the video as well as the image of him and Theo. *Are you kidding me? This is your song. It was meant for you.*

No. It's yours. You wrote it. Now you just need to own it in here. Theo's voice came through just as clear as he tapped the middle of his chest in the video. *Just remember a time when you found love and didn't want to lose it.*

Kendra pressed pause on her phone. "Will this help?"

"Yes!" Standing behind Gable, Brooke threw her arms around him and kissed his cheek.

At the same time, Keith's voice came through the speaker on Gable's phone on the counter. "Hell, yeah."

Lou grinned from behind the bar counter. "This calls for free drinks on the house."

Gable turned to Kendra sitting next to him. "This helps tremendously. Thank you. And please thank your boyfriend. Would you send me a copy of this video?"

"I'll tell him." Kendra smiled. "And I'll drop the video to you now."

Keith interjected, "And make sure you send it to me, Gable. I've already got a plan."

"Hold on." Gable accepted the video on his phone that Kendra had just sent him then took Keith off speakerphone. He put the phone to his ear. "Go ahead."

"First, the attorneys. Melonie secured one, planning to make a payday if you signed a recording contract. She's not getting anything now but a cease and desist notice, and we're demanding she make an online apology as loud as her accusations have been. We need to get some influencers in the mix for a signal boost. We can work with my PR person, or if you have someone else in mind we can use them. And it's a good time to get your philanthropy arm in motion. What do you think about setting up a foundation honoring Theo that supports young musicians?"

Something like that would reflect Theo's generosity and be a good way to remember him. Gable accepted a shot of Uncle Nearest whiskey from Lou and clinked glasses with him. "That's a great idea, but I haven't committed to restarting my music career." He tossed the shot back.

"Not yet. We'll talk more about that later. Right now, let's work on clearing your name and giving Melonie a taste of what she's been giving you these past few days. Send me the video, and we'll post it in as many places as we can."

The slight burn of alcohol made Gable's tone a little huskier. "Hold on. Giving Melonie a taste of what?"

"A lot of those people who've been trolling you and calling you a thief are going to be looking at her in a different way."

The comments he'd received had been cruel. Sure, Melonie had been harsh toward him for months, and she'd jumped to the wrong conclusion about the song, but she'd made a mistake.

What did Wes use to say? Was it two wrongs don't make a right?

"No," Gable said. "She doesn't need to receive the hate that I did. Two wrongs don't make a right. Actually, I want to be the one to tell her about the video."

"What's the point in calling her? She'll just hang up on you."

"I'm not going to call her. I want to see Melonie on my own, face-to-face."

Brooke and Lou paused their conversation to glance at him. The look they exchanged with each other reflected the disbelief in Keith's voice.

"Are you nuts? The things she said to you. The things she's said about you. Why would you even want to see her?"

Gable toyed with his empty shot glass as he sifted through his thoughts about why he felt so strongly about speaking to Theo's wife. "If we had talked after Theo died, maybe Melonie and I wouldn't be where we are now. I need your help arranging the meeting."

"That's not in my job description." Keith sighed heavily. "But I'm motivated. If settling things means I might get you behind a microphone again, I'll try."

Hours later, Gable found himself facing the unexpected. He hadn't envisioned Keith working this quickly on his request, but there he was, sitting in a chair in Melonie's living room. They weren't alone. Her attorney, who was also one of her good friends, was present.

The professional-looking Black woman in a plum-colored suit stood behind Melonie, who sat on the couch. Theo's wife wore a neutral expression on her light brown face, but her gray eyes shot daggers at him.

Her attorney broke the silence. "For the record, I'm not in favor of this meeting, but Melonie wanted to see you."

"No," Melonie retorted, smoothing light brown hair from her forehead. "I'd hoped to never see your face again, but this meeting gives me a chance to tell you how I feel. I think you're horrible and definitely weren't my husband's friend." Her attorney rested a hand on Mel's shoulder. "Wasn't it enough that you drove Theo to an early grave? You had to steal from him, too?"

Her words were like a slap Gable had already anticipated, but they still stung. But Brooke had helped him realize that so many factors had played a part in what happened to Theo. He was ready to accept that but Melonie wasn't.

He responded. "I cared about Theo like a brother, and if I could roll back time to save him I wouldn't hesitate. But I also realize there's nothing I can say to make you believe that. As far as stealing from him, I never would." Gable opened the tablet he'd borrowed from Brooke. "There's a video you need to see before it gets posted tomorrow. I didn't want you to be blindsided by it."

The attorney frowned. "What kind of video?"

"It proves that I didn't steal anything from Theo. 'Chances' is my song." He set the tablet up on the coffee table. "I'd like to play it for you."

Melonie huffed, "People can deepfake a video."

"It's not, and the people who made the video and witnessed it being made are willing to vouch for it."

"Let's see it." The attorney rounded the couch and sat next to Melonie. She picked up the tablet and hit Play.

Rusty pipes? As Gable heard his voice, the vision of him and Theo at the piano played in his mind. *Are you kidding me? This is your song. It was meant for you.*

No. It's yours. You wrote it. Now you just need to own it in here. Once again, Theo's voice brought up the memory. *Just remember a time when you found love and didn't want to lose it.*

"Turn it off." Melonie stabbed her finger to the screen of the tablet, stopping the video. "I don't want to watch anymore." She got up and walked to the nearby bay window behind her.

As he went to speak, the attorney raised her hand and stalled him. She turned and spoke to Melonie. "I think you should listen to the rest of this."

"No." Melonie shook her head. "Hearing Theo's voice… It's too painful."

"I know." The attorney sounded less like a lawyer and more like a friend. Her expression turned empathetic. "But I think you really should hear the rest of what Theo had to say."

Melonie hugged herself. "Fine…play it."

The attorney rewound a brief segment of the video, then pressed Play.

Theo was speaking. *Just remember a time when you found love and didn't want to lose it. For me, that's Mel. My life wouldn't be the same without her.*

Mel's breath audibly caught. Still facing the window, her shoulders rose and fell with a shaky breath.

What about your love for music? We used to talk about cutting albums, being headliners, winning awards. Is working here enough for you? Gable hung his head, a part of him ashamed for asking Theo those questions. He almost sounded callous.

Absolutely. Would I jump at the chance of being a headliner at Coachella? Of course I would, but for me, being famous isn't what it's all about. The certainty in Theo's voice sounded even clearer to Gable now. *I have my wife and son, a good job that allows me to support my family, and now I have this place where I can connect and share my music with an audience a few nights a week. Thanks to you, I have the best of all worlds.*

"Oh, Theo…" Melonie dropped her head into her hands and sobbed. "I miss you so much."

The attorney put down the tablet and went to Theo's wife. As she embraced and comforted Melonie, the attorney whispered something to her.

Melonie nodded, and as the attorney walked down a nearby hallway, she went back to looking out the window. She swiped tears from her cheeks. "An apology video is in order. The comments I'll receive once the post goes up will be rough, but I'll get through it." She paused. "After all I've done and said about you, this moment must feel like sweet revenge."

"There's nothing sweet about it." An idea that might soften the blow for her came to him. "We can do the video together. That might change the focus of the comments to something more positive."

She stared at him. "You would do that for me? Why?"

"The last thing I want is you facing harassment over a social media post. I've experienced it firsthand."

Melonie nodded. "I'll do it. My attorney just told me that finding closure on this situation between us would help me to focus on what's important." She pointed out the window. "Him."

Gable joined her at the window.

Outside, Theo Jr. laughed with glee as he chased bubbles with a young woman in the backyard. With his wide smile, he looked exactly like his father. As the boy got older, hopefully he would know how much Theo had loved him, and that Theo had also been loved. He'd expressed that through his life and his music.

Melonie glanced up at him. Grief and shades of inner turmoil were in her eyes but also sincerity. "In the video you just showed me, you told Theo the song was meant for him, probably because of the way he sang it. The video I watched of you singing the same song, you have what he had. Talent. It's a gift. Don't forget that. And I hope you hold on to whoever caused you to sing 'Chances' that way. Feeling that way for someone—" she swallowed hard as tears welled in her eyes "—that's a gift, too."

Gable watched the boy play and considered what she'd told him. A new clarity emerged about what Theo had been trying to tell him about love and the lyrics in the song. Never take love for granted. Hold on to it if you find it. Success, ambition, they meant nothing. Love was everything.

It was nighttime when Gable returned to the hotel room he and Brooke shared.

As he walked inside the space, seeing her curled up sitting on the king-size bed watching television made his heart beat faster with a rush of happiness. He'd missed having the woman he loved by his side. A small part of him had questioned the four-letter word that had slipped so easily into his thoughts about Brooke. He'd never thought he'd find that something real, but he had and he wouldn't deny it. He loved her, and he wanted to do exactly what the lyrics in his song said. He wanted to take that chance with her and move to the next step. A real relationship. Hopefully,

Brooke felt the same way about him, but she couldn't stand Bolan, and she was such a free spirit. Getting to that next step in their relationship would require compromises. Like maybe letting her go explore the world until she was ready to come back to him. It would be hard, but he'd wait for her.

But this wasn't the time to tell her how he felt. He'd save all of it until they returned to Maryland and do it right.

"How did it go with Melonie?" She rose from the bed.

All he could do was stare at her. Her long, toned legs were on display in a pair of shorts. The loose T-shirt she had on hinted at the curves of her breasts underneath the fabric. The light from the lamp on the bed table shone through her loose curls, creating the same halo of light that the sun had formed that day he'd fallen off his horse and she'd come to his side. She was his beautiful sun angel. His one and only sun angel.

Overcome by how he felt about her, for a moment, Gable was lost for words, He set the tablet and his things on the dresser. "Better than expected. We made her apology video together. Both of us are posting it tomorrow. Keith is actually pleased."

"Wow. That's wonderful." She wrapped her arms around his waist and looked up at him. "What's wrong? You don't look happy?"

"I am. Everything that happened today was just so unexpected."

Melonie had told him to hold on to the person who caused him to sing "Chances" the way he had at the Montecito. Brooke was that reason. He wanted to hold on to her so badly it shook him. Gable's hand was unsteady as he traced his finger down her cheek. He might have to let her go soon, but tonight she was still his.

He cupped her face in his hands and softly kissed her.

With each brush of his mouth over hers, he memorized the shape and plushness of her lips. When she welcomed him in, he thoroughly explored every curve and hollow, hoping to never forget how wonderful it was to kiss her.

As he lifted her shirt and took it off, he traced over her skin, memorizing the silky smoothness of it beneath is fingertips. As Brooke helped him with his, he seared the warmth of her touch into his mind. He kissed her, drowning in all of the sensations he tried to capture, but his need for her jumbled his thoughts. Her soft moans reflected her own desire. Motions fueled by urgency and anticipation, they stripped off the rest of their clothes.

He backed her up to the bed and followed her down on the mattress. Hoping, wishing for more minutes, hours, days like this with Brooke, he forced himself to take his time, kissing and caressing every inch of her that was available to him. As he kissed down her belly and lower still, Brooke arched up to meet his mouth as he lost himself in sweetness that was better than honey.

Long moments later, they joined together as one…moved as one. He tried to delay what imminently waited for both of them, but gut-clenching need drove him. When he finally saw pure ecstasy wash over her face, he let go. *Release.* His heart felt as if it would burst with the force of it.

Later that night, lying wide awake, holding Brooke close, Gable knew without a doubt they had to find a way to make it work. He knew he couldn't just let her go.

Chapter Twenty-Four

Brooke pulled the blue sheet taut on the bed and tucked it in on the side of the mattress. As she moved to Gable's side of the bed, she picked up the cord to his charger that had fallen to the floor and put it back on the nightstand.

Where was he?

She'd been half-awake when he'd slipped out of bed before dawn, and he hadn't returned. This wasn't the first time he'd disappeared early in the morning.

Ever since they'd gotten back from Jacksonville a week ago, he'd been acting a little strange and preoccupied.

One time, when she'd asked him where he'd been, his answer had been vague. The next time, he'd claimed he was taking soil samples. Really? In the dark? And then there was that day she'd awakened in the living room from a nap, went looking for him and found him singing and playing his guitar in the barn. Sheets of music in various forms of completion had been on the ground. He'd rushed her out, claiming he was practicing outside to soothe Pepper, but if horses could be bored out of their minds, Pep had looked it.

But Gable had also been extremely happy. He smiled a lot. Hummed around the house. He'd also been super attentive. Checking in about what she wanted to eat, giving her awesome foot rubs as they relaxed on the couch. She en-

joyed all of the things he was doing, but it also made her…
uneasy. She'd never experienced something like this with
a guy before—near domesticated bliss. She'd only ever
strived for completeness in a few short moments with someone, like the ski instructor she'd met the winter before last.

The guy had actually slid into her DMs the other day.
He'd been asking but not asking, just hinting around the
question of whether or not she was going to be at the ski
lodge this coming winter. He'd also included subtle but not
so subtle, *supposedly* candid photos of his adventures since
she'd last seen him. The photo array had a theme. Him,
shirtless, chopping wood. Shirtless on a boat. Shirtless on
a ski slope. Shirtless on a beach. Shirtless with a teacup
Yorkie that looked a lot like pre-zombie Mitzi. Yeah, that
one had given her a weird vibe. She'd deleted them all. The
ski instructor couldn't compete with Gable shirtless. He
couldn't compete with Gable. Period.

As Brooke finished making the bed, he strode in with a
towel around his waist.

She looked him up and down. He looked a little sweaty.

As if he'd read her mind, he said, "I was doing some
work outside. My clothes were dirty so I took them off in
the laundry room." Before she could ask more questions,
he slid his hands around her waist to her back, brought
her closer and kissed her. The scent of the clean outdoors
mixed with cedarwood and his own unique scent wafted
from his skin.

Just as she started to slide her hands up his chest, her
stomach growled.

He leaned away from her. "What time do you have to
get to the farm?"

"Not for a couple more hours."

"Perfect. I have time to make you breakfast?" He let

her go with a final kiss, leaving her empty-handed as well as hot and bothered as he hummed his way to the shower.

A little later, as promised, he served her breakfast at the counter of the galley kitchen—a fluffy stack of French toast along with crispy bacon.

Just as she was about to ask for a bottle of syrup, he snapped his fingers as if he'd forgotten something. "Be right back." He hustled through the archway to the main kitchen and came back with a warmed carafe of syrup with butter melting into it. "Here you go."

She drizzled syrup over everything. "Thank you. This smells delicious. Where's your plate?"

Standing in the galley kitchen, he leaned back against the opposite counter and sipped a mug of coffee. "I had oatmeal this morning. I'm good."

"It's no fun eating alone." She held up a piece of bacon as an offering.

Gable walked over to her and leaned down, and she fed it to him. When he finished, she kissed away syrup from his lips. "Thank you. I was starting to feel abandoned."

"The one thing I'll never do is abandon you."

His earnest tone made her lean back to see his face. His expression was just as sincere and way too serious.

She forced a snorted laugh. "You don't have to twist my arm. If you want more bacon just ask."

"More is a good start." He gave her a small lopsided smile before he turned away to refill his mug.

Were they still talking about bacon? The feeling of unease she'd been battling over his behavior reared to the surface. His "more is a good start" comment could have been referring to anything, like more time in bed together. More...well, more anything that maybe didn't relate to their relationship. Or he really did just want more bacon. Gable's actions were probably normal, and she was the one being strange. She should stop wondering about him treating her so well and enjoy him while she could. *Ten days.* That's all the time they had, and he knew that. All of his extra attention was about making the most of it, that's all.

After she finished breakfast, they cleaned up the kitchen together. As she washed dishes, he dried them. The normal, mundane task settled her anxiety. See? Everything was good. It was just her making a big deal about nothing.

Done with the kitchen, she prepared to leave.

Gable asked, "Before you go, there's something I'd like to get your opinion about. I'm thinking of planting a garden, and I'm not sure if it's the right spot."

"A garden? When did you decide this?"

He shrugged. "It's been on my mind. I've decided to bump it up on the list. This won't take long."

They went out the back sliding door and took the path toward the left. It was a cool morning, but the sun was already adding a layer of warmth.

"Are you thinking of putting the garden near the gazebo?"

"Maybe. Do you think it's a bad spot?"

"Not if you pick the right plants. And maybe use a few raised plant beds like Mrs. Davies's had in her bee garden. A layering effect could be nice."

He nodded as they rounded the curve in the path. "I can see that."

"And you could also…" Brooke stared at the unexpected sight a couple of yards ahead. He couldn't just see what she explained. He'd already done it.

Her dream gazebo that she'd told him about that day over lunch, before the incident at Mrs. Davies's, sat nestled in the trees.

A garden of colorful plants in pots and raised beds sat on both sides of the rectangular-shaped structure. Cushioned bench seats bordered the inside of it, and he'd built a firepit in the middle and filled it with aqua and white glass rocks.

As they walked up to it, she had a difficult time keeping her mouth from hanging open in amazement. "This is beautiful. You've created a gazebo hideaway for yourself."

"And you."

Feeling touched and confused at the same time, she almost added, *only for the next ten days*, but she didn't want to ruin the moment. "Is this why you've been disappearing so much?"

He grinned. "Yeah, I wanted to surprise you. Tristan and Mace have been coming by early in the morning to help me out."

She smacked him playfully on his arm. "I can't believe you were able to keep this from me."

"Luckily, you've been sleeping in lately." He led her to the steps.

As they climbed up, she spotted his guitar lying on one of the cushions. "Have a seat."

She sat down. "You're giving me a morning serenade? I love it already."

"I hope so." He took a seat next to her then strummed the melody of "Chances" on his guitar.

Smiling, Brooke settled back to listen. She really liked this song.

Gable lifted his head and closed his eyes. As he sang the familiar chorus, his voice was like a beautiful offering to the clear blue sky.

"What I'm feelin' for you I just can't hide. I'm standing here for as long as it takes...for a chance at something real with you...my Sun Angel..."

Wait. He'd changed the lyrics. Gable wasn't the type to say what he didn't mean. He wasn't just singing the song for her. He was singing it *to* her. He was asking for a chance at something real with her. A chance at something more than a temporary relationship.

A sweet vision of that very possibility started to emerge in her mind, but remembered grief steamrollered through it and so did panic. No. Something like that could lead to a chance she couldn't risk facing ever again…heartbreak.

One day, he could leave before dawn and not come back. She could lose him…just like she lost her parents. When that happened to her, it had felt as if her heart was about to shatter into a billion little pieces, but she'd held herself together. If she let herself love Gable, which she could easily do, and she lost him, her heart would definitely shatter and she might not be able to put herself back together again.

Gable's voice faded away at the end of his song, and he strummed a final note on his guitar. Setting the instrument aside, he slid closer and took her hand.

Just as he was about to speak, she waved him off with her other hand, stalling him. "Don't ask me what you're about to say. We're not doing this. A fling was the plan."

"Brooke, I know, but what we have—"

"Can't go any further. If we try to turn this fling into something more, you're going to get hurt. I'm going to get hurt."

But he'd already crossed the line by raising the question of more. They couldn't unring that bell. It would resound for the remainder of their time together, reminding them of what they couldn't have. They wanted different things.

"I have to go." She slipped her hand from his. "It's for the best."

"Wait, what are you saying?"

Brooke stood. The hurt look on his face, and the tender emotion she felt for him but wouldn't let herself label, almost made her sit back down. She didn't want to hurt him, but she had to do this…for both of them. "I'm saying it's over."

Chapter Twenty-Five

Brooke woke up miserable. Putting on her clothes and makeup as she got ready for work felt nothing short of a chore. She had a tasting to attend at Brewed Haven Café that morning. Philippa, Rina and Pat were bringing samples of some of the items they'd planned to feature during National Honey Month.

She hadn't slept well for the past two nights. She kept seeing Gable's stricken face as she left him standing in the gazebo.

My Sun Angel...

Why had he changed those lyrics? Why couldn't he have left well enough alone? Gable hadn't reached out to her so she could ask him. She had to admit, she'd expected him to show up and make her talk. But she had told him it was over. That had felt like the best thing to do at the time, but now, she wished she'd explained things better to him so they could have parted as, what? Friends? But that word sounded hollow and it was the wrong one to describe them. Strangely, the one thing her and Gable did agree on was that they weren't friends. Whether she wanted to admit it or not, their situationship had already grown into more, but she just couldn't do more with anyone.

An hour later, in the upstairs meeting room at the café,

Brooke sampled the food and tasted nothing but her own sadness. If she could have, she would have drowned her sorrow in the cocktails Pat had provided.

Conversation flowed as Philippa, Rina and Pat traded ideas. The promo for National Honey Month was coming together while her life had just fallen apart.

After the tasting, she went downstairs to the café. She was exhausted on every level. She needed a strong hit of caffeine to give her energy for the drive back to the bee farm.

Peggy, the real estate agent, stood in front of her in line for coffee, talking on the phone. "Yes, I'm on my way to look at the house now. I can't believe he's already moved out."

Brooke tried to tune Peggy out, but she was so loud.

"Uh-huh. No, he is gone, gone. He's not coming back. He left this morning and took his horse with him. I'm starting to think that house is cursed. First the Rosses, now him. But on the other hand, he didn't own the house. He was only renting…"

The Rosses? Took his horse? Only renting? Brooke followed the thread of the conversation. Gable had moved out. He was gone?

Suddenly nauseous, Brooke left the café and drove home. By the time she got there, her temples throbbed. Her chest felt hollow and her heart ached. Knots in her stomach pulled tighter and tighter.

She walked into the kitchen.

Harper looked up from where she stood at the counter by the refrigerator, pouring a glass of juice from a carton. "Hey, you're back. How did the tasting go? Do you want some?" She held up the carton.

"The tasting—everything's on track. My stomach is a

little upset, not because of the food. Do we have any ginger ale?"

"No, I'm sorry. It's all gone."

Gone. The word echoed in the hollow space in her chest, filling it until it was hard to breathe. "Oh, that wasn't what I expected to hear at all."

Concerned, Harper put down the carton. "You're not talking about ginger ale, are you?"

"No… Gable. He left town for good."

The empathy on Harper's face as she approached her and the fierceness of her embrace pulled Brooke's sorrow more to the surface.

"I'm so sorry." Harper gave her a squeeze. She leaned back and looked into Brooke's face. "Do you want to talk about it?"

"I…" Brooke swallowed hard. "This wasn't supposed to happen this way."

Harper led her to the kitchen table and they sat down. "What happened?"

Brooke started from the beginning. Partway through the saga of her situationship with Gable, her sister brought orange juice to the table. Then vodka. By the end of the story and her bottomless screwdriver, Brooke's head and her heart felt floaty and numb.

She stared at her empty glass. "How much alcohol did you put in here?"

"Enough. You should probably lie down for a while." Harper stood. "Come on. I'll help you to your room."

Good thing Harper was there for her to lean on. Brooke's legs felt a tad wobbly. It wasn't all about the alcohol. Knowing that Gable was gone had knocked her off balance in every way. She was supposed to leave Bolan with Gable happily tucked away at his house while she drove into the sunrise with the happiest memories of her life safely tucked away in her mind.

As Harper pulled the comforter over Brooke lying on the bed, Brooke realized what she hadn't gotten from her sister. Judgment about how she'd handled things with Gable.

"When I was talking, why didn't you say anything?" she asked. "Why didn't you tell me how I royally screwed up a temporary relationship with the best guy I'd ever met?"

Harper sat on the edge of the mattress. "Because you have your own compass, and you've always followed it where it leads you."

"Where do you think it led me with Gable?" Brooke wasn't sure anymore.

Harper stood. "That's not for me to say." She paused at the door and looked back at Brooke. "But the way you travel from place to place, never wanting to settle in, I've always wondered, is that inner compass your fear or your heart?"

At his parents' house, Gable led Pepper into the pasture next to the barn. He secured the gate behind him then unclipped the lead rope from Pepper's rope bridle.

The horse did a full body shake from head to tail as if relieved to finally be free.

Gable patted the horse. "Go on, Pep. You know where you are." After the drive from Maryland, the horse deserved to stretch its legs.

Pep chuffed and nudged his shoulder as if reluctant to leave him. Perhaps he knew Gable was leaving for Nashville and they were about to be separated.

Gable rubbed the horse along his neck and shoulder. "I'm not leaving for a day or two. We'll go on a nice long ride before then."

After that, Pepper would be in the capable hands of his

mom and her husband, Seth. Between recording his debut album, promotion and possibly being the opening act for a major music tour, it was hard to say when he'd be able to keep Pepper with him.

He'd called Keith the same day Brooke had walked away from him at the gazebo and told his talent manager he was signing the contract.

Anticipating the possibility of him calling, Keith had already had the plan half in motion. After that everything had happened so fast. They wanted him in Nashville immediately, and he was available. He didn't feel led to stay in Maryland. What he really wanted in his life, Brooke, wasn't there for him anymore.

Pepper ambled off in search of grass to eat.

Gable stood by the fence, watching him.

"He looks good." His mother, Andrea, stood on the other side of the white ladder fence. He'd gotten his height from his dad, but his coloring along with his eyes came from his mom.

"He does. He really thrived in Maryland."

"So why did you leave? I thought you had a girlfriend out there?"

"I never told you I had a girlfriend." He'd done that intentionally. Every time he was with someone, his mom got her hopes up that he was finally settling down.

"But you were seeing someone?"

"Yes, I was seeing someone."

"So are the two of you going to do the long-distance thing?"

Disappointment sank deep in his chest. He'd been ready to go any distance with Brooke. Boy, he'd really misread the situation. No, actually, he'd misread their situationship and forgotten what they'd outlined their first night together. No strings.

Realizing his mom was still waiting for an answer, he said, "No, it didn't work out."

"What happened?"

It just didn't. That would be the easy answer, and his mom would probably let it go. But he needed to release the pent-up words filling his chest. The ones making it hard to breathe when he lay in bed at night thinking of Brooke and how much he missed her.

Gable gripped the top of the fence then loosened his grasp. "The woman I was seeing, Brooke. We agreed on just a short-term relationship..." He told his mom about Brooke's spontaneity, her smile, her laugh. Her loyalty to the bees. How smart she was. Her unwavering support when Melonie had accused him of stealing Theo's music. How he couldn't imagine not supporting her in any way he could. About his first time seeing her in a field of flowers. About the times their paths had randomly crossed and about writing those lyrics for her...and how she'd left him in the gazebo.

Empty of words, but filled with memories, his shoulders dropped with a long breath. "We agreed to stay together for a few weeks. I should have been satisfied with that. Singing her that song in the gazebo was a big mistake."

"I agree. It definitely was," his mom said.

Surprise at her response made him raise his brow. "Isn't this the part where you're supposed to offer motherly guidance and support?"

"I am, but with it comes honesty and tough love. Don't give me that look. You asked for my opinion."

Actually, he didn't, but by telling his mom about Brooke,

he'd opened the barn door, so to speak, and now he had to deal with whatever came out of it.

His mother rested her arms on the top of the fence railing. "So when you and Brooke talked about a short-term thing, did you sing to her about it?"

"No. Why would I do that?"

"Exactly. A deeper relationship is a lot more serious, but you chose to put your feelings into a few catchy lyrics?" His mom shook her head. "A commitment like that takes at least one conversation, maybe two or three, to figure it all out."

Catchy lyrics? No, they were heartfelt. Gable opened his mouth to object, but he stopped. As good as the words sounded in his song, they didn't encompass everything that needed to be said, not just from him, but Brooke, too.

He released a heavy sigh. "I cut her out of the most important part of the conversation—the beginning. It's just that I saw us being together so clearly. The entire time we were together, we just clicked. I assumed she felt the same way."

"Possibly, she does. But in a way, you blindsided her. Maybe even scared her a little with that oh-so-smooth voice of yours."

As his mom gave his arm a playful nudge, he huffed a wry chuckle. "Smooth or not, I really screwed up."

"It was more of a miscalculation than a screwup. Where Brooke wants to be right now and where you want to go isn't the same place. I'm sorry things didn't turn out the way you wanted, but I'm also proud of you."

"For what?"

"A few months ago, you were struggling to find your way, but you did. Not that I was worried. I always knew you would."

"Not worried? You were either calling or texting me

once, sometimes twice, a day until I convinced you I was okay."

"Alright, maybe I was a little worried." Motherly love softened her expression. "I can't help it. You'll always be my baby boy, but I've always remembered what Wes told me when you went to stay with him. He said you were hard-headed, which I already knew." She laughed. "But he also said you had good instincts. As long as you trusted them, you'd come out okay."

Wes's stoic expression had been hard to read. He'd always hoped to gain his great-uncle's approval. "He said that?"

"Yes, he did." His mom laid her hand on his shoulder. "Your instincts sent you to Bolan for a reason. Maybe it was to remember your time with Wes, but being there led you to two important things—to Brooke and back to music. You care about her, and I know losing her is hard, but just because two people are headed in different directions doesn't mean their paths won't cross again. Think about the times you and Brooke landed in the same place over the years. Maybe it's not random but meant to be."

Hearing his mom say something similar to what Mrs. Davies had said caught his attention, but... "How do I know that us ending up in the same places even means something other than it was all a coincidence? And even if it's not, I don't know what to do about me and Brooke."

His mom gave him a small shake by his shoulder. "The key is to follow your instincts about which path to take. If you trust yourself, you'll always know where you're supposed to be."

Days later in Nashville, looking out the window of his new high-rise apartment, he pondered what his mother told him. Instead of the bustling city of his dreams in front of him, he envisioned a blue sky over pastures and sun shining over a field of flowers…and Brooke. He missed all of it, especially her. Gable laid his hand on the window as the vision dissolved in his mind. Were his instincts telling him that this was where he was supposed to be?

Chapter Twenty-Six

Her last night at the house in the Hollywood Hills, Brooke floated on her back, staring at the darkening sky. It had been a quiet two weeks, and while she'd been there, she'd done a lot of thinking about Harper, the farm and what happened with her and Gable.

She didn't have an answer to Harper's compass question, but it remained stuck like an earworm. It wouldn't go away. It had stayed on her mind her entire last week at the farm and traveled with her to California. It remained with her along with what felt like a hole carved into her chest. Her heart ached in the hollow space. She missed the bees. She missed her sister. Most of all she missed Gable. Sharing meals with him. Sitting on the couch watching television with him. Waking up to him and seeing a just-woke-up-sexy smile on his face. As regret started to overtake her, she closed her eyes, blocking out the vision of him. She'd forget him in time, right? As she kicked her arms and legs to stay afloat, doubt pinged in the hollowness that her aching heart couldn't fill.

The housesitting job in Spain hadn't come through yet, but the dude ranch in Texas wanted her back. She was considering it. She wouldn't mind working with horses again. Where was Pepper? Was he boarded somewhere close to

Gable's new place in Nashville? He was living in a condo downtown with a view just as spectacular as the one she had here. She'd watched his video of the place on social media.

Whoever was in charge of his social media posts deserved credit. They were the right mix of personal glimpses into his private life, time in the recording studio and promo for the upcoming release of his single, "Chances." An EP was also in the works. She had mixed feelings about "Chances" being shared with the world.

I'm standing here for as long as it takes...for a chance at something real...my Sun Angel...

The remembered lyrics from that day in the gazebo intertwined with Harper's question. With Gable, their needs for mutual distraction, maybe even their own fears had been their compass, but where it led them hadn't been anticipated.

Brooke got out of the pool. Sitting on the edge, she kicked her feet in the water, trying to erase her reflection and the sadness she saw on her face. Did she regret her decision to be with Gable? She didn't, but she hated how she'd ended things with him. They should have talked it out. If they had, she and Gable would have arrived at the same conclusion—going their separate ways was the only answer. It would have been the right ending instead of a messy one. That's why she felt so bad. That's why Gable stayed on her mind. Along with the fact that she'd fallen hard for him. More accurately, she was in love with him, but he'd already moved forward with his singing career, and she had...nothing. Sure, she had a new list of hot job prospects. That used to excite her, but it didn't feel meaningful anymore. She'd pushed everything away that mattered. Gable. Ownership in the farm. And even the last single tie that had kept her close to her mom. The apiary. The reality of that made her swallow hard.

Early next morning, she locked up the house using the front door keypad. As she drove down the winding road with gated homes, the area was just waking up. She had a long drive ahead of her to Florida. She was staying at Nellie's apartment just outside of Jupiter Beach.

Day one to Phoenix went fairly smoothly. The next day, on her way out of the city, the interstate turned into a parking lot with bumper-to-bumper traffic. Construction had already slowed things down considerably. Based on the police cruisers speeding past, a car accident had most likely occurred.

Needing a way to pass the time and take her mind off of her bladder suddenly hinting she needed to find a ladies' room soon, she called Nellie.

Her friend's voice came through the car speakers. "Hey, where are you? How's the drive going?"

"I'm in Arizona stuck on the interstate." Brooke sighed in frustration. "I'll have to push it if I want to make it to my planned stop. This delay is throwing me off."

"No, don't push to get to your next planned stop. It's better to be safe than sorry. You can start again early tomorrow morning."

"True." She really should put safety first. Brooke picked up the cup with her remaining iced caramel macchiato. Rolling the dice on her ETA to a pit stop, she took a small sip. "So what are you up to today?"

Nellie released a stifled yawn. "Recovering from the baby shower I worked last night. Ooh, do you remember the runaway groom-to-be?"

"Runaway groom?" The car in front of Brooke rolled forward. As she grappled with the sudden topic switch, she eased off the brake and came to a stop just inches ahead. "You mean the runaway groom movie you mentioned where he gets eaten by an alien."

"No, I'm talking about a real-life person. Do you remember that engagement party where the love triangle was going on and you saved the bee? Well, the bridal shower was for that bride-to-be. And guess what?" Nellie paused dramatically. "She's pregnant."

Brooke waited for the punch line. "And?" The bride-to-be wouldn't be the first who was expecting before her wedding day.

"*And* she's not marrying the guy we thought was going to be the runaway fiancé. It's his baby, but they broke up right after the engagement party, and he happily took a job on the North Pole. Now she's engaged to the guy in the navy suit who was trying to save her from the bee. They're getting married in a month. Isn't that bonkers?"

"Good for her. It sounds like things worked out like they should."

"I know, right? Oh, but it gets even better. Someone overheard pregnant bride-to-be arguing with Momzilla on the phone. She told Momzilla if she didn't want to show up to the baby shower, that was fine. But if she couldn't handle who she was marrying, Momzilla could consider herself uninvited to the wedding. Pregnant bride-to-be also said she didn't care if she was disinherited. She was done following the plan. She was following her heart, and then she hung up on her mom." Nellie cackled. "I wish I could have been a fly, no, a bee on the wall where Momzilla was so I could see her face."

As Nellie chatted on about more highlights from the party, Brooke half listened. All she could think about was the bride-to-be's courage. She'd followed her heart instead of the plan and she'd found happiness.

Brooke knew the answer to Harper's question. She had been following her fears on a lot of things. It was time to follow her heart.

The next day, as she drove down I-40 headed for Dallas, she slowed down near an exit. As she read the sign, her heart beat so hard in her chest it felt as if it was leaping into her throat. It was telling her something, so she followed it and the exit toward Oklahoma City.

Chapter Twenty-Seven

Buzzing from all the caffeinated drinks she'd consumed during her long stretches of driving over the past few days, Brooke pulled into the driveway of Bishop Honey Bee Farm. It was nearly ten at night, and except for the porch and security lights by the garage, the house was dark, but the lights were on at the office cottage.

It felt good to be home. But technically, this wasn't her home anymore, it was Harper's.

Brooke parked in front of the smaller building. She got out and walked to the door. It was locked, as it should be. Her sister was alone. She knocked. Moments later, the door flung open.

Harper stared at her in disbelief. "Brooke? What are you doing here?"

"You shouldn't have just opened the door like that. I could have been anyone."

"I saw you on the door camera feed on my phone. Aren't you supposed to be in California or somewhere else?"

"I…" Brooke didn't know what to say. She'd been so focused on getting there. She hadn't thought that far ahead. Ignoring her confused inner compass, she spoke from her heart. "I don't want to go anywhere else. I want to be here at the farm. I know I signed over everything to you, and I don't have a right to be here."

"Will you stop." Harper pulled her into an embrace. "You have every right." Her tightening hold reminded Brooke of Aunt Ivy's fierce welcoming hugs. "This is your home and it always will be."

Hours later in the wee hours of the morning, Brooke stood in the threshold of Ivy's office.

After she'd arrived home last night, she and Harper had gone back to the house. The combination of a caffeine crash, exhaustion from the long trip and the relief of Harper welcoming her home had left her in a daze.

Harper had helped her make up the bed in the guest room, and shortly after that, Brooke had promptly conked out. But something, a dream she couldn't recall or a feeling, had nudged her awake. She'd felt led to come to the home office. Was it her heart leading her again to what truly mattered? It had brought her back to the farm and Harper; now it seemed to beckon her to do one of the hardest things she'd ever done. To truly embrace the past and all of the memories that came with it.

She entered the room. It was blanketed in silence and the semidarkness of twilight. Walking to the chaise, she lowered herself down on the cushion and released a sigh.

The first time she'd entered this room, she'd prided herself in being able to compartmentalize her memories. But she hadn't been honest with herself. She hadn't walled them off in their designated space. They'd cluttered her mind, buried under the distraction of her adventures. There was one memory—she really needed to let it in starting now.

Brooke's hand slightly shook as she picked up the throw blanket. It had the same soft feel as the one her mother had wrapped herself up in. Bringing it to her nose, she inhaled the clean scent of laundry soap, but she recalled the light floral scent of her mother's perfume. She only wore it at night since she couldn't wear it around the bees.

Boots, jeans and T-shirts had been her mom's attire during the day, but when she went to bed, she'd preferred satin or silk gowns and robes. Most had been in the beautiful shade or pattern of cobalt blue, delicate, sumptuous and elegant. Brooke and Harper were both their mother in different ways. She'd inherited her mom's willowy build and sense of adventure. Harper had inherited their mom's coppery-brown eyes and her relentless determination.

Closing her eyes, Brooke let her mind continue to drift through memories of her mom. On most mornings, when her mom had lounged in the chaise before sunrise drinking her first cup of coffee, a softness would shadow her gaze as she looked out the window or while she watched Brooke's dad snore softly in bed. Either way, a small, happy smile would be on her face. It would grow larger when Brooke pushed the door farther open.

In her mind's eye, Brooke recalled how her mom would put a finger to her lips, cautioning her not to wake her dad, then beckon her inside. Crawling into the chair with her, she would eagerly snuggle in close, soaking in her mother's warmth and her scent. As her mom stroked her hair, they would watch the sun creep across the grass or sparkle in the snow.

As she let the vision fade, tears welled in her eyes, forcing her to open them.

Sunlight gleamed on the gold and silver picture frames. The oval-shaped frame holding the picture of her dad carrying her mom across the threshold of the house at the farm shone the brightest. Her parents both smiled broadly as if they'd accomplished something wonderful. Her gaze rested on the two square gold frames hinged together. Instead of focusing on the frame's imperfection and the photo bubbling up, she held it and allowed herself to just take in the images.

In the photo with her and Harper she'd been around seven, maybe eight years old. Her hair was blowing loose in the wind, and she had a gap-toothed grin as she held a jar of honey in her hands. Harper stood next to her, hair tied in two neat braids, giving her an adorable, purse-lipped, side-eyed look as only someone that young could.

The attached frame held a decades-old photo of two young girls dressed in summer shorts and T-shirts. Her mom and Aunt Ivy. The sisters were both laughing with childhood abandon as Aunt Ivy blasted her sister with water from a garden hose.

Brooke laughed, sniffing as she wiped tears from her cheeks. She fully related to the mischievous look in Aunt Ivy's eyes. She would have done the same thing with the hose.

A soft knock made Brooke glance to the door.

Harper walked in. With her hair down, dressed in satin peach-colored pj's, she reminded Brooke of their mom. "I'm surprised you're up. As tired as you were last night, I didn't expect to see you until at least noon."

How could she explain it? "I was awake. I thought I'd watch the sunrise."

From the way Harper met her gaze, she understood what Brooke couldn't or wasn't ready to explain. "This is a great spot to do it. Sometimes I sit here and do the same." She glanced at the picture frames. "I'd never seen that photo of Mom and Aunt Ivy before until she put it there."

"Neither had I. I really didn't look at it until today. And this photo of us, I vaguely remember taking it."

"I remember it clearly. You were practically covered in honey, but I was the one who got stung by a bee."

"You did? I definitely don't remember that."

"Of course not." Harper huffed a laugh. "You were too excited about Mom letting you help her spin the honey extractor. You slept with that full jar by your bed the entire weekend until Mom and Dad convinced you it was better to eat the honey and not stare at it."

The recollection became a bit clearer in Brooke's mind. "That's right. But we didn't just eat it. I also put some on your bee sting."

They both looked down to where Harper had been stung near her wrist. Harper rubbed the spot. She looked to Brooke and smiled. "It actually helped."

Helping, that's what Brooke wanted to do now when it came to the farm. She wanted to be there for Harper. "Last night, you said this is my home, but I want you to know that I understand where I fit when it comes to the business. You own this place. You're the boss. I'll work as your employee."

Harper stared at her a moment. She pointed to the joined frames on Brooke's lap. "Can I see those a minute?"

Brooke handed them to her.

As Harper separated the frame from the picture of Aunt Ivy and their mom, a small envelope slipped out, solving the mystery of why that side of the frame had been crooked and the photo had been bubbling up in the middle. She offered it to Brooke. "I found this one day a few months ago when I knocked over the frames by accident. There's a card inside of it."

"Who's it from?"

"Just read it. You'll see."

Brooke slipped out the small folded card with balloons on it. As soon as she opened it, she recognized her mom's neat script and the nickname her mom used to call Aunt Ivy at the start of the note.

Happy Birthday, Vivie! Instead of jewelry, I'm send-ing you liquid gold—one of the first jars from our first honey harvest. It was amazing.

When some of the bees died, I had doubts, but now I know moving here was the right choice. The girls are thriving. Brooke is a natural with the bees. Harper hasn't quite warmed up to them yet, but she's magical with flowers. They're opposites, just like us. They even argue like we did when we were their age, but someday, their passions as well as being oppo-sites will be their strength in running this place and for each other. I can see it. This farm is their legacy. Visit soon. I miss you!
Lexy

Brooke looked to Harper. "Why didn't Aunt Ivy ever show us this?"

Harper offered up a delicate shrug. "I don't know. I won-dered if I wasn't supposed to find it. This was her office. Her personal space. I didn't want her to think that I was snooping around, so I never admitted I found it."

Brooke closed the card. "Aunt Ivy followed through. She built Mom's dream, bees, flowers and all."

"For us."

"You were right about the legacy part. I thought you made it up. Why didn't you just show me this to begin with?"

"You were so set on leaving, and I didn't think it would

change your mind." Harper turned more toward her. "What made you come back?"

Brooke's thoughts went to the engagement party and the forager bee she'd saved, knowing it would instinctively find its way home.

"You asked me before if my inner compass was my fear or my heart? It was both. Every year, my heart brought me home to take care of the bees. I told myself it was because I felt obligated to Aunt Ivy, but it was more than that. I belong here, but my fear drove me to leave." Brooke swallowed hard, working up the courage to say what she'd never admitted to anyone, including herself. "I was afraid of loving you, Aunt Ivy and the farm too much. That one day, the rug would be pulled from under me, and I could lose you forever...like Mom and Dad." Surprised to feel tears, she swiped her cheeks. "I know, that sounds foolish."

"No, it doesn't. Now I understand why you wouldn't stay. I thought..." Harper shook her head as if dismissing the thought. "I'm here for you. Yes, that could change in an instant, but because there are no guarantees about having another day, or another year, we have to dive into every moment we have. And right now, we're here and we have this farm."

"So you forgive me for bailing on you?"

"Only if you can forgive me for saying you didn't care about the bees."

"Yeah, I guess that comment does make us even."

Harper gave her a side-eye look that almost matched her expression in the picture except she was smiling. "So do you want to be my partner again or not?"

Smiling back, Brooke bumped her sister's shoulder with hers. "Of course, I do. Partners for life."

Chapter Twenty-Eight

Brooke stood in the kitchen waiting for the kettle to heat up on the stove. She put a tea ball strainer in her cup filled with tea leaves that promised to boost her mood and energy levels. Longingly, she stared at the coffee maker on the counter. She would have preferred to start the morning with her usual boost of caffeine, but she'd end up crashing from exhaustion by noon. Since she'd gotten home two weeks ago, she wasn't sleeping well.

It wasn't that she didn't feel happy about returning to the farm. She had no regrets about settling down in one place. Resuming her partnership with Harper in running their family enterprise felt more than right. But passing by the house next door, remembering her time with Gable was harder than she'd anticipated. It would become even harder when the new owners moved in. She'd heard a few days ago the property had been sold.

"Hey, good morning." Harper walked into the kitchen carrying a small cardboard box. She had a pep in her step that Brooke envied. "I was just coming to find you. We got a special delivery this morning. The samples of our line of honey with the new Symphony branded labels came in."

Gable's face flashed in Brooke's mind and she forced a smile. "How do they look?"

"I don't know. I cut the seal, but I didn't look. I thought you should do the honors." Harper offered her the box.

With a mix of excitement and bittersweet feelings, Brooke set it on the counter and opened it.

Six jars were tucked into dividers. The top of the musical-note-shaped honey dipper was visible from the side of each container.

She removed one of them. Her smile naturally grew on her face as she took in the label of musical notes floating above a background of wildflowers. "This is lovely. It turned out even better than I expected."

Harper held one of the jars up. "You definitely nailed it—the name, the theme. You did a great job. Aunt Ivy will be excited to see this when she gets back."

Happiness filled Brooke as she thought of Aunt Ivy holding the jar in her hands.

Their aunt had hopped on another cruise. This time she was on her way to Mexico. From her texts and voicemails, a life of travel was agreeing with her.

"We need to find out when she'll be back so we can send her one," Brooke said.

"I'll reach out to her today," Harper replied. "And what about Gable?"

Brooke looked away and slipped the jar back into the box. "He's busy making an album. I'm sure he's forgotten all about this. Besides that, I don't know where to send it to him."

"You could bring him a jar in person." Harper set the jar in her hand in front of Brooke on the counter. "I saw a moving van pull in next door. And I also think I might have spotted Gable's truck in the driveway."

Gable? Was he next door? Feigning disinterest, Brooke picked up the whistling kettle and poured water over her tea. A slight tremor in her hand nearly gave her away. "Oh really? That's nice."

"Oh really—that's all you have to say about him possibly being next door right now?"

Brooke shrugged away Harper's question and her sister's direct stare. "What else am I supposed to say?"

"How about the truth? You've been miserable since you came back. I think you miss him."

"No, I haven't. And I don't miss him. I'm happy for him." Brooke took a sip of weak tea and grimaced. She'd meant to let it steep longer and add some honey to it.

Harper crossed her arms over her chest. "So the heartbroken sighs you've been making whenever you look toward the house next door are about you being happy for Gable?"

Denial was at the ready, but truth won out. Brooke put down her mug. "It doesn't matter how I feel. I told him our relationship was just a fling, and I didn't want anything more from him. He left right after that, and I don't blame him for moving on so quickly."

"But it wasn't just a fling to you."

"No, it wasn't," Brooke said. "But trust me, he has definitely moved on." She'd kind of, sort of stumbled across one of his posts while checking out the farm's account on social media. "His career is on the rise in Nashville. He's signed a contract and he's cutting an album. There are even rumors about him opening for a major music tour. That moving van next door just solidifies he's left Bolan for good so he can concentrate on what's important to him. His music. That truck you saw parked outside probably belongs to someone interested in buying the house."

Harper started to speak then hesitated. "But what if he is there? Gable could have come back to tie up a few loose ends with the house. The only way you'll know for sure is if you go next door." She gave Brooke's arm a squeeze. "If he is there, as hard as it will be to see him, once you do, you'll be able to have closure. I know you need that."

Seeing him again would be hard, but maybe Harper was right. She needed closure so she could move on. Honestly, she hadn't yet. At least not all the way. Brooke breathed against the dull thudding of her heart that was close to an ache. "So if he does happen to be there, what do I do? Just walk up and tell him I just wanted to say hi, so long and good luck?"

"He did suggest the new name for the honey. Bringing him a jar would be a nice way to say thank you." Harper gave her an empathetic look. "If there's anything else you need to say, I'm sure it will come to you."

Close to twenty minutes later, armed with a Bishop Honey Bee Farm boutique bag and a jar of the Symphony labeled berry honey, Brooke drove next door. She parked next to the moving van in front of the house then got out.

After tucking her car keys in the front pocket of her jeans, she rubbed her damp palm over her thigh, silently rehearsing a snippet of what she'd practiced on the way over. *I wanted to say thank you and good luck with everything...* That wasn't a lie. She was grateful for meeting him and the good times they'd shared, as well as all of the good things he'd added to her life. She also wanted the best for Gable, whatever that may be.

As she walked toward the front door, it took a second for her to process what was odd about the scene. The movers were carrying furniture *into* the house instead of out of it. Also Gable's truck wasn't there, but a car from the real estate office was. Just like she'd thought, the new owners were the ones moving in.

A strange mix of relief and disappointment came with her as she started to turn back to her Jeep.

"Brooke." Peggy walked out the open front door. The real estate agent smiled as she came down the porch steps. "Are you here to greet the new owner of the house?"

"Yes." Remembering the bag, Brooke awkwardly held it up. "I mean, Harper and I wanted to give them a small welcome gift. But I shouldn't have come here with this in the middle of moving day." Not in the mood to be neighborly, Brooke offered Peggy the bag. "Maybe you could pass this along for me?"

"But don't you want to do it yourself?"

"I wouldn't want to intrude. I'm sure they're busy."

"No, I'm sure he'll want to talk to you." Peggy looked past Brooke's shoulder to the driveway and smiled. "Perfect timing."

Behind Brooke, a car door opened then closed.

Meeting someone new hadn't been the plan, but she couldn't walk away now. As Brooke turned around to meet her neighbor, she conjured up a smile and took a step. She almost faltered as her legs grew weak.

As Gable approached, dressed in dark boots, jeans, a dark T-shirt and his Stetson, he had sexy cowboy written all over him. His shoulders looked a little broader. His chest more muscular. Even his legs looked longer. Had he gotten taller? No, that was impossible.

Why had he come back to the house? He'd probably forgotten something.

Whatever Peggy was saying as she walked back to the house was drowned out by the echo of Brooke's heart flip-flopping against her rib cage.

Gable paused in front of her. "Brooke…hi. I didn't expect to see you."

"Hi. I just brought this by." Held by his gaze, she was at a loss for words. When she'd first met him, sadness had been in their depths. Maybe a hint of it was still there, but she also saw something else. Peacefulness. His new path, pursuing his music career, was clearly a right fit for him.

He glanced down at the bag and looked back up at her face. Waiting.

"Oh, right. This is yours." Brooke handed it to him.

His fingers brushed hers, and wild and magnetic tingles bloomed where they touched. That feeling. That connection, it hadn't gone away. On a reflex her hand tightened, and his did, too. They both held on to the bag. Neither one of them seemed to want to let go, but she had to end this. She needed to find closure like Harper had suggested.

Brooke released the bag. "I also wanted to say I'm sorry. That day at the gazebo, I shouldn't have run off the way I did. I should have stayed so we could talk and end things properly."

"I shouldn't have put you in that position by singing to you. It was a mistake. It wasn't what you expected."

He was partially right. It was unexpected because she hadn't anticipated what it revealed to her about herself. She'd fallen in love with him, hard and fast, and her feelings for him had scared her and rocked her to the core. But that didn't matter now. For him, he viewed that moment in the gazebo as a mistake.

"I understand." Afraid he would see disappointment in her eyes, she looked to the movers unloading furniture "So, it's official. You've moved out and the new owners are moving in. Have you met them?"

"I have. Their horse is a little ornery at times, but I know for a fact you'll win him over."

She smiled. "You said Pepper was ornery and he wasn't at all. Where is he by the way?"

Gable tipped his head. "In his permanent home in the barn."

"You sold him?"

"No. He and I are both home. I'm not moving out. I'm moving in. This is my house now."

"But what about your condo in Nashville with a spectacular view?" The question slipped out. So much for playing down her feelings. Now he knew she'd been stalking him online.

He took a step closer as he looked at her face. "The condo is where I need to be for work, but this place is where I belong."

"It is? That's good news. I'm really glad you're back." Regret that it was over between them. Loving him. It hit her all at once. She looked down, trying to steel herself against the onslaught of emotions.

"Do you mean that?" he asked softly. "Are you really glad I'm back?"

It would be much easier to lie, but she couldn't do that to herself anymore. Or him. "More than you know."

"Brooke, look at me. Please."

Unsure of herself or what was to come, she took an unsteady breath and met his gaze. What she saw in the depths of his eyes seemed to mirror all she felt, and her heart stumbled through a few beats.

Gable's chest rose and fell with a deep breath. "At the gazebo, I tried to express my feelings for you in a song instead of telling you what I wanted outright, and I won't make that mistake again." He took another step closer, and his warmth radiated over her. "Yes, I consider this house my home, but, more than anything, I would like this to be *our* home. I'm not trying to rush us into anything. We can take it as slow as you want. Building something meaningful takes time and effort, and I'm willing to put in both if it means I can have another chance with you. A real chance. Whatever we build, I want us to make it strong enough to support a marriage, our careers, and when it's right, a family. I know I'm asking a lot, but that's what I want, and I only want it with you."

"Oh…" His words were sweeter than any lyric she'd ever heard him sing or any honey she'd ever tasted. Filled with the desire to have all that he'd just said prompted Brooke to press her mouth to his.

Gable wrapped his arm around her and kissed her back, passionately, lovingly.

But then, he eased away. "Don't get me wrong. I could kiss you all day. But what's your answer? You and I giving it a shot together. Is that what you want? I know with my career ramping up and you traveling for work, it won't be easy…"

She smiled up at him. "I thought you were trying to talk me into a relationship with you, not out of it?"

"I am."

Brooke rested her hands on Gable's chest. His heart was beating just as fast as hers, maybe faster. "Well, since I'm back here at the farm for good, that eliminates me traveling all the time from the equation. We'll still face goodbyes and separations because of your career." She waited for her doubts and fears to rise, but they didn't. "But we'll have homecomings to look forward to, and when I'm not needed here, I don't mind traveling to see you."

Gable leaned in. "So, Sun Angel, can I take that as a yes?"

Joy enveloped her from the inside out. They were on

the same path, committed to making it to the same destination. Forever.

Smiling, Brooke looped her arms around his neck and brought her mouth a hairbreadth from his. "Definitely."

Chapter Twenty-Nine

Three months later

Dressed in an oversize T-shirt, Brooke climbed the lighted stairs at Gable's house, carefully holding a full porcelain cup. He'd built a coffee station in the galley kitchen, and since then, she'd experimented with making different drinks to kick off her day. She almost had espresso making down to a science. The foam heart at the top of her cup was only a little wonky. By the time Gable returned from the recording studio in Nashville, she would have it mastered. One more week. That's how long she had to wait to see her fiancé again.

Brooke's gaze traveled to the ring on her left hand. She didn't risk wearing the engagement ring with a marquise cut diamond working around the bee farm so she took advantage of the moments when she could, especially first thing in the morning when she missed him the most. She and Gable had sped from zero to one hundred, becoming engaged only two months after finding their way back to each other, but the speed of their relationship felt more than right.

She reached the bedroom, walked to the glass-enclosed balcony with a modern teal love seat chaise. A just-because gift from Gable, it had arrived a few days ago. A wood table with a vase of wildflowers completed the space. After setting her cup there, she opened the balcony window, reveling in the cool air. Just like her mom had done in her favorite spot, she looked toward the sunrise.

As she stood at the window, the room grew brighter as rays of soft white transformed to pale yellow and orange. The sun crested the horizon, illuminating a blue nearly cloudless sky.

Brooke smiled in the warmth of the light. The only thing that would have made the moment more special was...

"Good morning, Sun Angel."

Had she imagined Gable's voice? Hopeful, she turned around.

Smiling, he walked toward her.

"You're here!" Brooke's heart soared with her as she leaped at him.

He caught her.

As she wrapped her arms around his neck and her legs around his waist, she pressed her mouth to his, and they indulged in a long welcome-home kiss.

She felt his heart thumping with hers as he eased a hairbreadth away and said, "I missed you."

"I missed you more. I thought you couldn't come home until next week?"

"We're ahead on recording the album, and my voice needed a break." Aside from working on his debut album, he had opened for a few concerts on the East Coast when another performer had dropped out of a tour with a popular country artist. Gable glanced over her shoulder. "I'd planned on joining you for coffee, but it looks like a visitor beat me to it."

"What visitor?"

He set her down, and she followed his gaze to the table.

A lone bee flew between her espresso and the vase with flowers.

Brooke walked over to the table and said softly to the bee, "Just land. I've got you." As the bee landed on a bud, she slipped the flower from the vase. Turning toward the window, she released the bud into a light morning breeze. As it gently floated in the air, the bee took flight and flew away.

Gable wrapped his arms around her from behind. "A sun angel and a bee charmer. I'm a lucky man."

She turned in his arms, losing herself in the depths of his eyes as she remembered the day he'd fallen from his horse. That was the moment he'd captured her heart, even though she hadn't realized it. Just like the forager bees in the hive, she'd traveled and explored and found her way home to Gable.

"We're both lucky." Brooke met him halfway for a kiss. It deepened with something real. A passion and a love meant for a lifetime...together.

* * * * *